BRENDA JACKSON

Follow Your Heart

HQN

ISBN-13: 978-1-335-14797-4

Follow Your Heart

Recycling programs
for this product may
not exist in your area.

For questions and comments about the quality of this book,
please contact us at CustomerService@Harlequin.com.

HQN
22 Adelaide St. West, 40th Floor
Toronto, Ontario M5H 4E3, Canada
www.Harlequin.com

Printed in Spain

To the man who will always and forever be the love of my life, Gerald Jackson, Sr. My hero. My everything.

To my sons, Gerald Jr. and Brandon. You guys are the greatest and continue to make me and your dad proud.

"Delight thyself also in the Lord: and he shall give thee the desires of thine heart." —*Psalms* 37:4

Follow Your Heart

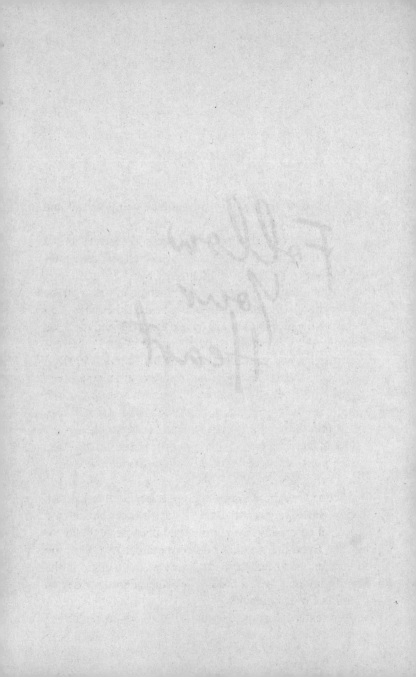

PROLOGUE

"KAEGAN AND BRYCE, I now pronounce you husband and wife. Kaegan, you may kiss your bride."

Victoria Madaris swiped at the tears in her eyes as she watched the couple at the front of the church seal their marriage vows with a kiss.

Kaegan Chambray and Bryce Witherspoon—now Bryce Witherspoon-Chambray—made a beautiful couple. You could see the love in their eyes when they'd recited the vows they'd written. When Kaegan, a member of the Pointe-au-Chien Tribe, had spoken to Bryce in his Native American tongue and she responded in that tongue in kind, it had been the most touching thing. Although Victoria was certain she wasn't the only one who hadn't understood what they'd said, the important thing was that *they* had understood.

A handkerchief was suddenly shoved in her hand. "Here. I can't believe you're carrying on like this at a wedding, considering your fate."

Victoria fought the urge to glare at her brother Corbin. Today was Kaegan and Bryce's day. It had been such a beautiful ceremony. Everything had been perfect and romantic. Even the weather had cooperated. Although the forecasters had predicted rain, there wasn't a cloud in the sky. Today had been a totally awesome February day in Catalina Cove, Louisiana.

"Honestly, Corbin, do you have to be so negative?

There's nothing wrong with falling in love and getting married," she said as people began exiting the church. When she'd received a wedding invitation for the same weekend he'd planned to visit, she'd invited him to be her plus-one.

"So says the woman whose single days are numbered," her brother grumbled. "Glad it's you and not me."

Victoria decided not to point out that he better be glad it was her, otherwise it would indeed be him. "I'm going to tell you the same thing I told Nolan. I have no problem with our great-grandmother finding me a husband if she's inclined to do so. Mama Laverne has an astounding track record as a matchmaker, and whomever she chooses will be well vetted. It will certainly save me the time of trying to figure out if the man is worth my time and attention."

"You honestly want a husband?" Corbin asked, as if appalled at the very thought.

"No, but if Mama Laverne has chosen one for me, I'll take him. I trust her judgment. She's the best."

It was a well-known fact that at ninetysomething, the matriarch of the Madaris family was determined to marry off her great-grands before she left to go with the Lord. It bothered Victoria whenever Mama Laverne would say such a thing because Victoria couldn't imagine a world without her great-grandmother in it.

Over the years, Victoria had seen her work her magic on some of the staunchest bachelors in the family. They had fought her all the way. But then the next thing she knew, they had fallen in love with the women Mama Laverne had chosen for them.

The last match had been Victoria's brother Nolan, and everybody knew that Nolan had had no intention of ever getting married. He was singing a different tune these days with Ivy. The two would be celebrating their second wedding anniversary soon, and people suspected a baby was on the way. Victoria hoped so. She was looking forward to the day that she became an auntie.

"This is a pretty nice town, Victoria."

She glanced around when they reached her brother's car. "Yes, it is. I love it here. It's so peaceful and the people are friendly. Mom and Dad came to visit last month and said the fishing here was great."

"So I heard, but don't get too attached to the place. You're a Texan. Remember that."

Victoria rolled her eyes. Like there was any way she could. The Madaris family had settled in Texas seven generations ago, back in the 1800s, after acquiring a ten-thousand-acre Mexican land grant. At a time when most newly freed Blacks were still waiting for their forty acres and a mule from the United States government, Carlos Antonio Madaris, half Mexican and half African American, along with his wife, Christina Marie, were shaping their legacy on land they used to raise cattle. A parcel of land they named Whispering Pines. Today Whispering Pines was a huge cattle ranch run by her uncle Jake.

"Now tell me why you're living here and not in New Orleans when that's where your job is," Corbin said as he pulled out of the church's parking lot.

Victoria knew he'd heard the reason from their parents, but if he thought there was another version that he hadn't gotten wind of, she had no problem bursting his bubble. "I came to Catalina Cove to cover a story about the shrimp festival they hold each year. It took me less than an hour to get here. I loved the place immediately and decided although I worked in New Orleans, I didn't have to live there when I liked this place better."

Corbin nodded. "You've only been here a couple of

months and already you've made friends who invited you to their wedding?"

She smiled. "Bryce was one of the first people I met. She's the Realtor I contacted to find me a place to lease in the cove. And you have to admit my place is nice."

"It's small."

She figured he would say that, since his condo in Houston was bigger than most houses. "It's big enough for me, Corbin. And I love that apple grove in the back. There's nothing like waking up to the smell of apples every morning."

"How's your job going?"

Victoria glanced over at him. She knew that her brothers hadn't particularly liked the idea of her taking a job as a news reporter in New Orleans when a similar job had been offered to her in Houston. She tried to get them to understand it was time for her to spread her wings. Besides, the Madaris name was well-known not only in Houston, but also in the entire state of Texas. She didn't want to worry about taking a job and being treated differently because her last name was Madaris.

"My job is going great, although I miss being out on the beat." Six months ago, she'd been promoted from a beat reporter to coanchor one of the morning shows.

"I'm glad the political season is over. I couldn't take interviewing one more politician," she said. There was no reason to explain to her brother why she felt such deep animosity toward politicians. Most of the family already knew why. To change the subject, she asked, "So what's going on with your love life, Corbin?"

She laughed when he let out an expletive. She knew one sure way to get her brother riled was to ask about his love life. Like most single Madaris men, he intended to stay a bachelor forever.

"Don't worry about my love life. You need to be concerned with your own. I'm not the next person on Mama Laverne's list."

"Not for long. I've been summoned. I got a call from Mama Laverne. She wants to see me, so I'm going to Whispering Pines next weekend."

Stopping at a traffic light, Corbin glanced over at her with an arched eyebrow. "Do you think she's going to tell you who she's chosen as your husband?"

"Probably, since I can't think of any other reason for her to want to meet with me, especially when I spent time with her over the holidays. It has been almost two years since she told Nolan I was next in line. You know what that means, right?"

Corbin shook his head. "No, what does that mean?"

Victoria smiled. "It means since I don't plan to give Mama Laverne grief about anything, I'll probably have a June wedding and then she can turn her attention to you, since you're next on the list."

Corbin frowned. "Like hell."

Victoria laughed at her brother's reaction. "I suggest you start enjoying your final days as a bachelor, Corbin."

The following weekend

"UNCLE JAKE AND Aunt Diamond, how are you?" Victoria asked as she entered their home on Whispering Pines and gave both huge hugs. She adored her grand-uncle and grand-aunt. She also loved Whispering Pines, the place everyone in the family considered the Madaris homestead.

Whispering Pines was an hour drive from Houston and

encompassed hundreds and hundreds of acres of land for grazing cattle. The ranch was renowned for raising only the highest quality grass-fed Texas longhorn cattle. Victoria thought the ranch house, a massive hacienda-style villa where Jake and his family lived, was a real piece of art. It had always been beautiful, and since marrying former actress Diamond Swain, who'd put her special touch here and there, it was even more so.

Jake, a distinguished rancher, had once made the cover of *Time* magazine when they'd applauded his efforts in aiding the British government with England's cattle industry's mad cow epidemic. Not only was her uncle a great rancher, but he was also highly intelligent when it came to investments. Thanks to him, all the members of the Madaris family had a hefty amount of stock in the family business. He managed the portfolios for all his nieces and nephews, and they all had lucrative trust funds. Jake was well-respected in numerous circles and his name carried a lot of weight in Texas. As far as Victoria was concerned, he was the best grand-uncle in the whole wide world.

"I hope I didn't arrive during the time Mama Laverne is napping," she said.

"No. She's expecting you and delayed her nap until later," Diamond said.

Jake studied his grand-niece. "I guess you have an idea why you're here."

Victoria nodded. "Yes, I have an idea."

"You're not bothered by the fact Mom is about to interfere in your life?" he asked.

Victoria saw the concern in her grand-uncle's eyes and decided to tell him the same thing she'd been telling her brothers and cousins. "I'm fine with everything, Uncle Jake.

Even you have to admit Mama Laverne's track record for hooking people up successfully is astounding."

"Well, just as long as you're okay with it."

Victoria touched her grand-uncle's arm to reassure him. "I'm okay with it, and I'm really anxious to know what man she's chosen for me."

A few moments later, Victoria was knocking on the door to her great-grandmother's suite.

"Come in."

Opening the door, Victoria found her sitting in her favorite chair, knitting. Felicia Laverne Madaris had taught Victoria to knit when she'd been eight, and for her great-grandmother to still be able to use her hands to knit the way she did, and as often as she did, was amazing.

"Hello, Mama Laverne," she said, leaning down to place a kiss on the older woman's cheek.

"And hello to you, Victoria."

Her great-grandmother was wearing a pretty floral button-front dress with her signature pearls around her neck. Perched on her nose was a pair of reading glasses. While growing up, Victoria thought her great-grandmother was one of the most stylish women she knew. She still thought so.

"You look pretty today, Mama Laverne."

"Thank you and so do you. Would you like some of the Madaris tea?" Mama Laverne asked as she placed her knitting aside and removed her reading glasses.

Victoria loved the Madaris tea. The recipe was known only to certain Madaris family members. "Yes. You want me to pour?" Victoria asked.

"That will be fine, dear."

After pouring them both cups of tea, Victoria noticed Mama Laverne studying her intently. She knew there was a reason for her doing so and figured if she was patient, her great-grandmother would tell her what was on her mind.

After taking a couple of sips of tea, Mama Laverne said, "I'm sure you know why I wanted to meet with you."

Victoria nodded. "Yes, I do have a good idea."

Mama Laverne took another sip of tea. "I know some of you merely see me as a meddling old woman, intent on destroying your lives. But as you can see, I haven't steered anyone wrong yet."

Victoria chuckled. "No, you haven't. Nolan is happy with Ivy, Lee is happy with Carly, Reese is happy with Kenna, Luke is happy with Mac…need I go on?" All the cousins she had mentioned—Lee, Reese and Luke—had their marriages prearranged by the woman sitting before her.

"Heavens no. You don't have to," Mama Laverne answered. "I just want you to believe that you will be happy with the person I've chosen for you, as well."

Goose bumps formed on Victoria's arms and butterflies began floating around in her stomach. "Who is he, Mama Laverne?" she asked excitedly.

Felicia Laverne Madaris placed her teacup down to give her great-granddaughter her undivided attention. "Now *that* I can't tell you."

Victoria lifted an eyebrow. "You can't?"

"No. Nor can I tell you when he will make the first approach to you. He's a very busy man and falling in love is the last thing on his agenda. At least so he thinks."

Victoria's forehead bunched in confusion. "I don't understand. Why can't you reveal his identity? It's not like I'll have a problem with whoever you've chosen because I know you will look out for my best interests."

Mama Laverne reached out and took Victoria's hand firmly in hers. "Yes, I will, and I appreciate your faith and confidence in me. It's refreshing to have a willing partici-pant instead of an unwilling one like your brother and male cousins have been."

She paused a moment and then said, "The reason I am withholding his identity for now is because although you might be ready to accept him as your mate, the man I've chosen for you might not feel the same. If he knew what I had planned, he would fight it all the way and become ex-tremely difficult."

Victoria shrugged. "But don't they always fight it, any-way?"

"Yes, but he needs to feel that he's fallen in love with you on his own and not because he's being manipulated. For that reason, keeping his identity from you is the only way. You're going to have to trust me on this."

Victoria did trust her great-grandmother, although she wasn't sure this was the best approach. "Is it someone I already know?"

Releasing Victoria's hand, Mama Laverne picked up her teacup and took a sip, then said, "I can't tell you that, either."

Victoria released a deep sigh. "But how will I know it's him?"

Mama Laverne smiled. "Trust me, dear, you will know."

PART 1

Your heart knows things that your mind can't explain.
—Anonymous

CHAPTER ONE

Six months later

VICTORIA MADARIS ENTERED Susan's Bakery and immediately inhaled the aroma of beignets. They smelled divine, which wasn't a surprise, since this was a favorite shop for so many New Orleans locals—the line at the counter was long. She glanced at her watch to make sure she had time before heading over to the television station to prepare for her show and saw that she didn't. The line was moving at a slow pace and waiting wasn't an option today.

She had been elated when her boss, Mr. Richards, had called her into his office last month to let her know that due to her hard work and dedication, as well as her popularity with the television audience, she was getting promoted and would be switching from the morning slot to the noonday hour. She would be joining two other women in a very popular talk show called *Talk It Up.*

Guest slots had already been filled for the next six months and she was very impressed with the lineup. She knew the other two women, Debra Morris and Icelyn Crews, had been doing the show for a while. Debra was a veteran with the network and Victoria was eager to learn from her.

Victoria was about to turn around to leave when she hit what felt like a solid wall. It was only when a hand reached out to steady her and keep her from falling that she realized it hadn't been a wall, but a man.

"Hey, you're 'Little Nolan,' aren't you?"

Victoria cringed. She hated when people who knew her oldest brother referred to her as if she didn't have her own name or identity. She looked up into the smiling and handsome face of Tanner Jamison. Tanner was good friends with her brothers and male cousins. She was surprised he recognized her since it had been years since she'd last seen him.

She figured most women would have felt honored to have been recognized by one of the most eligible bachelors in Houston, and he was certainly that. Tanner was extremely good-looking. She remembered that he was best friends with her cousin Blade Madaris. In fact, she recalled that Blade, Tanner and another one of their close friends, Wyatt Bannister, had been known as notorious bachelors. Years ago, in her late teens, she'd eavesdropped on a conversation between one of her brothers and male cousins to learn just how notorious Blade, Tanner and Wyatt were.

Blade had since settled down and married Samari, and they had a beautiful little girl. However, last she heard, Tanner and Wyatt were still out there on the prowl and sowing their wild oats. "Yes, I'm Nolan's sister, *Victoria*."

His smile widened. "Victoria, that's right. Now I recall Ms. Felicia Laverne mentioning that you were here in New Orleans."

Victoria lifted an eyebrow when a red flag suddenly went up. When had he talked to her great-grandmother and why would her name come up in their conversation? "You talked to Mama Laverne?"

"I sure did. I dropped by Blade's house earlier this year and she was there visiting. She'd made her delicious bread pudding and invited me to talk to her while we ate some

and drank coffee. At least I drank coffee—Ms. Felicia Laverne had tea. We had a nice chat."

"You did?"

"Yes."

Victoria wanted to ask what their chat had been about,
but knew that wouldn't be the proper thing to do. However,
she did want to know when their conversation took place.
"And when exactly was this? I know you said earlier this
year, but do you remember the exact month?"

If he found her inquiry odd, he didn't say so. "It was in
January," he said. "I specifically remember the month because I dropped by to watch the NFL playoffs with Blade."

Victoria nodded. Her grandmother had summoned her
to Whispering Pines in February...the month after her chat
with Tanner. Interesting.

"Ms. Felicia Laverne even gave me a couple of gift cards
to this bakery," he said, and nodded. "She said the owner
was the granddaughter of an old friend who'd sent her a
few gift cards as a Christmas gift. Since she knew I was
headed this way, she passed those gift cards on to me."

Umm...interesting. Her great-grandmother had given
some of the same gift cards to her, as well. Had she done
so hoping that she and Tanner would run in to each other
here? "That was nice of Mama Laverne."

"I thought so, too. She knows how much I like sweets
and was looking out for me."

Victoria shook her head. The man was being played and
didn't even know it. She was about to ask him more about
his meeting with her great-grandmother and the gift cards
when he asked her a question.

"How do you like New Orleans, Victoria?"

She couldn't help but notice all the female attention
Tanner was getting. Because of her brothers and older male

cousins, she was used to seeing women's reactions to them. Some things never changed when it came to a good-looking man and she had to hand it to him. Tanner was definitely good-looking.

"I like it. I've been working at a television station here for almost two years now, but I live in Catalina Cove. That's an hour drive from here."

"I'm familiar with the place. It's a beautiful little town."

"Yes, it is," she agreed. "Are you in town visiting or sightseeing?" she asked him.

"No. I'm opening a new club in town."

"You are?"

"Yes, it's the third Gentlemen's Club to open and the first one outside of Texas."

Victoria had heard all about the Gentlemen's Clubs that he co-owned with Blade and Wyatt. From overhearing her brothers talk, the members of the all-male club were far from being gentlemen of any kind. She'd heard what went on in their clubs, especially about the strippers who were hired to entertain the men. All legal, but definitely pushed to the extreme. Women who went to the club had to be invited by the members. "Congratulations on the opening of your new club. I'm sure it will do well. Now if you will excuse—"

"How about dinner?"

She tilted her head. "You're asking me out to dinner?"

He chuckled. "Yes. Nothing wrong with that, is there? You're the sister and cousin to several of my close friends. That's the least I can do since it's like I'm practically a member of your family, anyway. And I did tell your great-grandmother while I was here that I would check on you." He chuckled again. "In fact, she all but insisted I did."

Oh, she did, did she? From the sound of it, Mama Laverne was making sure that their paths crossed here in New Orleans. Was Tanner the man Mama Laverne had chosen for her? A man who wore bachelorhood like a badge of honor? A man who'd been just like her brother Nolan and several male cousins that Mama Laverne had successfully married off? Did Mama Laverne actually believe Tanner Jamison would give up his man-whore ways for her?

"Victoria?"

She looked up at him. "Yes?"

"Will you have dinner with me? I just flew in today and haven't had a chance to go grocery shopping yet."

She blinked. "You're moving to New Orleans?"

His smile widened and she noticed several women in the bakery who weren't hiding the fact they were listening to their conversation, and seemed to be holding their breath waiting for his answer.

"Yes. We bought an old nightclub that needs renovations. It's easier for me to move here temporarily while the work is being done than to fly in two to three times a week."

She nodded. How convenient for Mama Laverne. "And how long do you think the renovations are going to take?"

"Our plans are to have the club open and ready to jam with a New Year's Eve party."

There was no doubt in her mind it would be one wild party. "Then I'm sure it will be ready."

He glanced at his watch. "So are you free for dinner tonight?"

Honestly, she wasn't. However, if he was the man Mama Laverne had chosen for her, then the opportunity would present itself for them to run in to each other again. Tonight she already had plans. Her cousin Christy was flying into town to attend a conference, and Victoria promised she'd pick up Christy from the airport and have dinner with her.

"I'm sorry, Tanner, but I have a prior dinner engagement. Maybe some other time." If he was disappointed, he didn't show it. In fact, his smile widened even more.

"How about a rain check?" he asked.

"A rain check will be fine."

"What's your phone number?" he asked her, pulling out his cell phone.

Victoria told him her phone number and he punched it into his phone. When she heard her phone ring in her purse, he said, "And now you have mine, as well. If you ever need anything, just call." He slid his phone back inside his jacket. "You take care, 'Little Nolan.'"

She was about to remind him that her name was Victoria and not "Little Nolan," but decided not to waste her time. "You take care, too."

She then quickly left the bakery to get to work on time.

A SHORT WHILE later Tanner Jamison walked out of the bakery smiling. Women. He just had to love them, and he did. While standing in line, he'd gotten numbers from four different women. All nice-looking, single ladies with bodies he couldn't wait to try out. He had a feeling he wouldn't regret the six months he would be living in New Orleans.

His phone rang when he reached his car and he quickly clicked on, recognizing the ring tone. "What's going on, Blade?"

"Just checking to see if the renovations are on schedule."

Blade Madaris and Wyatt Bannister were his partners in several financial ventures, including the nightclubs they owned. They had purchased their first club years ago, when all three had been single men on the prowl. They'd figured if women could have a place like Sisters, a nightclub in Houston that catered to females, then there was nothing wrong with them establishing a club that catered to men. Blade was the only one of the three who'd since gotten married. Although he didn't frequent the club like he used to, he was still a partner.

"I met with your construction manager earlier. I went straight there from the airport," Tanner said, opening his car door to get in. "I think we might be ready by New Year's Eve." Since Blade and his twin brother, Slade, owned a construction business, they would be using Blade's company for the renovations.

"Let's hope so. The construction manager I've assigned for the job, Hank Brighton, is good. He's going to make sure we dot every *i* and cross every *t* to open on time. By the way, have you checked in to your condo yet?"

"Not yet, but already I've checked out quite a few beauties here in New Orleans. My black book is filling up. I definitely won't get bored while I'm here."

Blade chuckled. "I'm sure you won't. I don't know who's worse, you or Wyatt."

Tanner grinned. "You mean since you got married and removed yourself from the picture? Wyatt has always been worse than the two of us put together, because he takes after his old man in his younger days."

"Yes, you're right about that," Blade agreed.

"Oh, and by the way, guess who I ran in to at the bakery a short while ago?" Tanner then said.

"Who?"

"Your cousin. 'Little Nolan.' It's been quite a while since I've seen her. She looks good, man. Definitely not a kid anymore. I asked her to dinner, but she had other plans."

"You asked Victoria to dinner? Are you crazy? You know better than to hit on any of my female relatives, Tanner. They're off-limits."

"Relax, Blade, my invitation was nothing more than a friendly gesture. I wasn't coming on to her. I had told Ms. Felicia Laverne that I would look her up when I moved to New Orleans."

"Damn, man, I hope you haven't fallen into my great-grandmother's trap."

"Trap? What are you talking about?"

"After taking Nolan off the singles market, Mama Laverne has made Victoria next on her 'to marry off' list. So unless you want to be the man Mama Laverne marks as Victoria's future husband, I suggest you keep your distance."

Shit, Tanner thought. Everyone knew about Blade's great-grandmother's matchmaking track record, even when marriage was the last thing on their minds. Blade was a prime example of the older woman's shenanigans.

"Come to think of it, I noticed that you and Mama Laverne talked for a long time that Sunday when you dropped by and she was here."

Tanner swallowed. "Yes, but we were talking about a lot of stuff, mainly about some cruise she plans to take this fall and how good she was at playing bingo."

"Are you saying Victoria's name didn't come up, not once?"

Tanner swallowed again. "When I mentioned my plans to move to New Orleans to oversee the club renovations, she mentioned Victoria worked here. That's when she suggested that, being a family friend, I should look her up."

Tanner then recalled something else. "Oh, and that bakery that I just left after running in to Victoria…"

"Yeah, what about it?"

"Your grandmother is the one who told me about it.

Suggested I try out some of their baked goods. She even gave me a few gift cards for free coffee and Danish rolls."

"Umm, did you not wonder how a little old lady in Texas would know anything about a bakery in New Orleans?"

Tanner shrugged. "Yes, when I asked, she said the owner was the daughter of a friend of hers."

"That's how it always starts," Blade sighed. "She connives with the old cronies in her church group who want to marry off their grands or great-grands, as well. That's how she arranged for Lee to marry Carly."

Tanner didn't like the sound of that.

"I bet you anything that she gave Victoria some of those same gift cards with the intention of the two of you running into each other. It appears her plan worked. She's set you up real nice like."

Tanner resented the amusement he heard in Blade's voice. "Ms. Felicia Laverne might manipulate her family members into marriage, but she can count me out of it."

"Nice try, Tanner, but you and Wyatt have been my best friends for years, so don't think she doesn't consider you as part of the family. So the way I see it, it's too late to count you out."

Tanner disagreed. Sex was sex and a serious relationship with a woman was something altogether different. They were mutually exclusive in his book. He only had time for sex and nothing more. Engaging in a relationship for a specific purpose—like marriage—was way out of the league he intended to keep playing in.

"It's not too late, and since now that I'm on to what she's trying to do, I will keep my distance from Victoria."

"Not sure you can at this point," Blade said.

Tanner frowned. "Watch me."

CHAPTER TWO

SENATOR ROMAN MALONE got into his car, then checked his phone and saw a missed call from Mint Stover, his political manager and best friend. They'd known each other since their days together at Harvard. It was there, on the university's campus, where they'd made a pact. Roman would follow his father, Roman Sr., into politics, and Mint would be the campaign manager who made sure Roman won every office that he ran for. So far, he had. Over the years Mint's duties had expanded to include such things as consultant, opposition researcher, lobbyist, fundraiser and polling analyst. Mint was good at everything he did and kept Roman on track.

Returning the call, he said, "Hey, Mint, what's up?"

"First of all, how did your meeting with the majority leader go?"

He wasn't surprised that would be number one on Mint's mind. Keeping him electable was Mint's goal. "It seems they hired a consulting firm to provide names of party hopefuls for the next decade. My name made the list."

"That's great, but as far as I'm concerned, they didn't need to pay a consulting company to tell them of your qualifications to be considered for president one day. All they had to do is look at your voting record and popularity, which I can only see getting better over time."

"You would, Mint."

"No, seriously. In a few short years you've become the rising star of the party. You're vastly popular and well-liked…especially among American women, who, need I remind you, still maintain the largest voting bloc."

"Well, that might be true, but they thought the need to call a potential problem to my attention."

Mint got quiet for a minute, and then he asked, "And what might that potential problem be?"

"My marital status. It's been strongly recommended that I give thought to not dating all over the place, settling down and begin thinking of securing a wife who is worthy of one day becoming a first lady. Of all the names on that consultant's list, I'm the only one still single."

"And what do you think about that, Roman?"

"You, of all people, know how I feel about that. I've never felt the need to marry for the sake of boosting one's political career. People should marry for love."

Roman figured he would fall in love and marry one day, but he didn't plan to rush the process. According to his father, he'd known the moment he'd met Traci Kinsey that she was the woman for him and had fallen for her immediately. The same thing had happened to his older sister, Erika, and the man she'd married. Erika swore she'd known Silas was the man she loved after less than a month.

Roman figured that's how it would be for him. He would know the woman he was destined to love when he saw her, or soon thereafter. For him, marriage was a lifetime commitment, and he wouldn't marry for any other reason than love. His parents were great role models.

"Over the years, you have dated quite a number of beautiful, intelligent and sophisticated women."

"That might be the case, but I'm not ready to settle down to just one woman, Mint," Roman said. "I'm flying to Texas tonight to visit my parents in Austin for a couple days. Before returning to DC, I think I'll make a pit stop in Houston and seek counsel with Senator Lansing."

Senator Nedwyn Lansing had been in the US Senate for over twenty years and when he'd been ready to retire, he hadn't wanted to turn his seat over to just anyone. He had called Roman and convinced him he was the most qualified person to take his seat to represent the good people of Texas. Because of Senator Lansing's support, Roman had won in a landslide victory seven years ago. Last year Roman had been reelected to that same senate seat.

"I think talking to Senator Lansing is a good idea," Mint said. "And don't forget about that interview in New Orleans next Wednesday. You're to appear on a morning talk show."

"Thanks for the reminder."

"While the senate isn't in session, now is the best time for you to get away. I've cleared your calendar for the next three weeks to take some much-deserved R and R. It will start right after that interview in New Orleans, which means you won't return to Washington until a week and a few days after Labor Day."

Roman grinned. "That sounds good to me."

"I figured it would. There's a shipping town an hour outside of New Orleans and it's reputed to be the best place for fishing and boating. A place called Catalina Cove."

"Umm, I've never heard of the place, but that's great. Just make sure you book me somewhere close to the water so I can get a lot of fishing in."

"I already have. And another thing, Roman, the Capital Ball at the Kennedy Center will be in a couple of months. Should I add Audria's name to the RSVP as your plus-one, or will you be taking someone else?"

"Audria will not be my date, Mint. You can be sure of that."

Audria Wayfare, daughter of Senator Wayfare, had somehow convinced herself that she was the woman Roman needed in his life, saying she had the right pedigree to be a senator's wife, especially one with aspirations to live on Pennsylvania Avenue. He'd known it was time to end things between them after she mentioned in a magazine interview that they were contemplating marriage. That had been a lie.

"Okay, then let me know who it will be before the end of next month."

After Roman ended the call with Mint, he snapped on his seat belt thinking he wasn't even sure he would take a date. He had no problem attending the ball alone if he chose to do so.

No matter what, he would not be taking Audria.

"TANNER JAMISON? SERIOUSLY, VICTORIA. Do you honestly think he's the man Mama Laverne has chosen for you?" Christy Madaris fixed Victoria with her gaze and took a sip of wine.

Victoria sat across the table from her cousin. She had picked up Christy from the airport and they were sharing dinner at Sloan's, a popular restaurant in New Orleans.

Although Christy was six years older, the two of them had always been more than just cousins. They'd been gal pals. Victoria thought Christy was beautiful, with her high cheekbones and abundance of reddish-brown hair that flowed down to her shoulders. The mother of three was, and always had been, absolutely stunning. And it was a known fact that she was adored by a husband whom Christy had loved since her early teens.

Victoria could credit Christy with helping her through those growing years, when her three older brothers, Nolan, Corbin and Adam, would get on her nerves by being so overprotective. Christy had also been the recipient of such overprotectiveness from her own brothers—Justin, Dex and Clayton—while growing up. Christy had made things easier by becoming Victoria's mentor.

With Christy's help she was able to pretty much ignore her brothers' protectiveness and come up with her own agenda—focusing on her studies and career goals. Victoria had graduated with a master's degree in communications, broadcasting and journalism, and a bachelor's degree in public relations.

"All signs lead to Tanner," Victoria explained. "And it really wasn't a coincidence that we ran in to each other at that bakery when Mama Laverne gave us both gift cards. Tanner also mentioned that he and Mama Laverne had a nice chat, during which time she mentioned to him I worked here and told him to look me up. That's the only reason he asked me out. All that sounds suspect to me."

Christy nodded. "I hate to admit it, but it sounds pretty suspect to me, too. Tanner is such a ladies' man, I can't imagine him changing, not any time soon."

"Honestly, Christy, do you think Mama Laverne cares if he's ready to change? Consider who else were ladies' men. Namely, Blade, Lucas, Nolan, Lee… Need I go on? Mama Laverne has a knack for transforming notorious bachelors into perfect husbands, whether they want to or not."

Christy didn't say anything for a moment as she took another sip of wine. "You do have a point. If what you think is true, how do you feel about it?"

Victoria shrugged. "Right now, nothing. Possibly once I get to know Tanner, I'll feel an affinity toward him or something. I certainly didn't feel anything today. Not even a smidgen of sexual chemistry. All the other women in the shop were practically drooling, but I didn't feel even the tiniest bit of an attraction."

"It could be that you were too busy trying to rationalize things about him. Your mind was too occupied questioning if he was the one."

"Possibly. But I would think if he was going to be the man I was to fall in love with, I should at least feel something, shouldn't I?"

Christy smiled over at her. "You're asking the wrong person because I've always felt something for Alex. I've loved him forever. But if you were to ask Sam, she would tell you that she couldn't stand Blade at first and can't pinpoint exactly when she fell in love with him. She just knows that she did."

Victoria tilted her head. "Are you saying there's a chance I might not fall in love with Tanner right away?"

"That's a strong possibility. There's also a good chance he will fight falling in love with you until the bitter end. That's the way it works with die-hard bachelors. You have to be patient. You're looking at a lifetime commitment."

Victoria had no problem being patient since falling in love seemed to take a lot of work and she had enough on her plate. And why did the thought of spending a lifetime with someone suddenly have her feeling apprehensive? She and Christy paused in conversation when the waiter brought their meals.

When he walked off, Christy said, "You're not having second doubts about all this, are you, Victoria? Possibly thinking you've given Mama Laverne too much control and you're not ready for what she has planned for your future?"

That was exactly how Victoria was beginning to feel,

but she knew such thoughts and feelings weren't warranted. All she had to do was spend time around Luke and Mackenzie, Blade and Samari, Lee and Carly, and Nolan and Ivy to know when it came to matchmaking, her great-grandmother knew what she was doing. Victoria had to be patient and believe the rest—all that love, passion and romance stuff—would follow.

"I'm all right, Christy. It's the unknown that had me somewhat concerned. But now that I know the identity of the man Mama Laverne has chosen for me, I'll be okay."

"Good. Just so you know, even with his womanizing ways, Tanner is a nice guy. All you have to do is look at all those charities he's involved with to see that. We shouldn't judge him because he wants to enjoy life before settling down. Some of our brothers and cousins did that same thing and they turned out to be great husbands. You've never spent any real amount of time around Tanner. Maybe now you'll get to see a side of him you wouldn't expect and didn't know."

Now that was an uplifting thought, Victoria mused. She was twenty-seven and she figured Tanner was at least nine years older than her. There had never been a reason for her to get to know him. Now there was.

"I suggest you continue to enjoy your freedom while waiting for Tanner to start noticing you," Christy said.

"So you think I should date like normal?"

"I don't see why not. The last thing you want Tanner to think is that you're waiting for him to finally accept your place in his life. Heck, now is the time to have a hot, steamy affair if you'd ever thought about having one."

"Christy!" Victoria said, throwing her hand to her mouth to keep from laughing out loud.

"Why not? I'd thought about it and was about to act on it

that time when Alex rejected me. I refused to let him think he was the only man I could want, or who could want me. That brought Alex to his senses real quick when he saw how friendly I was getting with other guys. Like I said, there's nothing wrong with making Tanner jealous to kick-start feelings he might be fighting hard to suppress."

"I'll keep that in mind."

"You do that. Sooner or later, Tanner will begin noticing you to the point where all those other women will mean nothing to him. That's when he will only have eyes for you. When that happens, he'll start monopolizing your time. Then it won't be your time alone."

Victoria understood everything Christy was saying, and she much preferred all that happen later, rather than sooner. She didn't want any man to start monopolizing her time. She liked the way her life was now and loved the place she was renting in Catalina Cove. She enjoyed leaving work and driving home each day while listening to music or one of her favorite books on tape. It was such a pleasant and scenic drive and traffic wasn't all that bad once you left the New Orleans city limits. When she got home, she didn't have to worry about anyone but herself.

"Well, I know of one particular person who will appreciate the slow process of me and Tanner getting together," Victoria said.

Christy lifted an eyebrow. "Who?"

"Corbin. He knows once I'm married off, Mama Laverne will turn her undivided attention to him. I can't wait to see how he deals with it."

Christy chuckled. "I can't wait to see, either. After Corbin, there's Chancellor, Emerson and Adam. I can just imagine how much trouble they will be in going along with any plans she has for them."

Victoria took another sip of wine, then said, "You seem rather calm about leaving the babies in Alex's care."

Victoria could see the look of love that immediately warmed Christy's eyes at the mention of her husband. "Alex will handle the kids just fine. He's the perfect dad." Christy and Alex had three kids. A daughter and two sons. They'd always wanted a large family and everyone figured they weren't through making babies yet.

Alex Maxwell was a private investigator, and after they married, Christy became his assistant, doing the research for his cases. That's where her skills as an investigative reporter had come into play.

"Of course, I'll check periodically to see how they're doing," Christy added. "It pays to have family living close by if he needs them. However, I doubt he will. Alex is wonderful at almost everything he does."

Victoria didn't say anything as she smiled at her cousin and hoped things would be like that for her and Tanner. Of course, they would be. Mama Laverne wouldn't be getting them together otherwise.

"Let's do a toast," Victoria said, holding up her wineglass. "To the man you love and to the man I'm destined to love."

Laughing, Christy and Victoria clinked their glasses together.

CHAPTER THREE

"ARE YOU COMFORTABLE, Senator Malone? Would you like a glass of water or anything?" It was the third time the young woman who'd introduced herself as a production assistant had asked him in the last twenty minutes.

"No, I'm fine," Roman said, smiling at her. "Thanks for asking."

He'd been told the interview would last less than ten minutes and he was glad of that. Afterward, he would return to the hotel and check out, and then head to Catalina Cove. He couldn't wait to get there. A whole month to himself—no media of any kind, social or otherwise, and if he was lucky no one in the small coastal town would recognize him.

And, more importantly, no women.

Because the media had practically hounded his tail throughout the entire campaign last year, and then after the election both the Senate Select Committee on Intelligence and the Senate Committee on the Judiciary, of which he was a member, had frequent committee meetings that had meant putting his active social life—and getting laid—on the back burner. Now he needed rest more than sex, since all his combined political activities had taken a toll.

He was about to get the production assistant's attention to ask for a glass of water after all when a woman approached her. He figured he wouldn't interrupt their conversation and would wait it out, hoping it would be short. He switched his gaze to the television monitor displaying the person being interviewed ahead of him, when for some reason, he glanced back to where the women were standing and still conversing.

He told himself he'd only glanced back to see if the production assistant was now free, but deep down he knew that wasn't the case. Especially when his gaze lingered on the other woman.

She was beautiful in every sense of the word, and she looked damn good in that pencil skirt and blouse. He liked a woman with curves, and she had some pretty nice ones. The snug fit of her blouse indicated a pair of nice-size breasts, as well.

He studied her features and thought there was something about her that looked oddly familiar. It was as if he knew her from somewhere. A campaign staffer perhaps? Possibly not, because he would have definitely remembered her.

Whatever the two were talking about had the woman smiling. He was mesmerized by the dimples that showed in her cheeks, and the thick mass of dark brown curly hair that flowed to her shoulders seemed to highlight her almond-colored complexion. She was young and he would probably put her age at midtwenties.

There was something uniquely sexy about her. It didn't help matters that she was standing under one of the bright ceiling lights and the beam seemed to highlight every single seductive thing about her...and yes, she did look seductive. Sensuously so.

Suddenly she glanced over at him and her smile widened, catching him off guard and making his pulse quicken. She was even more beautiful than he'd initially thought. Especially since he was getting a better view of full shapely lips and a gorgeous pair of brown eyes. A slow-moving stir was taking place in the pit of his stomach.

Could it be because he hadn't had sex in a while? He thought it over. The last time would have been over ten months ago—right after the election—when he'd successfully ignored Audria's attempts to resume their "lovers only" arrangement.

He studied the woman's features again, almost convinced he knew her from somewhere. Had they met before? On the campaign trail, perhaps? Evidently, she possibly thought the same thing because he saw a flash of recognition in her eyes.

She left the production assistant and walked over to him. He stood upon her approach and when she reached him, she extended her hand. "Senator Malone, I'm not sure if you remember me."

He tilted his head, wondering how any man could forget a woman who looked like her. "Your face looks familiar, but I just can't place you at the moment."

She chuckled. Roman thought even the sound of her soft laugh was sexy. "It's been years so let me help. Your godparents, Jonathan and Marilyn Madaris, are my uncle and aunt. I'm Victoria Madaris."

The moment she'd mentioned the name Madaris, he knew he'd seen her before. Probably at one of his godparents' parties or cookouts. But that had to be quite some time ago. She was right. It had been *years*.

"Of course. I remember you now. And you're right, it's been years," he said, finally releasing her hand.

"Yes, probably not since I was in my teens. Over the last few years, I was away at college a lot, getting both bachelor's and master's degrees at Oklahoma and Florida. And when my uncle Jake and aunt Diamond held a fundraiser for you last year, I was out of the country. I heard it was a success and congratulations on being reelected to your senate seat."

He liked the sound of her voice. "Thanks. You work here?"

"Yes. I've been here for almost two years now. I'm one of the hosts of the noonday show, *Talk It Up*. How are your parents and your sisters?"

"Everyone is doing fine. I saw the folks last week and I hope to see Erika and the twins, Spring and Summer, over the holidays. They're coming home for Christmas. How is your family?"

"As far as I know, all the Madarises are great. I saw your parents at Aunt Marilyn and Uncle Jonathan's last Christmas party."

He nodded. "I haven't attended one in a couple of years. I was hoping to attend the last one, but the senate had a special session that lasted through most of the holidays."

"I understand. The one in December was the first I'd attended since leaving home for college. I was lucky and got a college roommate who enjoyed traveling as much as I did. We used our time out of school around the holidays to travel." She chuckled and then added, "My family threatened to disown me if I didn't start coming home more often."

"Don't feel bad because I love traveling, as well. Now as an elected official, I don't get to do it as often, but I plan to get away for three weeks. My political manager found me a quiet place not far from here. A coastal town called Catalina Cove."

"You'll be in Catalina Cove for three weeks?"

"Yes, but I'm not telling a lot of people. I need some

R and R so I'm keeping it on the down low. You've heard of the place?"

"Yes, in fact I live there. I stumbled on to it when I covered their seafood festival a couple of years ago and loved it. I decided it was worth the hour drive into work every day and was lucky enough to find a place to rent that was perfect for me."

"How long have you lived there?"

"I moved in right before Christmas last year."

He nodded. "Is the town as nice as my political manager claims?"

"Yes. I am definitely Team Catalina Cove. The people are friendly and respect a person's privacy. So even if you are recognized, they will understand your desire to be left alone. And if you're someone who likes to fish, which I am, then you'll—"

"You like to fish?" he asked, surprised. Most women didn't.

"I go fishing every chance I get, which means when I'm not working or sleeping, I'm on the dock with my pole. I'm Nolan Madaris Junior's daughter, and I got to go on all Dad's fishing trips with my brothers. Fishing relaxes me."

Roman smiled. "It relaxes me as well, and I definitely need some relax time. Things have been crazy in DC."

"Do tell. I've noticed the politicians have a lot going on."

The politicians? "You say it like *politicians* is a bad word."

She shrugged. "Wish I could apologize, but I can't. They're not my favorite people. No offense, Senator."

"None taken, but one day you'll have to tell me why."

"Maybe one day I will." She glanced at her watch. "I need to go to a meeting. Good luck on your interview, and maybe I'll see you around in the cove. It was nice seeing you again."

"It was nice seeing you again, as well, Victoria."

Roman watched as she hurried off and noticed that she had an eye-popping walk in those stilettos. It was only when she rounded the corner and was no longer in sight that his heart stopped racing.

"They'll be ready for you in five minutes, Senator Malone. Do you need anything?"

The perky production assistant's question intruded into his thoughts. It was on the tip of his tongue to tell the woman that a cold shower would be nice right about now. Instead he said, "I'd like a glass of water, please."

"Will a bottle of water be okay?"

"Sure."

He watched her walk off, thinking she didn't have that seductive bounce in her step like Victoria Madaris had. And there was no sway in her hips, either. He could tell Victoria's walk wasn't done to intentionally grab anyone's attention. It just came naturally to her.

Just to think of all the Christmas parties Marilyn and Jonathan had given that he'd missed. He could easily envision what might have happened had their paths crossed at one of them. He would have definitely asked her out. But then, hadn't she said she'd missed a number of those parties herself? Obviously, it hadn't been meant for them to meet again until now.

"Here you are, Senator." The production assistant handed him the bottled water.

"Thanks." He unscrewed the top and took a long swig. He glanced at the woman and saw her watching him. "Is anything wrong?" He racked his brain trying to recall her name and was glad when he finally remembered it. "Terica?"

She quickly shook her head. "No, there's nothing wrong. And they are ready for you now, Senator."

Senator. A number of people addressed him as such, and he was okay with it. But for some reason he hadn't cared much for it when Victoria Madaris had done so. If their paths crossed while he was in Catalina Cove, he would make sure she called him by his given name, Roman. For some strange reason he wanted to hear her say his name.

The production assistant broke in to his thoughts. "Senator Malone? Please follow me."

He followed her, and a part of him wished he'd been following Victoria Madaris instead.

VICTORIA LEFT THE meeting she'd had with her boss to find several people—all women—gathered around one of the television monitors mounted on the wall. "What's going on?" she asked Bronwyn Lewis, the producer of the evening news show.

"Take a look."

She glanced up at the monitor. Senator Roman Malone was being interviewed by Norma Roadie, the person who'd replaced Victoria on the morning talk show, *Hello, New Orleans.* She liked Norma and was glad Mr. Richards had acted on her recommendation for Norma to replace her.

"That man is definitely good-looking," one of the women said. "Hell, I would have voted for him just on looks alone."

"Hey, don't forget his body. He is so friggin' built. Why is he still single?" another woman asked.

"You should have seen how he drank water straight from the bottle. It was such a turn-on," Terica added. "He caught me staring."

Victoria said nothing as she stared at the monitor like everyone else. They were right—Roman Malone was good-looking. She had noticed that right away, even before Terica had told her who he was. He had looked familiar, but she couldn't place him at first. And just to think their families were close. Small world. How long had it been since she'd seen him? She was certain the last time she'd been in her teens and wearing braces.

"Don't tell us he has you speechless, as well," Roxanne Chambers said to her, grinning. "Too speechless to answer my question."

Victoria turned her attention to Roxanne. "Sorry, what did you ask?"

"I wanted to know what you thought of his body?"

Victoria glanced back at the screen, as if she needed to check it out again in order to give her opinion. "It's nice."

"Nice? Is that all you have to say?"

"Yes, that's about it." She definitely didn't want to say that in addition to how great he looked in his suit, the senator had smelled good, as well. Then they would want to know how she'd managed to get close enough to get a whiff of him.

"We know you don't care for politicians, Victoria, but even you have to admit Senator Roman Malone is one handsome man. I wonder if he has a steady girl."

Victoria ignored the conversation around her as she kept her attention on Senator Malone. Unlike the others, who were ogling his body and wondering about his love life, she was listening to the way he was handling the interview and what he was saying. He was definitely a charmer and was even answering questions that the last politician they'd had on this show had evaded. Roman had no problem stating his opinion on any subject Norma asked him about, regardless of whether his position was a popular one or not. She liked that. She also liked that most of his positions reflected hers.

She also liked that he looked directly at the person he was taking to. So many times, people would look at the camera, as if they wanted to make sure they were seen.

"Well, his interview is almost over," Terica said, grinning. "I think I'll just wait out here in the hall, just in case he needs something else."

Victoria rolled her eyes. Sometimes it amused her how women could get carried away at the sight of a good-looking man. Looks were good but they weren't everything. She much preferred a man who not only looked good, but *was* also good character-wise.

She had grown up surrounded by good-looking men. So much that in some cases their looks had gone to their heads. At least her brother Nolan was no longer out there, but she didn't want to think of the number of other single Madaris men still left in her generation.

Deciding to leave the gathering and go to her office to get prepared for her noonday show, she said, "Well, I'll be going to—"

"So the two of you do know each other." Terica presented it as a statement rather than a question.

Victoria noticed it got quiet and all eyes were on her. Leave it to Terica to share that with everyone. "Yes, our families are close. My uncle and aunt are his godparents. However, I haven't seen him in years, which is why I didn't recognize him."

"So you never had a crush on him or anything while growing up?" Monica, the meteorologist, asked.

"Nope. To be honest, while growing up, good-looking guys turned me off. I was surrounded by too many of them."

They all nodded since they'd met her brothers and a few of her cousins when they had helped her move from New Orleans to Catalina Cove. "I'll see you guys later. I need to get ready for the noon show."

Before walking off, Victoria glanced back at the monitor. She was glad the others had returned their gazes to the screen, as well. Otherwise, they would have seen her drool when she caught sight of Senator Malone smiling. He had such a gorgeous smile and it matched the rest of him. The man was simply eye candy in a suit.

As she headed to her office, she found it strange that she felt a tingling sensation in her stomach when she thought about the senator. However, whenever she thought about Tanner Jamison, she felt nothing at all.

CHAPTER FOUR

Two days. That was all it took for Roman to conclude he was in paradise. There was no other way to describe Catalina Cove, the quaint shipping town located on the Gulf and surrounded by the Moulden River, Lafitte Harbor and other waterways in between. The August weather was beautiful—sunny through the days with a little breeze off the water in the evenings. Each morning, he awoke to see the sunrise over the Gulf, and then in the evenings, he had a front row seat for the sunset.

From the locals, he'd learned the parcel of land the cove sat on had been a gift from the US government to the notorious pirate Jean Lafitte for his help in the fight for independence from the British during the War of 1812. Some people didn't believe Lafitte was buried at sea in the Gulf of Honduras like history claimed, but that he was buried somewhere in the waters surrounding Catalina Cove. Due to Lafitte's influence, the cove had become a shipping town. It still was, which was evident by the number of fishing vessels that lined the piers in what was known as the shipping district. The Moulden River was full of trout, whiting, shrimp and oysters. Locals boasted that tourists would come from miles around to sample the town's seafood, especially the oysters.

Mint had known exactly what he needed and had delivered. A gorgeous forty-foot yacht that was docked in the perfect location was his exclusively for three weeks. He took it out both days and appreciated that the weather had been great and the fishing even greater. He returned in the evening and discovered there was always something to do in the marina. There were numerous restaurants, game rooms, a coffee shop and a variety of other shops to patronize. The distance between each slip was ample, so each boater had the space and privacy they needed. That also made leaving and returning the boat to the pier easier.

The refrigerator and pantry had been packed with food items Mint knew he liked. For the past two days, Roman had lived the life of a sea bum, and hadn't even bothered to shave. He was enjoying being alone in his element doing nothing. He hadn't known just how much he'd needed this time to just chill. Yesterday he'd gone to one of the restaurants to pick up his dinner and had roamed around. He noticed the locals respected his privacy. He was here for R and R. The last thing he wanted to do was talk politics. Then again, there was a chance no one had recognized him because of the beard. Whatever the reason, it was nice not to have a slew of reporters on his heels.

The boat had both upper and lower decks, as well as a main cabin. The main cabin was too luxurious for words. Covered in marble flooring, there was a spacious bedroom and a small galley, a sitting room, an eating area and a nice-size bathroom with a shower. Everything was just the right size for a crew of four, with all the amenities.

The one thing he hadn't planned to do while he was here was watch television. He figured that he could keep up with the news on his cell phone. However, he hadn't been able to resist the temptation to turn it on at noon to watch Victoria Madaris's hour-long talk show.

Seeing her on the show sparked a fire within him. Not

everybody looked good on camera, but she did. He thought the other two ladies looked good, as well, but his focus was on Victoria. She had a way of relaxing her guest and not making them feel intimidated, even when he figured she didn't agree with what the person was saying.

At the end of his second full day in Catalina Cove, Roman was sitting on the upper deck of the boat, drinking a beer and looking out across the water after watching a spectacular sunset. Moments later, his attention was drawn away when he saw a woman strolling on the boardwalk beneath a cloudless evening sky.

Victoria Madaris.

Dressed comfortably for the weather in a pair of blue shorts and white tank top, it appeared she was headed to one of the restaurants lining the pier. The moment he caught sight of her, he felt his blood surge. He thought the same thing now that he'd thought when he'd watched her earlier—she was an absolutely beautiful woman. He'd been in the company of beautiful women before, but there was something about her that kept him spellbound.

He had hoped to see her that day after his interview, but hadn't. When he'd asked the production assistant about Victoria, he'd been told she was preparing for her noonday show. He had regretted leaving without seeing that smile and dimples.

As he continued to watch her stroll along the pier, he wondered if she was involved with anyone, and figured she probably was. She was so beautiful that she had to be involved with someone, seriously or otherwise. He saw her stop to chat with several people and concluded that she was definitely the friendly type.

When she began walking again, he felt what seemed to be an awakening in the lower part of his stomach with every step she took. The very sensation unnerved him because lusting after a woman was definitely not something he had time for. He needed to rest and relax, because when he returned to the nation's capital, he would be busier than ever.

But still...

Roman watched her walk into Lafitte Seafood House and slowly returned his gaze back to the water. Moments later, he glanced at his watch. He hadn't eaten dinner yet and figured now was just as good a time as any to do so. And a seafood dinner sounded pretty darn good about now.

He knew the only reason he suddenly had a taste for seafood was because of that restaurant Victoria Madaris had walked into. That was fine, he thought as he stood. He would call himself all kinds of fool later. Right now, he didn't want to be alone in his element. He wanted to share it. And with her.

It then occurred to him that she might be meeting someone for dinner. If that was the case, then he would not intrude. If it wasn't, then today would definitely be his lucky day.

"I ENJOYED TODAY'S SHOW, Victoria."

"Thanks," Victoria responded to Neil Surrey, the owner of Lafitte Seafood House, as she looked around for a vacant spot. "You're busy today."

"Yes, we are. A lot of people are in town for the wedding of Nina Murray and Arnett Staples. They both grew up in the cove and moved away after college," Neil explained. "Last Christmas they came back to their high school reunion and have been a couple ever since."

"Oh, that's wonderful." When she saw a couple leaving their table, she said, "I think I'll grab that table in the back, Neil."

"Go ahead and get seated. I'll send a busboy over to clear off the table."

A short while later one of the busboys had cleaned off the table and a waitress handed her a menu. She liked coming here and was glad Bryce had recommended it to her when she'd first moved to town. This was one of her weekly drop-ins, and she'd gotten to know a few of the regulars.

Instead of studying the menu to see what she would eat today, her thoughts shifted to Senator Malone. Had he gotten settled in? She wondered if he was staying at Shelby by the Sea, the beautiful inn that sat on the Gulf. That would make perfect sense if he was, since he'd indicated he liked to fish.

She couldn't help but recall how good he'd looked that day at the television station. Several of the women were still talking about his visit. She wasn't talking about it, but she was still thinking about it. She'd even downloaded the interview to watch the entire episode and had enjoyed it. Judging by the number of calls the station had received from viewers, he'd been a favorite that day. Out of curiosity, she'd done her research and saw that he was well-liked among other politicians and his constituents.

Her thoughts shifted yet again, this time to Tanner. She'd honestly expected him to have connected with her for that rain check to dinner by now. It had been a little over a week. She knew exactly where the nightclub he was renovating was located and had been tempted to stop by to see if he was there, say hello and ask to look around.

But then she figured doing such a thing would make it seem as if she was chasing after him, when she wasn't. If Mama Laverne was right—and there was no reason to think she wasn't—he would eventually come around. And like Christy said, she had to be patient.

"The place is packed and there's not a vacant table. Mind if I join you?"

Victoria looked up to find Senator Roman Malone—at least she thought it was him. Gone was the clean-shaven, suit-wearing, suave and charismatic senator of a few days ago. Standing at her table was an unshaven man dressed in jeans and sporting a Houston Astros T-shirt. If you put a bandanna on his head and a loop earring in his ear, he could pass for a pirate. Why did this man have to be so breathtaking, even when he looked like a ruffian?

She deliberately broke eye contact with him. It was either that or let him see feminine interest in her gaze. Glancing around, she noticed that even more people were there than when she'd arrived. Returning her gaze to his, she said, "Yes, of course. I was lucky to get this booth when I did."

"Thanks."

She watched how he eased into the booth seat and wasn't prepared for the jolt of lust that raced through her. Where did such a thing come from and why was it affecting her with this man and not Tanner? Swallowing, she looked up to find him staring at her. Why? Had he said something and was waiting for a response from her? "Did you say something?"

He smiled as he shook his head. "No, and I apologize for staring. I was just thinking how much you and Christy resemble each other."

His words reminded her that Christy was his godsister. "People tell me that all the time. Only thing missing on my end is the red hair."

"True, but I think your brown hair is pretty."

She thought that was a nice thing to say. "Thanks, Senator."

He leaned across the table and in a low voice said, "For

the next three weeks I'm here to rest and relax so can we forget the 'Senator'? I prefer if you call me by my first name."

"Roman."

"Yes, that's me. That's also my dad, which is why some people call me RJ. I'll let you decide which you prefer."

"I like Roman."

He nodded. "Then Roman it is."

She decided she liked him, even if he was a politician. At that moment, a waitress brought him a menu and a glass of water. It was then that he glanced back over at her and asked, "What are you having?"

She picked up her menu and realized that after all this time she hadn't really looked at it to decide what she wanted. But she already had an idea. Placing it down, she said, "I got a taste for crab cakes tonight."

He nodded. "Are they good here?"

"Yes, they are delicious."

"Then I think I'll get the crab cakes, too," he said, smiling.

"You get to choose two sides with it."

His smile widened. "And what two sides are you getting?"

"Fries and slaw."

"That's sounds good to me, as well."

"You won't go wrong," she said.

"I'll take your word for it."

When he set aside his menu and began drinking his water, Victoria decided Terica had been right. There was something sexy about the way he drank water. Was it the way his throat muscles moved, working in unison with his mouth? Or was it the way his lips hugged the rim of the glass? She wasn't sure what it was, but it was definitely arousing.

Arousing? Yes, to her dismay, she found it pretty darn arousing to sit across from him and watch. Now she wondered how it would be when he ate his food. Would it have the same effect? For crying out loud, she did not understand her strange reaction to him. And she wasn't imagining it. Not when she was beginning to feel hot all over.

Quickly taking a sip of her own water, she decided to ask him about his accommodations. "So are you staying at Shelby by the Sea or an Airbnb while in the cove?"

He placed his glass down and looked at her. "Neither. I'm renting a yacht."

"A yacht?"

"Yes, and it's docked right off the marina—" he nodded in the direction of the pier "—and has everything I need. A spacious bedroom, bath with shower, galley and sitting area. However, my favorite spot is topside."

"I can imagine. Have you gone out in it?"

"I arrived two days ago and went out both days. You were right. Catalina Cove is a nice place. Quiet and quaint. Somehow it's been able to retain its small-town charm."

Victoria's lips stretched into a big smile. "You can thank Reid Lacroix for that."

"Who?"

"Reid Lacroix," she said. "He's one of the wealthiest men in town and owns the blueberry plant that employs a lot of people. I understand he stopped a multimillion-dollar tennis resort from setting down roots here. I'm told he hates change and has worked with the zoning board to block a lot of the new, more progressive developments from coming to town. His goal is to keep Catalina Cove as a small town. He doesn't mind the tourists—he just doesn't want large businesses coming in and overtaking all the mom-and-pop establishments. Some of those businesses have been here for generations."

He nodded. "You seem to know a lot about it."

"Only because I covered their seafood festival one year. It was my first time here and I was amazed by how this town was such a well-kept secret, free from rampant commercialism. I asked several locals about it. People around here see Reid as a hero for his vision to retain a small-town atmosphere. He's always looking out for the local business owners, making sure big businesses don't shoulder their way in and eventually shut down the smaller establishments."

They stopped talking when the waitress arrived to take their order. When she left, he asked, "When was the last time you saw Christy?"

"A little over a week ago. She was in New Orleans for a journalism conference. I talked her into staying the last night here with me in the cove and we had breakfast the next morning at Witherspoon Café. She fell in love with their blueberry muffins."

"The blueberry muffins are good there?"

"Yes, you've got to try them. Catalina Cove is considered the blueberry capital of the world. The blueberry plant ships berries all over the nation and abroad."

He nodded. "Do you eat at that café often?"

"I grab breakfast there a lot. Now that I do the noonday show I don't have to be at the station as early. That's how I got to meet so many of the locals. A number of them go to the café for breakfast, lunch and dinner. It's a nice place. You need to eat there at least once before you leave."

He smiled. "I think I will."

After taking another sip of water, she asked him, "When was the last time you saw Christy?"

"At that fundraiser Jake gave me at his ranch last year. Before that, I hadn't seen her or Alex for a couple years. Of course, I've been keeping up with her through Mom and Marilyn. I understand she has three kids now."

"Yes, she does, and it wouldn't surprise me if they want a fourth."

"She always said she wanted a big family," Roman said.

He was right. Christy always said that. "You've gone fishing both days since you've been here. How's the fishing going?"

"Great. I toss them back."

"And then you catch those same ones the next day," she said in amusement.

He laughed. "You're probably right, but it wasn't nice of you to point that out, Victoria."

Victoria's breath caught in her throat. There was just something sexy about the way he said her name. Sexy, just like the rest of him. Now she was reacting to him like the women in her office had. But then, could she really fault herself when he was so darn sexy? Still, her reaction bothered her.

"Just keeping you honest, Roman," she teased.

He leaned back in his seat. "And speaking of honest, would you like to tell me what you have against politicians?"

CHAPTER FIVE

ROMAN HADN'T BEEN able to believe his luck when he'd walked into the restaurant, found it packed and spotted Victoria sitting alone. When he'd asked to join her, she hadn't suspected that she was the reason he'd come here. He wasn't sure why of all the women he knew, he was so fiercely attracted to her, but he was.

"It has to do with Christy."

Her words drew his attention. "You have something against politicians because of Christy?"

"Yes."

She obviously saw the bewilderment on his face, because she added, "Remember that time she was kidnapped?"

He definitely did. A few years ago, Christy had been working as an investigative reporter and had exposed an international human-trafficking ring mostly run by US politicians. If it hadn't been for a family friend, Sheik Rasheed Valdemon, and Christy's husband, Alex, Christy would have been a victim herself.

"Yes, I remember," he said.

"It's truly somewhat of a miracle how things turned out," Victoria said. "Not only did she get the blockbuster story she went after, but she brought down an international human-trafficking ring that saved a lot of teenagers' lives. If you recall, there were several politicians involved."

"There were," he said. "I won't lie and say those senators involved didn't give politicians a bad name, but they weren't the only ones, Victoria. There were several businessmen involved, as well. Not only that, a few members of the clergy were arrested, too."

She didn't say anything, and he hoped he had gotten her to thinking. He was thinking, as well, but no longer about Christy's abduction. At that moment, he was struck by how the lamp on their table illuminated her features, making her even more beautiful.

She looked up at him and frissons of heat raced up his spine as he gazed into her dark brown eyes. "All you've said is true, but my opinion about politicians won't change overnight, Roman."

He liked the way she said his name, even when it came with a warning. "I understand and don't expect it to. All I can ask is that you not lump all politicians in the same bag. You know Senator Lansing, right?"

"Of course. He's married to Aunt Diana, so I consider him my uncle."

"Do you think of Nedwyn as corrupt?"

"No."

"There you have it. As you can see, there are honorable politicians, just like Nedwyn. I hope you don't see me as one of the bad ones."

She shrugged what he thought was a pair of beautiful shoulders. "I have no reason to think you are. But then, although I've always known who you were, I've never really gotten to know you."

He nodded. "I was just thinking the same thing about you. I've always known who you were, but my association with the Madaris family was limited to Jonathan and Marilyn's kids, your brothers and male cousins." He paused a moment and then said, "I know a way to remedy that."

She lifted an eyebrow. "How?"

"I suggest we spend time together while I'm in Catalina Cove to get to know each other."

VICTORIA HEARD WHAT Roman was saying and wasn't sure that was a good idea. Shouldn't she be concentrating on Tanner, and getting to know him better? But how was she supposed to do that when Tanner obviously wasn't concentrating on her? He still hadn't called for that rain check dinner.

"To get to know each other as friends?" she asked for clarification.

"Yes, of course," Roman said. "What other reason would there be?"

Now she felt embarrassed for having thought there could be anything else. From his bemused expression, there was no telling what he was thinking, and she felt maybe she should explain. "Sorry, but I had to ask because I'm promised to someone."

She saw him glance down at her hand before lifting his eyebrows. "You're engaged?"

She shook her head. "Not exactly. This guy and I were promised to each other."

Roman's brow furrowed. "Are you saying you've agreed to an arranged marriage or something?"

She figured he was even more confused. "Not exactly an arranged marriage, but he's someone my great-grandmother has chosen for me."

"Oh, I see."

Clearly, he'd heard of her great-grandmother's match-making shenanigans. It didn't surprise her since he was close to members of her family who would have enlightened him.

"Well, let me assure you, Victoria, that I'm here for rest and relaxation, not romantic entanglements. I just figured since we both know of each other, but never got around to really getting to know each other, now would be a good time."

He took another sip of water and then said, "Besides, I figured as a family friend, who's also a politician, I could get you to see that not all politicians are bad."

"I don't think they're all bad. And just so you know, you did get my vote last November. My family thinks highly of you."

"I appreciate that."

"There's something else that bothers me about politicians," she said, deciding to open up.

He gave her a quizzical look. "And what's that?"

"Their celebrity status. I know some who are followed about like they are the president himself. The paparazzi can be brutal and inconsiderate. You're one of the popular ones, so I'm surprised they aren't following you around now."

"The senate is on break, and they assume I'm resting on my ranch in Texas."

"Well, I don't see how you can tolerate it."

He shrugged. "It's all part of the career I've chosen. The media in some cases can be a necessary pain in the ass, but you learn how to grin and bear it."

He then asked, "What about you? I'm sure your face is recognizable since you're a television personality."

"Yes, but it's a local station and the show isn't even in syndication. New Orleans and Catalina Cove are the only parishes that can watch the show. So if I travel to Shreveport or Baton Rouge, no one will recognize me, thank goodness. I detest being in the limelight and don't see how you can deal with it."

"Like I said, you learn to grin and bear it."

"Well, that might work for you, but it wouldn't for me. I can only admire your tolerance for such things. I know how brutal the paparazzi can be." She paused a moment, then said, "They are the reason Jake and Diamond kept their marriage a secret for so long. Then there was the time they badgered Clayton's wife, Syneda, when it became known that Syntel Remington was her father. And when it was discovered that Skye's father was Senator Ryan Baines, they practically tried storming the Madaris Building to get a story." Skye was married to Blade's twin brother, Slade.

"Yet you became a news reporter," he said, as if pointing that out to her.

"I consider myself a journalist who reports the facts. Not a sleazebag reporter who distorts them. I offer accurate information, not sensationalism."

"Point taken."

They paused their conversation as the waitress delivered their food.

"Now, back to us getting to know each other," Roman said. "I just thought we could do what we're doing now—enjoy dinner or breakfast and talk. I'd love to catch up on how your brothers and cousins are doing. I haven't seen or talked to them in a while. And you did say you like to fish. Right?"

Victoria grinned. "Yes, I did say that."

"Tomorrow is Saturday. Do you have any plans?"

She shook her head. "No."

"Then how would you like to go fishing with me?"

"And recatch those fish you tossed out today."

He chuckled. "Hey, watch it."

Victoria chuckled, as well, enjoying his company. She

hadn't planned on doing anything tomorrow but lounge around and read a mystery novel. She smiled over at him and said, "I'd love to go fishing with you."

CHAPTER SIX

JUST LIKE THE day before, Roman was on the upper deck and caught sight of Victoria on the pier. He watched as she strolled toward his yacht. This time she was wearing a pair of jeans and a tank top, with a baseball cap on her head and a fishing pole in her hand. He thought she looked absolutely adorable.

The sun wasn't even in the sky but that didn't matter. She was bringing her own brand of sunshine with her, a brilliance that was shining all over the place. At least he thought so. Just from talking to her over dinner last night, he got the impression she was a rarity among women. A woman who was honest and expected honesty in return.

Like when she'd told him she was *promised* to someone, so he wouldn't be wasting his time if he wanted more than friendship. He was glad she'd been up front about that, especially when he was attracted to her. Every time she'd smiled last night and flashed those dimples, it had done something to him. Just watching her walk toward his boat, he felt a sexual hunger stirring to life in his lower region.

It was something he intended to get over. He'd meant what he'd said when he'd told her he was here for rest and relaxation and nothing more. Definitely not romance. But he did want to get to know her better. Why, he wasn't sure. He just knew that he did.

He knew the exact moment she saw him. She smiled

and he couldn't help but return it. Her smile caused desire to throb deep within him. When she threw up her hand in a wave, he waved back. He knew that somehow, today he had to focus his attention on fishing and not on her. Maybe it hadn't been a good idea to invite her. But then he had a feeling he would have spent the entire day thinking about her if he hadn't.

"Good morning, Roman," she greeted when she reached his boat.

He quickly moved to help her board. Extending his hand out to her, something happened the moment their hands touched. A charge sliced through him and he almost snatched his hand back. He quickly glanced at her at the same moment she drew in a sharp breath, which meant she had felt it, as well.

Trying to downplay what had just happened, he said, "Good morning, Victoria. Welcome aboard." The moment her feet stepped on the deck, he swiftly removed his hand from hers.

"Thanks. I hope I'm not too early for you."

"No, you're right on time. The sun hasn't quite come up."

"Good. I get to see the sunrise on the ocean this morning," she said excitedly. "Usually, I just see it peeking through the apple trees."

He lifted an eyebrow. "Apple trees?"

She smiled up at him. "Yes, the house I'm leasing backs up to an apple grove. I don't wake up to the smell of the ocean but of apples."

"Apples are delicious."

"Yes, and I love them. And what's really nice is the owner of the grove has given his permission for me to pick as many as I want. So now I have apples each day. I brought you a few," she said, taking off her backpack and pulling out two beautiful red apples.

"Thanks. And I got you something, as well," he said.

"What?"

"These," he said, grabbing a bag off the table.

She peeked inside and then flashed what he thought was one dazzling smile. "Blueberry muffins? From the Witherspoon Café?"

"Yes. I checked out the place on my laptop last night and saw they opened as early as five in the morning."

"And you went and got them?"

"Yes, I went and got them, along with coffee."

"Now aren't you a sweetheart," she said as he handed her a cup of coffee.

He chuckled. "I do my best. Come on. We can eat below before we take off. The Witherspoons were also kind enough to prepare us a box lunch."

"Hey, you thought of everything," she said, following him down the stairs. "So you got to meet the Witherspoons?"

"Yes, even with my less-than-polished look, the owner recognized me but promised not to make a big deal of my presence in the cove."

"That was nice of him, but since moving to town I've discovered the Witherspoons are nice people. Their daughter, Bryce, got married earlier this year. She's the local Realtor and the one who found the rental property for me."

When they reached the main cabin, she glanced around. He could tell from the look on her face that she was impressed. "Nice yacht, Roman. I love the setup."

"Thanks. I think I'll keep Mint around after all."

"Your political manager?"

"Yes."

"You were actually thinking of firing the guy?"

Seeing her serious expression, he wanted to assure her that wasn't the case. "Not hardly. Mint Stover and I have been a team since our college days at Harvard. He always said if I ever ran for public office that he would be my campaign manager. Mint does a great job, although sometimes he does get carried away with how he wants to direct my future."

She nodded as she followed him to the table. Glancing over his shoulder at her, their gazes met. He couldn't stop the electrical current that passed through him. He figured she had to have felt it, too. They could either ignore it or address it. It seemed she planned to ignore it, so he thought it would be best to follow her lead.

The last thing he needed was to become involved with a woman, no matter what advice the senate majority leader had given him. When he'd met with Senator Lansing, he'd pretty much agreed with Roman. When and if he ever decided to marry it should be for love and not politics. Roman was glad his mentor felt that way because he wasn't in a hurry to make any woman the future Mrs. Roman Malone.

However, he would admit there was something going on with him and Victoria. There was an attraction—he knew that, but he wasn't sure that was all there was. But then what more could there be? Hadn't she told him yesterday that she was promised to someone? He'd heard about her great-grandmother's matchmaking schemes from her brothers and cousins.

It just so happened that Felicia Laverne Madaris was also good friends with his father's sister, his aunt Nora. It seemed the old lady had a pretty good track record for getting people together. He wondered what kind of man she had chosen for Victoria.

"Thanks for breakfast, Roman."

He slid into the chair across from her. How could a woman who was about to spend the day fishing smell so good? "It's the least I could do since you might have a disappointing day."

She cocked an eyebrow. "You don't think I'll be able to catch anything?"

A smile touched his lips. "I'm keeping my opinions to myself."

"That might be best," she said, smiling back.

He tried not to stare when she bit into her muffin and then used her tongue to lick a crumb off her top lip. Hearing her moan afterward didn't help, either. "This muffin is so good."

Roman forced his heart rate to slow. Otherwise he might have a heart attack. She was affecting him just that much. He had to get a grip. He wasn't a man who lost his focus for any reason. But then there was a reason—a real good reason—and she was sitting across from him. "Glad you like it."

"Like it? I love it."

He wondered what else she loved. For some reason he was goaded into finding out. "Tell me about this guy you're 'promised' to. How does he feel about it?"

The sound of her chuckle seemed to float across him like he figured the caress of her hand would have done. "He doesn't know it yet. But then again, he might have figured things out, which is why he hasn't called for our rain check."

"Your rain check?"

"Yes, we ran in to each other over a week ago. He asked me to dinner, but I couldn't go because Christy was in town. He and I agreed on a rain check and exchanged phone numbers. He hasn't called."

In a way Roman was glad he hadn't. He then pondered what she'd said, which propelled him to ask about it. "You're promised to a man you don't know that well?"

She looked at him. "What gave you that idea?"

He took a sip of coffee, then shrugged. "You said you ran in to him and the two of you exchanged numbers."

"Only because Tanner and I never had a reason to have each other's phone numbers. Tanner Jamison. Do you know him?"

Roman shook his head. "No."

"I thought maybe you did since he's a good friend of Blade's. In fact, Blade, Tanner and Wyatt Bannister are thick as thieves."

Nodding, Roman said, "I know Wyatt Bannister very well since he's Marilyn's nephew. A lot of summers that I spent in Houston with Jonathan and Marilyn while growing up would often include Wyatt. He also lived in San Antonio, not far from my grandparents' home. Whenever I visited them, I got to spend time with Wyatt, as well. However, I don't recall ever meeting any friend of his and Blade's named Tanner Jamison."

Victoria nodded. "Probably because Blade, Wyatt and Tanner became close friends during their college years."

She then took a small bite of her muffin and added, "I'm sure Tanner assumed it was a coincidence that we ran in to each other at that bakery last week, but now I know our paths would have crossed eventually."

"Why do you think that?"

She licked a crumb from her lips again before leaning over the table. "Because we're dealing with my great-grandmother, Felicia Laverne Madaris. She never leaves anything to chance. Tanner told me she suggested he look me up when he got to New Orleans. And then she gave both of us gift cards to Susan's Bakery, the very place where I happened to run in to him. That's a clear sign of her handiwork."

Roman sipped his coffee. "You're not bothered that your great-grandmother is doing that? Selecting a man for you?"

"No. I'm going to tell you the same thing I told Nolan when he called to warn me after finding out I was next on Mama Laverne's 'marry off' list. I have no problem with our great-grandmother finding a husband for me. It frees up my time in doing so because I know Mama Laverne is going to vet him to the nth degree."

He leaned back in his seat. "So you're looking for a husband?"

She rolled her eyes. "Heck no. A permanent man in my life is the last thing I want now, but if Mama Laverne says I'm next, then I'm not going to buck the idea. She has an astounding track record and I hear about too many women out there who can't find a good man. I'm happy to let her find one for me."

He took another sip of coffee. "Are the people she put together happy?"

"They're extremely happy and in love, but believe me when I say that originally, they were upset with how she did things."

He didn't say anything as he thought about what she'd said. He could understand them being upset about it. Who would want their lives manipulated that way, regardless of the outcome?

He bit into his muffin and instantly decided he liked it. "This is good."

"I told you it was."

A short while later they cleaned up the trash from the table, and were now ready to get the day started. "I'm going to get the boat moving. You might want to join me. The sun will be coming up shortly."

"All right."

As he headed up the steps, he was compelled to look back over his shoulder at her. She was sitting at the table, sipping the last of her coffee with what appeared to be a wistful look on her face. Was she thinking about that guy Tanner? Why did it bother him that there was a good possibility that she was?

"Victoria?"

She glanced up and met his gaze. "Yes?"

"I hope Tanner Jamison is worthy of your affections."

She nodded. "He is. Mama Laverne would not have chosen him for me if he wasn't. She hasn't gone wrong yet."

He came close to telling her that there was a first time for everything, but decided not to. It really wasn't his business and he refused to think about it any longer. Nodding, he turned and went up top.

VICTORIA RELEASED A deep sigh when Roman left. It was hard to ignore the thrumming pulse rushing through her and the flutters that went off in her stomach whenever she was around him. That didn't make sense. How could she be promised to one man, but attracted to another?

She stood, then went to one of the portholes and looked out. It was destined to be a beautiful day and she hoped she wasn't making a mistake by accepting Roman's invitation to go fishing. She was attracted to him but that couldn't be helped. He was such a good-looking man. That couldn't be helped, either, since he looked a lot like his father, and she would have to say Roman Sr. was good-looking, as well.

She'd heard stories of how much of a ladies' man Roman's father used to be before marrying Roman's mother, Traci, who had been her aunt Marilyn's best friend while growing up. Did Roman inherit more than his father's good looks? Did he carry a player card in his wallet like her single brothers and cousins? Like Tanner? What if he did? Didn't he have every right to do so as long as he wasn't hurting anyone? He had told her yesterday that he was not looking for romance with anyone.

She figured any woman he did get serious about would come under close scrutiny with the media, because Roman was a well-respected senator. She'd noted during the television interview that Norma had asked about his future plans; more specifically, if those plans included a bid for the presidency. Instead of evading the question like most politicians would have done, he had given her an honest answer by saying that he had given it some thought, and that if he did such a thing it would be a decade or so away. At present, his main concern was the people of Texas and their welfare.

She thought the presidency was an awesome goal for him to aspire to and hoped he would be careful in choosing a mate. There would be women out there who'd want to be his wife, just so they could wear the title of first lady.

The thought of people using others to propel their own agenda made her think of Karl McDowell. He was the guy she'd dated her second year in college. She had loved Karl and he'd been the first guy she'd ever shared a bed with. He was the first and, so far, the last.

After they'd been seeing each other for about six months, he suggested that she take him home to meet her family over spring break. When she told him she didn't think that was a good idea, trying to spare him the misery of being interrogated by her brothers if she did such a thing, he got upset. In an angry tirade after downing too many beers, he'd admitted his only purpose for dating her was for her family's name. He said her last name of Madaris would open doors for him.

That's when it had become crystal clear that Karl was a man with high ambitions and saw her as nothing more than a meal ticket. She had gone home during that spring break with a broken heart. When she'd returned to campus, Karl had had the nerve to seek her out and asked for another chance, saying he hadn't meant what he'd said to her. She refused to believe him and all his begging and pleading for forgiveness hadn't moved her one iota. Victoria decided then that she wouldn't be so quick to give her heart to another man, and that she would make sure whatever she got in life was because she earned it, and not because of her last name. That was the main reason why, after finishing school, she'd sought a job some place other than Texas, where her family's name was well known.

That's why she had no problem with Mama Laverne finding her a husband. At least he would be vetted thoroughly, and she wouldn't have to worry about future heartbreaks caused by guys like Karl.

She knew Tanner's family—the Jamisons—had just as much money as the Madarises, although they weren't as well-known. Like her uncle Jake, Tanner was in charge of growing his family's wealth through investments, and from what she'd heard, he was good at it.

Not wanting to think of Tanner anymore, her thoughts returned to Roman. She had enjoyed sharing both dinner and breakfast with him, and discovered he was someone she could talk to easily. While waiting for Tanner to come around, it would be nice to have objectivity from a male's perspective, and hopefully, Roman could give her that.

Although she was close to her brothers, she dared not

ask them anything—especially any advice regarding a relationship with a man. The less they knew, the better. However, she had felt comfortable enough with Roman to tell him about Mama Laverne's matchmaking plans for her and Tanner. It had been good talking to someone about it other than Christy.

But then who would give her advice regarding Roman when she knew she was attracted to him? What kind of advice did she really need? She understood the principles of nature. Women were attracted to men and men were attracted to women for different reasons. Roman had a lot of sex appeal, along with a ton of charisma, which made a deadly combination. All she had to do was recall that day when all her female coworkers had surrounded the monitor and drooled.

She decided that if she got to know him better, the attraction would eventually wear off and she would think of him as another big brother.

Victoria glanced at her watch. She had hung back long enough. It was time to go up top. She hoped she would be able to keep the attraction she felt for Roman at bay until it wore off. And she was certain that it would.

CHAPTER SEVEN

FOR THE UMPTEENTH time that day Roman forced his gaze away from Victoria. Had she noticed him staring, she probably would have seen both admiration and attraction in his eyes. Admiration for how well she could handle a fishing rod and bait a hook. She'd caught just as many fish as he had.

Then there was the attraction. He wasn't sure what had gotten to him most—her looks, her smiles, her movements or her talent for conversation, which showed how well-versed she was in a number of subjects. For someone who didn't like politicians, she knew a lot about their world, both domestically and internationally. He actually enjoyed being around her.

Over lunch, she brought him up-to-date on Jonathan and Marilyn's sons and daughters. Although they lived in different cities, while growing up, their sons—Justin, Dex and Clayton, who were also his godbrothers—had been role models for him. Okay, Clayton, maybe not so much since he'd been known as the womanizer in the group. Roman had always liked Justin's easygoing approach to things and Dex's serious side. Dex had a way of letting people know how far to push and if pushed too far that he would push back.

"How are you doing over there? You haven't reeled in anything lately?" she said.

Victoria's question made him glance over and smile. "I don't see how you can talk when I've caught more than you so far."

She rolled her eyes. "The key words are *so far*. Today is still young."

Young? She had to be kidding. It was well past lunch and they'd been out here for close to eight hours. In another couple of hours, it would be time to head back to the pier.

"I meant to tell you earlier, that's a nice fishing rod," Roman said.

She smiled at his compliment. "Thanks. It belonged to my dad, but when he got a new one he gave this to me. He brought it to me when they came to visit a few months ago."

"They come to visit you often?"

She shrugged. "Often enough. Like my brothers, they weren't crazy about me moving away for a job when there are plenty of television stations in Texas. But then I heard the same thing when I left to attend college in Oklahoma— plenty of good schools in Texas. Thankfully, Aunt Marilyn came to my rescue and convinced them they'd been raising boys for so long and how different things were with girls."

He chuckled. "Marilyn's good at that. Forever being a peacemaker and diplomat. I think Justin got that from her."

"I do, too."

At that moment there was a tug on her fishing rod and he knew she'd caught something. Whatever was pulling was big. "What did you have on your hook as bait?"

She glanced at him while balancing her stance to hold tight to her pole. "Shrimp. A large one."

He nodded. He'd had shrimp, worms and minnows, and knew she'd preferred the shrimp. It was obvious this wasn't her first rodeo and he admired her skill as she stood firm and held tight, regardless of the pull on her fishing rod. But then, he couldn't help noticing how she arched her back and balanced her hips, determined not to let her catch get away. Why, at this moment, did he think she looked indisputably sexy as hell? Unmistakably and unequivocally.

When she let out an expletive, he blinked. "Need help reeling it in?" he asked her, placing his own rod aside in case she needed assistance.

"I don't know what I got, Roman, but it's big. It probably made a meal of all those fish you threw back."

"Whatever," he said, moving toward her as she began playing the fish toward the boat. She hadn't said she wanted his help, but he intended to give it to her. It was obvious whatever was on her line would be a challenge.

"I've never caught anything this size before," she finally said. He heard the amazement in her voice.

"You're doing a great job. You didn't play him too long, so he won't be dying from exhaustion."

She glanced at him. "Hey, it better not die. This is going to be our dinner tomorrow."

Our dinner... He liked that she included him in her dinner plans. He went to stand behind her. Not too close but close enough in case he needed to support her weight. She didn't need it, although her backside did brush against his crotch a few times. She probably didn't notice since all her concentration was on the fish...like his should have been.

"Easy," he said as he leaned close to her ear. "Be patient. Keep your line tight. You're doing a great job reeling him to the boat."

"Thanks."

"If you want, I'll land it for you." Moving from behind her, he went to the side of the boat. Leaning over the rail, he grabbed her fishing line and quickly yanked her catch out the water. The fish was a huge, feisty fellow, and using all his strength, Roman swung it onto the boat, making sure it stayed on the hook.

"And I did it!" Victoria said, jumping up and down with excitement. Roman couldn't help but throw his head back and laugh when she began doing a happy dance around the boat. It did something to him to see her so happy, proud and carefree. It felt good seeing a woman who enjoyed fishing as much as he did and was proud of her catch.

"Here, Roman," she said excitedly, her eyes twinkling with merriment as she handed her cell phone to him. I need you to take a picture of me and my fish. My brothers are going to be green with envy and Dad's going to be so proud. This is the biggest fish I've ever caught."

After helping her arrange the huge catch to be proudly displayed, he snapped the picture, definitely enjoying seeing her huge smile, which showed those dimples he loved seeing.

"I have to admit that this is the best-looking red snapper I've ever seen," he said to Victoria as he put the fish on ice in the cooler.

"And I intend for it to be the best tasting. Of course, you're invited to dinner tomorrow."

He grinned and said, "Thanks."

LATER THAT NIGHT, Victoria soaked her achy muscles in a hot bath. Although she enjoyed fishing, she had used muscles she hadn't put to work in a long time. But she had gotten the catch of the day and what a prize it was.

What she appreciated about Roman was that he hadn't been upset because she had caught it instead of him. She used to hate going fishing with her brothers. Just because she was a girl, they acted as if she had limitations. Roman hadn't behaved that way at all. When he'd offered to help, she'd known it was to offer his assistance if she needed it, and not because he thought she couldn't handle doing it herself. Corbin would have stepped in and tried taking over.

Sighing deeply, she dried herself off and quickly put on her nightgown. Deciding to have a cup of tea before bed, she went into the kitchen, opened the cabinet and found the canister her father had put there. It contained the Madaris tea. The special combination of herbs and spices was a secret that could only be shared between the men in the Madaris family, and only after they had reached their thirty-fifth birthday. The secrecy was due to one of her great-grand uncle's ex-wives trying to sell the recipe for profit.

Moments later, the soothing aroma of the tea filled the room. She sat down at the kitchen table to take her first sip when her phone rang. A number of her relatives had called to congratulate her on her big catch after her father had texted around that photo she had sent him.

Victoria smiled when she saw the caller was Christy. Other than a text letting Victoria know she'd gotten back to Houston, due to their busy schedules, she and Christy hadn't communicated since then.

"Hello," she greeted Christy.

"Hello to you, too. I heard you got some fishing time in today. Your dad sent everyone the photo. That fish was a big one."

"Yes, and I plan to cook it tomorrow. I can't wait for Roman to taste it and—"

"Roman? Roman Malone? My godbrother? RJ?"

Victoria chuckled. "Yes, *that* Roman Malone, your godbrother. I ran in to him at the television station when he appeared on one of the morning shows. He barely remembered me, but, of course, he knew my brothers and cousins. Anyway, he mentioned he was taking a month-long vacation in Catalina Cove. I told him that's where I lived."

"The two of you decided to spend some time together while he was there?" Christy asked.

"No. Even though Catalina Cove is a small town, I hadn't even thought about running in to him. But I did last night. We were dining at the same restaurant on the pier. It was packed so we shared a table."

She took a sip of tea and then said, "I mentioned how much I like to fish and he invited me to go out with him on his boat. He's living on a yacht while he's here and it's a beauty."

"Good for him. Mom and Dad have been worried about RJ. He hadn't slowed down since winning that election in November. I know Dad called him a few times to stress that he needed to take time for himself. I'm glad he's doing that, and he loves fishing."

"I'm the one who caught the big one today, but Roman didn't do so bad. We had fun," Victoria said.

"Sounds like it. Have you heard from Tanner?" Christy asked.

"No. I'm trying not to think about him, but it's disappointing that he hasn't called for that rain check and it's been well over a week."

"Well, I might know the reason. Some of the male cousins dropped by today to watch the preseason football game with Alex. I overheard Blade mention that he believes Tanner is the man Mama Laverne has chosen for you. That got some of them, especially your brothers, pretty pissed off since they all know Tanner's reputation with women."

Victoria rolled her eyes. "Like they didn't have a reputation before they settled down...or still have one now."

"Yes," Christy said, laughing. "Anyway, Blade assured them he had taken care of it."

Victoria lifted an eyebrow. "How?"

"By giving Tanner a heads-up on Mama Laverne's shenanigans. Tanner isn't ready to settle down and get married and told Blade that he refuses to be manipulated by anyone and intends to put as much distance between the two of you as possible."

Victoria nervously nibbled on her bottom lip. "What does all this mean?"

"It means the men in our family can be so dense at times. Especially, if they think putting distance between you and Tanner will keep the inevitable from happening. They are dealing with Mama Laverne, who so far has outsmarted them all. I'd like to see how she outsmarts them this time."

Victoria took another sip of tea. "What do you suggest I do? I'm not sure I want a guy who's avoiding me like the plague."

"If you recall, Nolan did the same thing to Ivy and look where it got him. In time, Tanner will come to heel. In the meantime, just enjoy life and don't worry about it. Tanner can only avoid you for so long."

Later that night, as Victoria was lying in bed, she thought about her conversation with Christy. Although she didn't like it, she figured Tanner keeping his distance made sense. She knew she should be patient like her cousin suggested, since it wasn't like she was in a hurry to give up her freedom and fall in love. It was just the thought of another man disappointing her. Karl had wanted her for all the wrong reasons, and Tanner *didn't* want her for all the wrong reasons. Go figure.

Deciding not to lose any sleep over it, she finally closed her eyes and drifted off.

NOT ABLE TO SLEEP, Roman got out of bed and slid into his jeans. He grabbed a beer from the fridge then went to the top deck. The night air felt cool on his naked chest and the scent of the sea was strong. The one thing he regretted was that the condo where he lived in DC was in Dupont Circle and not close to the water. For a man who'd grown up in a house with a lake in his backyard, that had taken some getting used to. That's why every chance he got, he would cross the bridge to the National Harbor on the Potomac River, or take a drive into Maryland and rent a boat to enjoy the Chesapeake Bay. Today he had enjoyed his time in Catalina Cove even more than either of those places.

All because of Victoria.

He smiled when he remembered her happy dance around the boat before he'd snapped the picture of her and that fish she'd caught. He had laughed harder than he had in years. Seeing her happiness and excitement had been contagious. And to think, he had arrived in town determined not to be bothered by anyone. Now he was glad she had kept him company today. She had reminded him how it was to have fun.

He took a slug of his beer and admitted to himself that there was still an attraction between them. It was one he hadn't been able to keep in check like he'd wanted to, but he figured with her being a beautiful woman such a thing couldn't be helped. It was what it was, and he was glad she hadn't brought up the topic of Tanner. For him, the man was out of sight and out of mind. He wondered if it was for her, as well.

Tomorrow they would dine together at her place. After returning to the pier, they had cleaned the fish together and she'd told him to get ready for an awesome meal. He was looking forward to it.

Roman had deliberately sent all his phone calls to voice mail as a way to monitor his incoming calls. There had been no calls from Mint since he'd arrived in Catalina Cove, so that was good. His friend was honoring his request not to be disturbed. However, Audria had been blowing up his phone like crazy. He'd finally listened to one of her numerous messages. She wanted to know where he was and why he hadn't called. Roman wondered what part of the talk they'd had a few months ago she did not understand. There was never an "us" between them. He had made that clear, yet she'd used that word twice in her message.

Shaking his head, he looked back over the Gulf and thought that he could get used to this. A few days spent in the cove and he was spoiled. He didn't want to imagine how things would be for him after a month. Then he would have to return to the rat race of politics in DC. He'd checked his news app every morning, and so far, no one was wondering where he'd taken off to. There had been positive comments about his television interview and that was all. It seemed both the tabloids and mainstream press were on good behavior.

In a way he was grateful. Maybe the press corps had finally accepted that they could leave the politicians they were intent on following, and sometimes harassing, alone. That the public didn't need to know what they did every waking moment, and that there was nothing wrong with letting them have their privacy every once in a while. Doing so wouldn't sell any fewer papers.

He knew the game and had understood it from the day he'd decided to enter politics. But even before that, since his father had been in politics all of Roman's life. Anyone serious about running for office or choosing a life in politics had to put up with the press whether they wanted to or not. It was the nature of the beast. A beast he knew not to fight, but to tolerate.

Tossing his beer can in the recycling container, he decided to return to bed. He wouldn't take the boat out tomorrow. He would do something he rarely did, which was sleep in late. He had something to look forward to when he did wake up.

Dinner with Victoria.

CHAPTER EIGHT

VICTORIA GLANCED ACROSS the table at Roman when he took his first bite. After a moment, she couldn't help herself as she asked, "Well, what do you think?"

He smiled at her. "This is delicious. Can I assume you attended the Felicia Laverne Madaris cooking school like the rest of your cousins?"

She couldn't help but chuckle since it was a known fact that Mama Laverne required all her grands and great-grands to attend her cooking classes. Of course, her male cousins had grumbled about it, but when they'd gotten older and discovered they could impress a woman with their ability to cook, or didn't have to rely on a woman who could cook, they'd counted those cooking classes as a blessing.

"I guess you heard about those cooking classes."

He laughed. "Yes. That's when I appreciated living in Austin and not Houston. I used to hear horror stories about those cooking classes from Clayton."

She rolled her eyes. "Probably because Clayton preferred using that time chasing girls and not learning how to follow a recipe. Personally, I enjoyed them. I learned a lot from her."

"You sure did. Like I said, this delicious. I've had fried fish before but this tastes different."

"I marinated it overnight in Mama Laverne's own special blend of herbs and spices. Trust me when I say Colonel Sanders has nothing on my great-grandmother."

"Is it a secret recipe like the Madaris tea?"

She wasn't surprised he knew about her family's tea. Clayton probably told him about that, as well. "Not that I know of, so if you want the recipe, I don't mind sharing."

"Great. I can pass it on to Rose."

She lifted an eyebrow. "Rose?"

He nodded. "Yes, Rose Solomon. She's been with me for over five years now. She's my cook and housekeeper, and also considers herself an adopted grandmother. Years ago, she worked for my dad as his secretary when he first went into politics, to help keep his calendar straight."

"How did she end up as a cook and housekeeper to you?" Victoria asked, intrigued.

"Her choice. She had three kids of her own and when they left for college, she felt useless. Since cooking and cleaning was something she was used to doing when she had them around, she offered to follow me to Washington to cook and clean for me."

He took a sip of his iced tea, then added, "She will be the first to tell me I'm not a slob. In fact, I'm a rather tidy person. Nor am I picky when it comes to food. She cooks it and I'll eat it, so I make her job easy. In fact, several of my colleagues have tried enticing her to leave me with the offer of higher pay, but she won't budge."

Victoria had gotten the distinct impression yesterday just how tidy he was. Everything on the yacht was in place, up top and down below. "I'm sure you can appreciate such loyalty."

"I do."

They finished off their meal of fried fish, rice pilaf and sautéed spinach. For dessert she had prepared baked cinnamon apples garnished with pecans, which she served with ice cream. She told him she had picked the apples from the grove out back.

He helped her clear off the table and volunteered to help with the dishes. "You don't have to do that, Roman. I'll load them in the dishwasher."

"And I'll help you do that."

He did, and she appreciated his help. He also disassembled and helped clean the huge fryer she had set up outside, where she'd cooked the fish. Once that was finished, he glanced over at her. "Do you want to take a walk?"

"A walk?"

"Yes. I think I might have overdone things at dinner and need to walk it off. In DC I have a membership at a gym, so while I'm here I try to walk every morning to stay fit. I didn't do so today because I felt lazy and decided to sleep in."

She smiled at him. "There's nothing wrong with feeling lazy and sleeping in every once in a while."

He chuckled. "I'm taking your word for it."

As she watched him store the fryer in a closet off her back porch, she said, "What about taking a walk around the apple grove so you can see how pretty it is?"

He looked down at her and smiled. "I'd love that, Victoria."

ROMAN KNEW THE moment he stepped on her back porch that he could see why she liked it so much. The apple grove was beautiful and the scent of fresh apples filled the air. The porch was screened in and when he saw the daybed, he wondered if she ever slept out here at night.

They left the porch and walked side by side toward the apple grove. Roman had suggested a walk because he'd wanted more time with her. He shouldn't want that, but he did. He didn't fully understand it, either, but at the moment that didn't matter. He had a little over three weeks to sort out what in the hell was happening to him where she was concerned.

He had enjoyed the food and he had enjoyed sitting across from her while sharing the meal. When he ate at home it was usually alone, except for those times Mint would drop by on the pretense of talking business to get a free meal. He didn't mind because he liked the company... not *enjoyed* the company. This evening he discovered there was a difference.

He had gotten little sleep last night, but had made up for it when he'd slept late. But even then, Victoria had been on his mind. Not only had he thought about her, but he'd also thought about that Tanner guy, the man she said she was promised to. He should be the one here, walking beside her in the apple grove, instead of Roman. But he wasn't. As far as Roman was concerned, the man had missed an opportunity that he should not have. Same thing about dinner.

She had gone fishing with him yesterday as a friend, but it should have been someone special who'd shared that meal with her today, and shared in her success yesterday. He wasn't complaining that he'd been her companion both times, he just found it odd that the man she was waiting to make his move...hadn't.

"What do you think, Roman? Isn't this beautiful?"

He slid his gaze first to her and then to where they were. They had walked a good hundred feet and she was right—the place was beautiful, but then so was she. He'd known he was in trouble the moment she'd opened the door wearing a pair of leggings and an oversize top that looked cute on her. She had pinned her hair up and back from her face. "Yes, it's beautiful."

She seemed pleased with his answer. "I thought so, too. It's one of the things that sold me on this place. It's different."

He nodded. "How often do you come out here?"

"Because of work, I don't come here during the week. However, I try coming on the weekends, mostly Saturday mornings. It's quiet, peaceful and I love the smell of apples. If I wasn't such a scaredy-cat, I would camp out here one night, but I haven't found the nerve to do so."

He knew she was probably familiar with camping out under the stars because of her uncle Jake's ranch, but the thought of her being by herself didn't sit right with him. He should find it strange how protective he felt toward her, but he didn't. Even though his sisters had been older, he'd still felt the need to look out for them.

"I think I'm going to grab that apple right there," she said, pointing to one of the branches.

"Can you reach it? Or do you need me to get it for you?"

"I can get it."

Roman watched her stand on tiptoe to get the apple while thinking she had been a gracious hostess. Over dinner he'd noted she'd not asked him anything about his work, and he appreciated that. His work was in DC, but he wanted to clear his mind of Washington and she was allowing him to do that.

"So what do you plan to do tomorrow?" she asked him.

"Take the boat out to a different spot. What about you? Tomorrow is a workday for you, right?"

"Unfortunately, yes. And Mondays are my long days because of meetings I have. I usually don't get home until after seven."

She was right—that was a long workday. A part of him wanted to make arrangements to see her again, but wasn't sure that was a good idea. He had enjoyed his weekend with her and wanted to do it again next weekend, but wasn't certain he could wait that long before seeing her again.

"I have an interesting show this week. Great lineup and interesting topics. Maybe you can catch it one day this week."

"I'll check out a show or two," he said, deciding not to mention he watched her show every day.

Then, because he couldn't help himself, he asked, "What do you do about meals during the weekdays?"

She looked up at him as if studying his features for a moment, concentrating on his eyes. He wondered what she saw in them. Did she see a man who was interested in her, but was fighting it? "Since I don't have to be at work until ten, I usually have breakfast at Witherspoon Café around eight. Not every day, but most days. I guess you can say I've become a regular."

He nodded, smiling. "You like their muffins that much?"

"I don't always get the blueberry muffins. They have quite an extensive breakfast menu. And depending on how tired I am in the evenings when I get home, which on most days is around four, I prepare something of my own here or I visit one of the restaurants in town or on the pier."

They walked around the grove for another ten minutes while she pointed out other interesting things on the property, including a huge tree reputed to be over a hundred years old. She also showed him the five-mile path that led to one of the waterways that fed into Moulden River. "I walked it one Saturday morning," she told him. "It was a nice place for a picnic. Are you ready to go back?"

"Yes, I'm ready." In all honesty, he wasn't ready because

he was enjoying being with her, but knew he couldn't dominate her time any longer. They turned and headed back toward her home.

When they had reached her house, he opened the porch's screen door for her. He liked the place where she was staying. It was an older home with a wraparound porch and a slanted roofline. The yard looked well cared for and she had mentioned the cost of lawn care was included in her monthly rent. The place was cozy, with two bedrooms, two bathrooms, a living room and a dining room. He definitely liked the back porch that was screened in and faced the apple grove. He could see her sitting out here and enjoying the view.

"Thanks for coming to dinner, Roman."

"And thanks for inviting me." Again, he just couldn't seem to stop himself, and he said, "I hear there's something special happening here starting Thursday night."

"It is. It's the week before Labor Day and they will have fireworks across the water every night, then on Monday they will have a beautiful light show."

"I bet it's beautiful."

"I've never seen it, but I heard that it is. Each night is dedicated to one of the primary colors, with all three featured together on Sunday. Then, Labor Day night is the grand finale with a fireworks display I hear is simply breathtaking."

"Sounds like it. Would you join me on my boat to watch it?"

She looked over at him. "Which night?"

"Any night you want or every single night."

She glanced down at her shoes before looking back at him. "I wouldn't want to wear out my welcome."

"You couldn't do that."

"Okay, I'll take your word for it. It would help if I had your number to call. I don't want to just pop up."

He took his phone out of the back pocket of his jeans and clicked it on. "What's your number?"

She gave it to him, and he called her. "Now you have mine and I have yours."

They had made it to her front door. "Don't work too hard this week," he said.

"I won't."

"And thanks again for dinner." He leaned in, wanting to kiss her to appease his desire for her, but he didn't. Instead, he placed a light peck on her cheek then stepped back. "Goodbye, Victoria."

"Goodbye, Roman."

Then he walked out the door.

CHAPTER NINE

"Where is Roman, Mint?"

Mint Stover looked up and stared into Audria Wayfare's not so happy face. How had she gotten past his personal assistant? He then recalled Tisha had left to do an errand. Most people would not have had the gall to just walk into someone's office like Audria had just done, but then she was special…or at least, she thought so. Daughter of a high-ranking senator, he knew her to be the self-centered brat that she was. She honestly thought she was entitled to Senator Roman Malone.

Like Roman, he had tried putting up with her haughty ways, tried to reason that she could somehow be an asset to Roman instead of a liability. She was twenty-six, attractive and well-educated. But the woman could leap from Dr. Jekyll to Mr. Hyde in a moment's flash. That wasn't good for a man with aspirations of one day becoming president.

She had deliberately gotten her name out there with Roman, a link that the press assumed meant something. They'd even started speculation about, of all things, an engagement announcement. Then, when Roman had stopped dating her, he had effectively thrown Audria's illusions under the bus. It was obvious she didn't like it one damn bit.

"Senator Malone is taking a little R and R," he said, leaning back in his chair.

"Don't 'Senator Malone' me, Mint. I want to know where Roman is."

Mint knew she had most people fooled, but he was glad Roman had seen through her facade and dismissed her. However, Mint didn't intend to dismiss her that easily. He didn't trust her and thought it was best to stay on her good side to keep track of what she was up to with regard to Roman.

"I can't tell you that, since he wishes not to be disturbed. You have his number. Have you tried calling him?"

"He's not answering my calls."

He nodded while thinking that would tell any logical person something.

"I'm sure the only reason Roman isn't taking my calls is because he's busy," she said, as if to explain why he hadn't called her.

Busy while on vacation? Yeah right. "If you think that then why do you want to disturb him?" Mint asked her.

"Because I need to verify that I will be his date for the Capital Ball."

He could dash her hopes now by letting her know she wasn't, but that was something Roman needed to tell her. "I have no idea. Roman will be returning to the office in around three weeks. I suggest you contact him when he's back."

"It will be too late," she said, actually stomping her foot like a bratty child. "I need to start shopping for a gown now."

It was on the tip of his tongue to tell her that it would make sense for her to shop for a gown whether or not she would be Roman's date, if she intended to go to the ball. But he decided to keep that opinion to himself.

"Why can't you tell me where he is, Mint?"

Evidently, she hadn't heard him the first time. "I have strict orders not to divulge his whereabouts to anyone. He's already told those who he wanted to know." *So in other words, if he didn't tell you, then he didn't want you to know.* "Like I said, he doesn't want to be disturbed, not even by me. However, if he calls in, I'll make sure to tell him you're trying to reach him."

She leaned over his desk. "Daddy told me about his meeting with the majority leader and what Roman was told."

Mint frowned. Senator Wayfare should not have told her anything. Such meetings were confidential. "And?"

"And I think it's great and he's going to need me to pull such a thing off. I have name recognition, and I've been in a political family all my life. Everyone loves my father."

But you, not so much, he thought. He'd overheard conversations between her father's staffers. Like him, they'd seen the transformation from lady to spoiled brat in the blink of an eye. But because they were loyal to her father, they'd never leak anything negative about her to the press.

He could see that she was taken with Roman. Most women were. However, he was beginning to think Audria was obsessed. Not just with Roman, but with the entire idea of one day becoming first lady. "Like I told you, Audria, if Roman checks in I'll let him know that you have an urgent need to speak with him."

"Yes, you do that." Audria turned and walked out of the office.

Mint released a deep sigh before picking up the phone to call Roman.

ROMAN FROWNED WHEN his phone vibrated. After setting aside his fishing pole, he pulled his phone out of his back pocket. "You better have a good reason to disturb my vacation, Mint."

"I think so, although you may not."

"What's the reason?" he asked, feeling both hungry and agitated. He'd pushed off from the dock before sunup and had yet to catch anything, and it was close to noon.

"Audria. She came here looking for you. Claimed she tried calling you several times and you haven't called her back."

"I think that will tell you a lot," Roman said. He put the call on speaker and set the phone aside while he picked up his rod again.

"It tells me everything. Unfortunately, it's not telling Audria anything."

"It doesn't have to. I spelled things out to her myself. She's heard it directly from me. If she chose not to accept it, then—"

"She knows you made the list. Her father told her. I guess that confidentiality clause Senator Wayfare signed doesn't mean a damn thing when it comes to his daughter."

"I guess not."

"You don't seem upset by it."

Roman frowned. "I'm not upset, Mint. I'm cranky because I haven't eaten breakfast and so far today the fish aren't biting. Yes, I'm disappointed that Senator Wayfare can't keep his mouth shut. And as far as Audria goes, she knows where we stand."

"Obviously not since she thinks she might be your date to the ball."

"There's no way that she will be," Roman replied.

"She wants to be FLOTUS one day, bad. Real bad."

"And she can, but not by my side."

"Maybe you need to return her call and reiterate everything to her again. I got some bad vibes coming off her today," Mint said.

Roman rolled his eyes. "Need I remind you that you're the one who thought she would make the perfect wife for me?"

"That was before I saw the true Audria Wayfare. At the time, I saw her as an asset more than a liability. I now admit I was wrong about that."

"Yes, you were." Roman knew that very few people rattled Mint, and for Audria to have done so meant she'd really gotten on his last nerve with this most recent run-in. "I'll talk to Audria sometime today, Mint."

"Thanks."

Roman ended the call and continued fishing. The only woman he wanted to talk to today was one he knew he wouldn't be talking to, and that was Victoria. Just the thought of her heated his blood. He had dreamed about her again last night and together they'd done all sorts of things. Things he had no business thinking of them doing.

And she didn't have a clue he was falling for her.

He drew in a sharp breath with that silent admission. He'd pretty much concluded the attraction he felt for her was more than his testosterone being out of whack. He was his father's son, after all. His father had fallen in love with his mother within a very short time. There was no reason the same thing couldn't happen to him...whether he wanted it to or not.

He threw his head back, sighing deeply. Victoria was all wrong for him. First of all, she disliked politicians. And she disliked being in the limelight. And, last, the main reason was because her great-grandmother had already chosen someone for her.

All those were good enough reasons for him to keep

his distance from her, but evidently no one had explained this to his heart, which was being tugged in her direction.

TANNER JAMISON STARED at the man standing in front of his desk, the man who'd just delivered news that he didn't want to hear. "What do you mean we need to install new wiring in parts of the club, Hank? Says who?"

"The code enforcement inspector from the fire department. They did their inspection today and said the old wiring in the kitchen and bar areas didn't pass, and before we can go to the next stage of renovations, new wiring has to be installed."

Tanner rubbed the back of his neck. That's the last thing he wanted to hear. That would result in more money and more time, and the club needed to open its doors and be fully operational by New Year's Eve. "Where's this inspector?" he asked Hank.

"In the lobby. And just so you know, that inspector is also saying that in order for them to approve a total capacity of three hundred for the club, we will need to put additional stalls in the women's restroom, or add an additional restroom altogether."

"Three restrooms for women in a club that will primarily be frequented by men? That won't be happening," Tanner said, grumbling as he headed out of his office. He and this inspector needed to talk. Negotiate. Do whatever needed to be done to remove any setbacks to the renovation process.

He rounded the corner that led to the main entryway of the club and bumped in to someone. "Whoa," he said, immediately extending his arms out. "Sorry about that."

After the person steadied themself and removed their hard hat, he saw it was a female. A very gorgeous female. Tanner knew he was staring, but he didn't care. The only thing he cared about was that just like that, his testosterone levels were spinning all over the place.

"Mr. Jamison, I presume?"

He could barely remember his name due to the rush of blood barreling through his veins. "Yes, I'm Tanner Jamison. And you are?" he asked extending his hand.

"Lyric Evans, code enforcement inspector for the New Orleans Fire Department," the woman said, taking his offered hand.

Tanner had the ability to size up a woman's body in a single sweep, and the one standing before him was absolutely gorgeous. Her breasts were a perfect size—probably a C cup. He particularly liked the way they were tilting upward against her shirt, showing how firm they were. And she had such a small waist that her shirt looked pretty damn good tucked inside her trousers.

Her facial features were striking. Almost too striking. There were her full lips, perfectly shaped chin and high cheekbones. Her eyes were a shade that reminded him of chestnuts and her hair was styled in short twists all over her head, making her face appear fuller. She looked to be in her twenties. Twenty-seven or twenty-eight. And he was convinced she had to be the sexiest woman he'd ever had the pleasure of meeting, and in his day, he'd met *a lot*.

"May I have my hand back, Mr. Jamison?"

He immediately released her hand. "Sorry about that." He quickly reclaimed his senses, which had gone tumbling to the great beyond the moment he'd seen her.

"No problem. I assume your foreman told you what I said."

Her words brought Tanner's attention back to the matter at hand. He and his partners had a lot at stake here, and everything hinged on the club opening on time. "Yes, and I'm sure it's something we can work out."

She frowned. "There is nothing to work out, Mr. Jamison. Unless the areas of the club in my report are re-wired, I can't sign off on the permit you'll need to continue your renovations. And then there's the issue with the number of stalls in the women's restroom."

The frown that appeared on his face was deeper than hers. "Is all that necessary?"

"I would not have cited them if they weren't."

Tanner was a man who knew the significance of his charm and when to put it to use. "Is it okay if I call you Lyric?"

She met his gaze. "No. I prefer to be called this," she said, tapping the name tag on her shirt that read *Inspector Evans*.

So she wanted to play hardball. He would just have to thicken the charm, knowing she would succumb eventually. "Inspector Evans, how about dinner tonight?"

"Dinner?" she asked, surprised.

"Yes, dinner." He watched her hug the clipboard to her chest as if she'd sensed his interest there. It wasn't his fault that his gaze had kept drifting to her breasts.

"Mr. Jamison, you do know there are penalties for trying to bribe me. One major one would be my recommendation that the city pull your permit to complete the work on this place."

Suddenly Tanner felt steam coming out his ears. "You wouldn't."

"I'll be doing my job, Mr. Jamison. So, yes, I would."

"Don't you think that's a little extreme?"

Lyric Evans narrowed her eyes. "What's extreme is risking people's lives in your club because of faulty wiring or there not being enough toilets in the ladies' restroom in case—"

"There won't be that many women patronizing this club," he interrupted.

She lifted an eyebrow. "Are you saying that you're opening an all-male club? Are you discriminating?"

Tanner felt a tension headache coming on. "What I'm saying is that this will be a *private*-membership, men-only club—however, men can invite women as their guests any time they want."

"I just bet they can."

Trying to keep his agitation under control, Tanner said, "And there is no way we can compromise?"

"None," she said, tearing off a slip of paper and handing it to him. "Have a nice day, Mr. Jamison." Then she turned and left.

"Have a good day, my ass," he muttered, watching her leave. And speaking of ass, he couldn't help noticing she definitely had a pretty nice one.

"REWIRING? MORE STALLS in the women restrooms? Are you kidding us?"

Tanner had known the news wouldn't go over well with his two business partners. "I know. I know. I don't like it, either, but that inspector, she's a real hardnose."

"Hell, Tanner, you're known to charm the panties off any woman," Wyatt Bannister said. "What happened?"

Tanner rubbed his hand down his face in frustration. "I tried, but like I said, she was a hardnose."

"Let's call in a second opinion," Wyatt suggested.

"We can do that," Blade said, "but we're racing against time if we want to have the club open for New Year's Eve.

Already we've reached membership capacity, and we do want people kept safe."

"Fine. I'll let you guys know the additional cost after I get an estimate," Tanner said.

After his call with Blade and Wyatt ended, Tanner moved around his condo, skirting boxes he had yet to unpack. There wasn't too much since the place was furnished. But just knowing he hadn't unpacked was pathetic. He'd had a date every night since arriving in New Orleans, and he smiled as he thought that, considering how each night ended, he truly couldn't complain.

His mind immediately went to Lyric Evans. There was something about her that had got to him. Yes, she had pissed him off, but she'd also gotten to him in another way, as well.

Curiosity propelled him to the laptop he'd set up on his kitchen table. Once it was booted up and ready, he went to Facebook to see if Lyric Evans had a Facebook page. He found hers immediately, since the name Lyric wasn't that common. There was a timeline photo of her and three other women. Lyric Evans was wearing a short dress with a pair of stilettos. Now he was seeing a pair of gorgeous legs that he hadn't seen today. He felt his groin tighten just looking at her in that outfit.

He studied the photo and it appeared to have been taken on a cruise ship. Tanner noted it was a private Facebook page so he couldn't see any other photos and her posts were hidden. Unfortunately, there wasn't any information about her available. Just as well, since the woman was bringing out an irregularity in him. Here he was stalking her Facebook page, a first for him. He'd never been this taken with a woman before, so why was he so interested in her? He wasn't a man who let a nice face and a luscious body go to his head, and he wouldn't start doing so now.

Tanner was about to click off the page when something captured his attention. Her profile picture, with the name of a gym on her T-shirt. Evans's Gym.

CHAPTER TEN

"AUDRIA. I UNDERSTAND you've been trying to reach me," Roman said when she answered his call.

"I have. I would think you would be checking your messages more."

Roman came close to saying he had been checking his messages, and he'd returned calls to those he'd wanted to talk to. Instead, he asked, "So what's up? Mint said it sounded urgent."

"I think you and I should talk."

"Why? What do we need to talk about?"

"Dad told me about your meeting with the senate majority leader and what he suggested about your marital status."

Roman frowned. "And this affects you how?"

"Because I'm the best person to be by your side. I've been groomed to be the wife of a politician."

He'd heard that before from her. Several times.

When he didn't say anything, he assumed she figured he was thinking about it, because she then said, "I have an idea—tell me where you are and I can join you to talk about it. We also need to make plans to attend that ball together."

"There's nothing to talk about. I told you months ago how I felt about things. You should not have alluded to us being a couple with marriage plans in that magazine article."

"Surely you can understand why I said that, because we were a couple at the time."

"Right. Well, we aren't now. Nothing has changed for me, Audria. We won't be seeing each other again as a couple, which means you won't be attending that ball as my date."

"You're making a mistake, Roman. I can help advance your career."

"I appreciate your offer, but I'll advance my career on my own. Thanks, and goodbye."

Being a gentleman, he waited until she had clicked off before ending the call.

AN ANGRY AUDRIA paced her bedroom a few times before snatching her cell phone off the bed and placing a call. A man picked up on the third ring. "Miller Investigators."

"John, this is Audria. I just got a call from someone and I want you to trace where the call came from."

SITTING AT WITHERSPOON CAFÉ Wednesday morning, Victoria's heart skipped a beat when she glanced up to see Roman walk through the door. If it was his intention to keep his identity well disguised, then he was doing a good job. With his bearded chin, long hair, flip-flops, jeans and a T-shirt proclaiming Nothing Beats Fishing, he looked even scruffier than usual. Scruffier, but in her book, even more handsome.

She hadn't seen or talked to him in two days. He smiled when he saw her and although they shouldn't have been, her senses were on full alert and her body tingled with full awareness. The last few nights, she'd dreamed about him—Roman, not Tanner. If Tanner intended to win her heart, he needed to stop messing around and step up his game.

Otherwise, when he did decide to seek her out, it would be harder to make her come around to his way of thinking.

"Good morning, Victoria. May I join you?"

Why did he have to sound so good? The deep and sexy sound of his voice oozed over her like sweet honey. And she loved honey. "Good morning, Roman, and yes, please join me."

She tried not to stare when he slid his tall frame into the booth seat. When he caught her staring, she tried to look away but couldn't when he said, "I was hoping to see you today."

Her heart skipped another beat. "You were?"

"Yes."

At that moment, Bryce Witherspoon-Chambray came to take Roman's coffee order. Before walking off, she looked at Victoria, gave her a cheeky smile and winked. Victoria chuckled.

"What's so funny?"

She glanced over at Roman. "Nothing." Then she decided to be honest. "At least I think it's nothing. That's Bryce Witherspoon-Chambray. Her parents own the café. I might have mentioned Bryce to you at one time. She's the one who found the place where I'm living now."

"And?" he asked, as if he knew there was more.

"And Bryce and I became friends."

There was no need to mention about the time, after Bryce's kidnapping, that she'd agreed to do a one-on-one special television taping with Victoria regarding the ordeal, to help other women who might one day find themselves in a similar situation. That show had received high ratings. Victoria was certain that was one of the reasons she'd gotten promoted to the noonday show.

"Remember the three couples I introduced you to that

night when we were leaving Lafitte Seafood? Sawyer and Vashti Grisham, Ray and Ashley Sullivan and Isaac and Donna Elloran?"

"Yes, I remember them."

"Well, when Bryce and I became friends she introduced me to them. They are all close friends of hers. When Bryce married, about six months ago, I was invited to the wedding. It was a beautiful Valentine's Day wedding. Since then she's always smiling and thinks marriage is bliss and there should not be any single people on earth. Sometimes I find humor in it because her attitude is so different from my brothers and single male cousins."

He nodded. "I see."

She wondered if he did really see. Most bachelors didn't. Deciding to change the subject, she asked, "So why did you hope to see me this morning?"

"Because I missed you the last couple of days."

Victoria knew his words should not have an effect on her, but they did, anyway. "You miss having someone to fish with?"

He chuckled as he glanced up from his menu. "Yes. The silence was unnerving."

She tilted her head. "Roman Malone, is that your way of saying I'm talkative?"

"No, it's my way of saying you have a knack for keeping things lively. Besides, I think the fish like you, which is why they hang around the boat. I haven't caught a single thing in the past two days."

"Change locations."

"I've tried that and still nothing. So you know what that means, right?"

Her eyes twinkled with a teasing glint. "No, what does that mean?"

"I need you for my fishing partner again this weekend. You game?"

"Yes, I'm game."

"Good."

At that moment Bryce returned with his coffee and to take his breakfast order. He ordered eggs, toast and Cajun shrimp and grits.

"Are you hungry this morning?" she asked him when Bryce walked off.

"Just a little," he said, grinning. After taking a sip of his coffee, he said, "By the way, I caught your show several times and enjoyed it."

"Thanks. I enjoy working with Debra Morris and Ice-lyn Crews on *Talk It Up*. I'm learning a lot from them. We have fun every day with our guests."

"I can tell. And you look good every day."

"Thanks."

He took another sip of coffee, then asked, "Are we still on for the rest of this week? To view the fireworks from my boat?"

"Yes, I think that will be awesome."

"I do, too, and I'm looking forward to spending more time with you."

His words made her feel good inside. At least he was willing to spend time with her when Tanner wasn't. It was then that she decided to ask him something. "Roman?"

He looked at her. "Yes?"

"Why is it so hard for men to accept their fate?" He didn't say anything for a moment, and it was as if he was giving serious thought to her question. She appreciated that because his answer was important to her.

He finally said, "By accepting their fate, I assume you mean falling in love?"

"Yes."

"You want straight facts and not BS?"

She nodded. "Just straight facts."

"It has to do with our makeup. Most men, but not all, are realists. Whereas most women are idealists. Most men are practical, sensible, levelheaded, and we like to think we're rational. We see everything in black or white. We like to think for ourselves and don't want others thinking for us."

He took another sip of coffee. "We never go looking for love. In fact, love isn't on our radar. It's our attitude that if it happens, it will happen. If it doesn't, it won't. We don't worry about biological clocks ticking." He grinned, then added, "As long as certain body parts are still functioning, we're good. Whereas most women are romantics, dreamers and visionaries. They are optimistic, and falling in love comes natural for them."

She nodded, pretty much agreeing with what he said. "Thanks."

"You're welcome. But just keep in mind that although it might take a man longer to fall in love, when a man does, he often falls harder than the woman. That's why heartbreak could be devastating to a man. Most men don't handle pain of any kind very well. And pain to their heart is something they rarely get over and seldom want to try love again. Whereas a woman will eventually get over it and move on."

He didn't say anything for a minute and then said, "Take my sister Summer, for instance."

Victoria knew he had twin sisters, Summer and Spring, who were older than him by a few years. Both were successful physicians living in California and, as far as she knew, were still single. "What about Summer?"

"She met a guy last year and fell head over heels in love. They broke up. I'm not sure why, but when she came home for Christmas, we could tell how unhappy she was. That was less than a year ago. I talked to her last week and she's met another guy who she really likes. Of course, she's being cautious with her heart, but at least she's willing to try love again, whereas most men would claim to be one and done."

Victoria sipped her coffee. "I can understand Summer being cautious. I dated a guy in college. In fact, Karl Mc-Dowell was my best-kept secret, at least for a while. We dated seriously for a little over six months and no one—not even my brothers and older male cousins—knew I had a boyfriend. I preferred it that way since the males in my family can be overprotective. In a way I wish I had told them about him after what happened."

At that moment, Bryce appeared with Roman's breakfast and a refill on coffee and blueberry muffins for her. As soon as Bryce walked off, Roman asked, "And what happened?"

"I discovered he was nothing more than an opportunist. When he suggested going home with me for spring break to meet my family, I told him that wouldn't be a good idea because I hadn't told anyone about him, and he would be subjected to intense interrogation by my brothers and older male cousins. Instead of appreciating me for looking out for him, he got angry—angrier than I'd ever seen him before. In that anger, he told me the only reason he was dating me was because of my family's name and the doors he felt the connection could open for him."

"He actually told you that?"

She could hear the anger in Roman's voice on her behalf and appreciated it. "Yes. He'd been drinking and practically confessed to everything."

Roman reached over and touched her hand. "I'm sorry, Victoria."

She liked the feel of his hand on hers. Though it felt

comforting, at the same time, his touch sent quivers up her spine. "Thanks. His admission was hard, and I went home on spring break with a broken heart. So much for my best-kept secret when Nolan came upon me crying my heart out one night, and I told him everything. Needless to say, he threatened to show up on campus one day and break every bone in Karl's body."

"Did he?"

She grinned. "No, my other brothers and cousins were able to talk Nolan out of it. The important thing is that I eventually got over it—and him. And like Summer, for a long time I operated on the side of caution where men were concerned."

"And now?" he asked, removing his hand to take another sip of coffee.

She felt a sense of loss when he pulled away. The rough texture of his hand had felt warm on hers, stirring something within her she only felt when around him. "I'm still cautious and less of an idealist," she said.

"Is Karl McDowell the reason why you're okay with your great-grandmother choosing a husband for you?"

Did she detect bitterness in his tone? He wasn't looking at her, but was sprinkling salt and pepper on his eggs, so she figured she must have imagined it. "Yes, that's why I'm okay with it. Like I told you, she has a pretty good track record, and if she thinks Tanner is my guy then I guess he's my guy."

"And what do *you* think, Victoria?"

Now he was looking at her with dark, intense and unblinking eyes. It was as if her answer was important to him. Why was she assuming that? And why were sensations curling inside her stomach? Why was an awareness of him filling every one of her pores? "To be honest, I think that although I know Mama Laverne has vetted Tanner well, I'm getting annoyed with him with every day that passes."

"Why?"

She swallowed. There was no way she could tell Roman that she was beginning to have feelings for him because of the time they were spending together—feelings she should be having for Tanner and time that she and Tanner should be spending together. But Tanner was apparently too practical, sensible, levelheaded and rational. Her brother Nolan was the most levelheaded person she knew...until Mama Laverne had made it obvious he was next in her matchmaking shenanigans. Then he began panicking like the dickens.

Knowing she owed Roman an answer, she said, "I am getting annoyed because I don't have the patience of Job, unfortunately. And while Tanner's off somewhere, probably in some woman's bed, while trying to come to terms with Mama Laverne's future plans for us, I'm losing patience. At some point he has to stop avoiding me. Or else..."

"Or else what?"

"Or else when he does come around it might be too late." She licked her lips and then nervously added, "Who knows? I might have fallen in love with someone else by then."

"Is that possible?" Roman asked.

She felt her pulse kick with his question. "I don't know. He's supposed to be my true love, like I'm supposed to be his. But like I said, he's probably out there sowing his wild oats until he comes to his senses."

"Does the thought of that bother you? That instead of spending time with you, he's spending time with other women?"

Victoria shook her head. "No. Maybe it should, but it doesn't. I have no feelings for Tanner."

"Didn't you say last week that although he was the guy your great-grandmother had chosen for you, he didn't have a clue?"

"That was last week. I have since learned that after Tanner mentioned to Blade that he'd run in to me, Blade gave him a heads-up about him being the man my great-grandmother had chosen for me to marry. I understand that freaked him out and he intends to put as much distance between us as possible. Now I know why Tanner hasn't made good on that rain check to take me to dinner."

She took a sip of coffee and said, "He's operating on the premise that under no circumstances will he marry me. I get that, and I'm truly not surprised with that decision. Nolan behaved the same way with Ivy. That's why it doesn't bother me about all the women he's probably spending time with. What he does before we acknowledge our love for each other is his business. He is free to do whatever he wants."

Roman nodded slowly, as if pondering her words. "And what about you, Victoria? Is what you do before the two of you acknowledge your love for each other your business, as well? Are you free to do whatever you want?"

Victoria thought about his question. While growing up, it always bothered her that the men in the family operated on the assumption it was okay to have double standards. They had tried monitoring whomever she and her sister Lindsay were dating, but hadn't given a flip about her brothers or single male cousins. They thought the more women they dated, the better. She didn't like the idea of double standards then and she didn't like it now.

"Yes, I'm free to do whatever I want. The way I see it, until I get a ring on my finger, all we have is Mama Laverne's assumption that we will one day get married and live happily ever after. And another thing—I won't accept

Tanner's ring until I've fallen in love with him. He definitely has his work cut out for that to happen."

Victoria checked her watch. "As much as I've enjoyed breakfast with you, I need to leave for the drive to work. What are your plans for today if you aren't going fishing?"

"I think I might just stroll around town and do some sightseeing. I understand there's a Jean Lafitte museum in walking distance of here with some interesting exhibits."

"There is. I visited there my first month here and liked it. Catalina Cove has some pretty interesting history. It's probably one of the most diverse places in the United States."

"You're going to have to tell me all about it tomorrow night when I see you. When should I expect you?" he asked.

"When do you want me?" Too late, she realized how that question might have sounded. She quickly amended, "When do you want me to show up at your place?"

He met her gaze. "I thought we could do dinner first at one of the restaurants on the pier and then go to my boat afterward. Text me tomorrow for an idea of what you want to eat."

"That sounds good. The primary color for tomorrow's fireworks is blue. I can't wait to see it."

He smiled at her. "Neither can I."

"JOHN? DO YOU have anything for me?" Audria asked the man who'd called.

"Yes. The phone call was made from a coastal town in Louisiana called Catalina Cove. It's about an hour drive from New Orleans."

Audria decided that made sense since the last time Roman had been seen in public had been when he'd done that television interview in New Orleans last week. "I want you to send one of your guys there. Let me know if Senator Malone is spending time with someone or by himself. Take pictures."

"Will do."

Audria ended the call. If Roman was with someone— a woman—she was determined to find out what woman thought she could replace her. That wouldn't be happening. When he made it to the White House, she, and no other woman, would be by his side. In time, he would come to see just how much he needed her.

CHAPTER ELEVEN

"It's beautiful, isn't it, Roman?"

Roman shifted his gaze from Victoria to the fireworks. Tilting his head back, he agreed. "Yes, it's beautiful." But then he thought she was beautiful, too. Even while wearing a cute baseball cap.

She had texted him earlier that day saying she had a taste for barbecue and he'd met her outside of Bennie's Rib Shack. The food had been delicious. They had eaten so much that afterward they felt compelled to walk around the marina a few times.

Now they had a front row seat on his yacht, and were drinking wine and looking at the fireworks that were illuminating the sky with the color blue in every shade imaginable. Several onlookers had their boats out watching, as well. It was indeed a beautiful sight.

"So how did your trip to the museum go?" she asked him.

"I thought it was fascinating to learn even more about the history of Catalina Cove. I hadn't known about the town before Mint suggested I come here."

"How did he know about it?"

"Not sure. I didn't ask. As far as my trip to the museum, in addition to seeing a number of artifacts representing Jean Lafitte's loot, I watched a video about the town's history. I found it rather interesting that whenever the pirate

Lafitte and his team of smugglers returned to the cove, it mainly was for downtime with their women. That's why several of the streets in the historical district were named after Lafitte's mistresses."

"I saw the same film and found that tidbit interesting, as well. Have you decided where we'll be fishing this time?" she then asked him.

So far he'd only been fishing in the Gulf. "I think this weekend we should find a spot on the Moulden River. I hear it's full of trout, whiting, shrimp and oysters. I understand a number of the restaurants on the pier will buy your catch of the day."

"I heard that, as well," Victoria said. "Just in the short time I've been here, I've discovered tourists come from miles around to sample the cove's seafood."

Roman could believe it. A short while later he regretted the fireworks show was coming to an end. That meant Victoria would be leaving, since tomorrow was a workday for her. He'd thought about what she'd said yesterday when he'd asked about being free to do what she wanted until Tanner was ready to claim her as his.

She had made several statements… *Yes, I'm free to do whatever I want… Until I get a ring on my finger… I won't accept Tanner's ring until I fall in love with him.*

Roman doubted she knew just how pleased he was with those answers. He didn't know Tanner Jamison and wasn't one to encroach on another man's territory. He hadn't liked what she'd told him about that guy she'd dated in college. Nor did he like how Jamison wasn't even giving her the time of day. She needed a man in her life she could trust, depend on and fall in love with.

"Well, that's it," Victoria said, standing when the sky went dark, signaling the end to the fireworks.

"I'll walk you to your car," he said, standing, too.

"Thanks. But you don't have to do that."

"Yes, I do."

He took her hand and led her off his boat.

VICTORIA WAS AWARE of when Roman took her hand. At first she'd assumed he'd held it to help her off his boat. But they were walking along the pier toward her car and he was still holding it.

She had dreamed about him every night for the last week, and in those dreams they had taken walks in the apple grove and along the pier, and he had held her hand. He'd also kissed her. It had been a real kiss and not the peck on the cheek he'd given her on Sunday. She tried not to let it bother her that he was the man of her dreams and not Tanner. Like she'd told Roman yesterday, she refused to sit and wait for Tanner to decide he was ready to fall in love with her.

"You're quiet."

She glanced up at him. "I was just thinking."

"About what?"

There was no way she could tell him what she'd really been thinking about, so she said, "How much I enjoyed tonight's show, and that I can't wait for the other nights. Tomorrow is the color yellow. I'm anxious to see what they will do. I bet the sky will be lit up so brightly, it will look like sunshine at night."

"We'll see," he said, chuckling.

Victoria knew she sounded excited, but she couldn't help it. She enjoyed being with Roman. He was someone she could talk to and have fun with. "So what are your plans for tomorrow?" she asked him.

He looked at her. "I'm hoping I could start off my day by

having breakfast with you at Witherspoon Café. I went there this morning hoping to see you, but Bryce Witherspoon-Chambray mentioned you'd been there earlier and had gotten your food to go."

Her heart began fluttering upon hearing he'd dropped by her favorite café hoping to see her. "Yes, I needed to be at work earlier today for a meeting. Had I known you'd wanted to share breakfast with me, I would have gotten out of bed early and dressed and met you there."

"I would always want to share breakfast with you, Victoria. Needless to say, I got mine to go, as well. So are we on for tomorrow?"

She smiled, feeling somewhat giddy that he wanted to spend even more time with her. "Yes, we are on."

They had reached her car. "Well, thanks for making sure I got to my car safe, Roman."

"I couldn't operate any other way. Remember I have three sisters."

Victoria wondered if that was his way of letting her know he placed her in the same category as his sisters?

"You're frowning," he said.

"Am I?"

"Yes. Everything's all right?"

"Yes, everything is all right. Good night, Roman."

"Good night, Victoria."

Neither made a move. He made no effort to step aside for her to open her car door and she didn't ask him to. Instead, they stood there and stared at each other. Then when he leaned down, instead of his lips touching her cheek, his fingers did. Her breath wobbled at the feel of the tips of his fingers caressing her skin. His touch was so gentle, it caused her eyes to close.

"Victoria…"

She reopened her eyes and glanced up at him. When she saw the dark heated look in his gaze, she felt a throb in her midsection as desire warmed her to the core. She wanted to touch him like he was touching her, so she slowly glided her hands up his abdomen to his chest, loving the feel of his T-shirt beneath her fingers.

"Say my name, Victoria."

She wasn't sure why he was asking her to do that. Not that she cared for the reason. At that moment, in her frame of mind, she would have granted him any request he made. "Roman."

"Say it again."

"Roman." And just in case he wanted to hear it for a third time, she said, "Roman."

As if three was a charm and that's what he'd needed to hear, he lowered his mouth to hers.

ROMAN TOOK VICTORIA's mouth with all the greed he'd felt over the past week and a half, since that day he'd seen her at the television station. Her lips and mouth had fascinated him then, so he couldn't help letting himself go, releasing all binds, tasting her as deeply as he pleased, while filling his senses with the essence that was uniquely her.

She was bringing out an intense sexual longing in him— wants, needs and desires that could only be assuaged by her. And she was allowing him to do so by parting her lips and reciprocating his need with her tongue, mingling with his in a way that only fueled the intense primitive need building within him.

He couldn't deny himself desire, nor could he deny her the same thing. They were caught up in a desperate joining of mouths. He knew at this moment that no matter what she thought, no matter what her great-grandmother assumed,

Tanner Jamison was not the man for her. He would figure out how he reached that conclusion later. For now, he just concentrated on this kiss.

Finally, when he knew continuing could lead to a risk he wasn't willing to take yet, for either of them, he pulled his mouth from hers, ending their kiss. But that didn't stop his tongue from licking around her mouth, from one corner to another.

Then he knew he had to stop, so he pulled her into his arms and rested his chin on the top of her baseball cap while drawing in a deep breath. He heard her draw in a deep breath a few times, too.

"Please don't ask me to apologize, Victoria," he said almost breathlessly. "But I needed to do that."

"And I needed you to do that, Roman," she answered softly.

He released another deep breath, this one of relief. He wished he could ask her to go back to his place, spend the night and sleep naked in his arms, but he knew he couldn't do that. At least not tonight. However, whether she knew it or not, this kiss—and her easy acceptance of it—gave him hope. He was beginning to feel emotions for Victoria that he had never felt for any woman. Maybe it was time to act on those emotions. Unlike Tanner Jamison, he had no problem claiming her as someone he wanted in his life.

"It's time for me to let you leave here, while I have a mind to do so," he said, dropping his arms to his sides and taking a step back.

She nodded and when he opened the car door for her, she quickly got inside. "We're still on for breakfast in the morning?" he asked her, hoping their kiss wouldn't scare her off.

"Yes, we're still on for breakfast. Good night, Roman."

"Pleasant dreams, Victoria."

As she drove off, he stood rooted in place until her vehicle was no longer in sight.

VICTORIA LICKED HER lips all the way home, certain she could still taste Roman on them. That had been some kiss and she had enjoyed every single moment of it. He'd said it had been something he'd wanted to do, and she'd been honest by letting him know it was something she had wanted him to do, as well.

A short while later she arrived home and was getting ready for bed. All types of emotions began taking over. Had that kiss meant anything? Where would it lead? Did she want it to lead anywhere? It hadn't bothered her that she'd shared a hot kiss with Roman and not Tanner.

As she slid between the sheets, she was still thinking about the kiss. It had been everything she'd dreamed it would be and then some. Now the major question was how they would handle the morning after, when they met at the café. She hoped she'd made it clear that she didn't regret tonight. If she needed to make it clear again, she would.

CHAPTER TWELVE

EARLY FRIDAY MORNING, Tanner walked through the doors of Evans's Gym with his duffel bag in hand and glanced around. Over the last two days he had done his research, and now concluded the gym located in downtown New Orleans was owned by Lyric Evans's parents, Jack and Leigh Ann Evans. And thanks to a rather chatty blonde he'd met when he had dropped by the NOFD yesterday to file the compliance paperwork, he learned that as a code enforcement inspector Lyric Evans worked out in the field ten hours a day, four days a week, and was off every Friday. He took a chance that he would find her here.

"Welcome to Evans's Gym," a smiling older woman said at the front desk. Her name tag said she was Leigh Ann. So this was Lyric's mother. He could see the resemblance around the eyes. "Are you a member or do you want to sign up for a membership?"

What he really wanted was to see her daughter, but, of course, he wouldn't tell her that. "A membership would be nice."

The woman's smile broadened. "Long or short term?"

"How short is short?" he asked. There was no need to come here any longer than he had to. Lyric Evans had rubbed him the wrong way and he didn't like it one bit.

"We have a three-month membership package."

"I'll take it," he said, whipping his credit card out of

his wallet. "And by the way, I want a personal trainer. I prefer a female and the only days I can come are Friday or the weekends." That's something he'd learned from his research. Lyric Evans helped out her parents as a personal trainer on her off days.

"Okay, let me see who I have available," she said, checking a file.

To save her time, he said, "Someone I know mentioned there was a Lyric who worked well with him, so if she's still around, I'll take her." He doubted the woman had any idea how badly he wanted to take her...in more ways than one.

"Let me check Lyric's schedule. She's usually full on Friday mornings."

He bit back from telling her that no one else would do when she said, "I do have a Friday morning slot from eight to nine with Lyric and a Saturday afternoon slot at three to four."

"I'll take the Friday morning. Starting today."

"All right. That will be an extra fifty dollars each week for Lyric. But I'll tell you now she's good so be prepared for a good workout each time."

He smiled. "I'm counting on it." It was on the tip of his tongue to tell the woman her daughter had a bad attitude, and it was about time someone put her in check.

WHEN VICTORIA WALKED into the Witherspoon Café, Roman was already there, seated at a booth. She smiled when she saw him. When she reached the table, he stood, leaned in and brushed his lips across hers. "Good morning, Victoria."

"Good morning, Roman," she said, sliding into the booth seat across from him. "How long have you been here?"

"Not long. I told Bryce I'd wait to place my order until you got here. Did you sleep well last night?"

She smiled, thinking it had been the best sleep she'd gotten in a long time. It was amazing what a kiss could do. "Yes, I fell asleep as soon as my head hit the pillow."

"That's good."

"What about you?" she asked him.

For a quick second their gazes locked, and she was certain every hormone inside of her came alive when he said, "My sleep last night was amazing...and all because of you."

He continued to look at her, and her body felt warm under his regard. She was tempted to ask for details, like how and why, but didn't. She would just use her imagination.

At that moment, Bryce came up to their table with coffee, blueberry muffins and menus. Victoria noticed she was all smiles—more smiles than usual.

"Good morning," Bryce said, pouring their coffee and placing the basket of muffins in the center of the table. "Are you guys ready to order?"

Victoria returned her smile. "Yes, and you're in a happy mood."

Bryce twirled around like she was doing a happy dance. "Yes," she said excitedly. "We've done a Harry-and-Meghan."

Victoria lifted an eyebrow, wondering what that meant. "What?"

Bryce laughed. "Kaegan and I are having a baby before our first anniversary and I am so happy."

Victoria was out of her seat to give Bryce a hug. "I am so happy for you and Kaegan. When did you find out?"

"A couple of months ago, but Kaegan and I wanted me to be further along before we shared the news with everyone. We figured we weren't getting any younger and there was no reason to wait since we both wanted children."

"Well, I am happy for you," Victoria said, smiling.

"Thanks."

After Bryce had taken their order and left, Victoria smiled at Roman. "She's happy."

He laughed. "Yes, I think that's obvious. Do you want children, Victoria?"

His question caught her off guard because he'd asked it like he wanted to know for a reason. "Uh-huh. Sure. What about you?"

"Yes. I want four, just like my parents."

"My parents had five, but I want to stop at two," she said. Then while it was on her mind, she said, "I'm getting off work early today, if you want to grab something to eat again before the fireworks to avoid the crowds. With Monday being a holiday, it will be a long weekend for me, and I can't wait for it to get started."

"Is there anywhere in particular you want to eat? Anything you have a taste for?"

Victoria fought back the urge to say "another one of your kisses would be great." Instead, she said, "I picked the last place, so I'll let you decide this time."

"Okay." Then he reached across the table and took her hand and asked, "About last night? Is there anything we need to discuss?"

She knew what he was referring to and shook her head. "No, there's nothing we need to discuss. Unless…"

He lifted an eyebrow. "Unless what?"

She wouldn't be so bold to say everything she wanted to say to him, but she would say this. "Unless you want to assure me that what we shared last night wasn't the first and the last."

He held her gaze for a long moment, and she felt her body practically convulse with sharp sexual energy when he said, "I can guarantee you, Victoria Madaris, that that kiss might have been our first, but it won't be our last."

She smiled, liking his answer.

"WE HAVE A new client."

"That's great, Mom," Lyric said, taking the folder her mother handed her.

"And he's a cutie if I say so myself," Leigh Ann Evans added.

Lyric rolled her eyes. "I told you, Mom, I'm through with men. Especially the 'cute' ones. They can't be trusted."

Now it was Leigh Ann who rolled her eyes. "Honestly, Lyric, it's not that you were all in to Westley, anyway. In fact, you told me that you planned to break things off with him."

"Yes, but that's beside the point. He should have waited until *after* I broke up with him before sleeping with Wendy. And she was my friend, for heaven's sake."

Leigh Ann frowned. "No, she wasn't your friend. A true friend would not have slept with your boyfriend, even if she knew you were getting ready to kick him to the curb. They were both wrong."

Lyric agreed with her mother. That's why she had given Westley his walking papers, just like she'd planned to do, anyway. And as for Wendy, she had deleted her from her Facebook friends page and dropped her name from her phone's contact list. Now that Wendy had taken a job somewhere in Canada, Lyric didn't have to worry about her ever coming back to the gym.

With Westley it had been a different story. He'd still come into the gym on occasion, trying to get back into her good graces. He'd discovered she didn't have any good graces where he was concerned and had finally stopped coming. She hadn't seen him in a couple of months and she honestly hoped she never saw him again.

"We'll discuss this some other time, Mom. I don't want to keep our new client waiting," she said, tucking the folder under her arm and heading toward the training room. First, she would give him a tour of the facility and then work out a schedule that was suitable for them both. Her mother mentioned the man only wanted Friday mornings and Saturday afternoons and that would work well for her.

She was just a few feet from the door when she paused to take a look at the folder. She went still when she saw the client's name. *Tanner Jamison.* No, it couldn't be the ass from a few days ago at that club that was being renovated. Hopefully it wasn't the same man who thought he could charm his way into getting her to overlook those two violations.

Lyric drew in a deep breath. If it was the same man, then it had to be a coincidence that he was here. When she walked through that door, he would probably be just as surprised to see her. She was sure of it. She decided she would give him a tour and then assign him to another trainer. There was no way she could work with him, a man who made it very obvious he thought he was God's gift to women and was used to them falling at his feet.

He'd discover the hard way that she didn't play that kind of game. She knew she had done more than stump him—she'd read it in his eyes and seen it on his face. She had bruised his oversize ego. Too bad.

Squaring her shoulders, she opened the door to find a man dressed in a workout outfit that clearly showed what great shape he was in. This man didn't need a trainer—he was already buff in all the right places. It was quite obvious he was already working out in somebody's gym. Muscular broad shoulders, firm chest, tight abs, sinewy thighs...

Why was he here?

He hadn't heard her enter as he studied the photos on the wall. They were of her father and had been taken years ago, when he'd competed in the Mr. Atlas competition.

"Mr. Jamison?"

He turned with a megawatt smile on his face, making it obvious he wasn't surprised to see her. "Ms. Evans. We meet again."

"WHAT ARE YOU doing here, Mr. Jamison?" Lyric Evans was glaring at him.

Tanner couldn't help but smile. "I prefer you call me Tanner."

"And I prefer you not being here."

"Why? I signed up as a client with you as my trainer."

"I get to pick and choose my clients. You knew I worked here. Do you deny it?"

There was no reason to lie. "No, I don't deny it."

"You're stalking me?"

Tanner frowned. "I don't stalk women. However, if there is one that I want to get to know better, then I make that possible."

He watched her cross her arms over her chest and thought the same thing he had that first day he'd seen her. She had a pair of nice-sized breasts. "Look, Mr. Jamison, if you think you can show up here and flash some sexy smile and believe I will drop those code enforcements, then you are mistaken."

She thought he had a sexy smile, did she? "My being here has nothing to do with the renovations. I filed the compliance paperwork yesterday. My partners and I will be doing everything you indicated needed to be done to bring the building up to code."

He saw the surprised look on her face. "Then why are you here?"

"Because I want to get to know you. Really know you."

"I can just imagine."

He chuckled softly. "No, I doubt if you can." He really meant that because he'd never spent a night dreaming about a particular woman. There were too many out there for a man to enjoy. Why would he think about getting hung up on just one? But he was hung up on her for some reason and the only way to get his senses back would be to sleep with her. It was as simple as that.

"Too bad, because I refuse to take you on as my client. We have several other trainers who—"

"I don't want them," he interrupted. "I want you."

"Well, you can't have me," she said.

He was very well aware she knew they were talking about the same thing, and it was not about her being his trainer. "Wanna bet? Don't discount my abilities, Ms. Evans."

"And don't discount mine."

Had she just dared him? Tanner crossed the room to her. "I'm up for the challenge. Are you?"

She glared at him. "There is no challenge. Goodbye, Mr. Jamison." She then turned and walked out the door.

AUDRIA WAYFARE WAS walking out of the spa after having spent the last two hours getting a facial, a body massage, a manicure and pedicure and everything else that made her feel like the beautiful person she was. Her father had an event on Labor Day at the Capitol building and she would be there with him when he delivered his speech. She was glad he had finally stopped talking nonsense about retiring.

Her mother had died of cancer when she was three. Four

years later, Matthew Wayfare had been elected as a senator for Florida—it was now twenty years ago. Although they would return to Florida to meet with his constituents, most of the time she and her father had made Washington their home. She had attended private schools there and had even gotten a degree from Georgetown University. Washington was as much a part of her as she was of it.

That's why she would always throw a temper tantrum whenever her father talked about retiring and moving back to Florida. She didn't want to live in Florida. She loved DC. So far, her outbursts had worked, but she knew it was just a matter of time before they wouldn't. That's why she'd had to come up with a Plan B.

Roman was Plan B. She'd known the first time he'd arrived in Washington that he was a young senator going places. Her father liked him and all the senior politicians from both parties liked him, as well. His other asset was that he looked good. Too good. Handsome beyond measure. Other women took notice and it had taken digging in to a few of their pasts and using blackmail to make them stay away. Most people living in DC had secrets. Luckily, she was blessed with the means to find out theirs before they could discover hers.

Through process of elimination, she was now one of the most desirable—and eligible—single women the nation's capital had to offer, and she made sure Roman knew that. But then he'd let her know he wasn't ready to get serious about any woman and wouldn't be for a long time. That he preferred a single life and his main concentration was on passing laws and bills that would improve the lives of his constituents.

She had accepted what he told her; however, she'd been determined to be more to him than just another woman he slept with. She wanted it all. Then, when whispers reached her of him being looked at as VP, or even president, she wanted it even more.

Okay, she would admit to getting a little ahead of herself in that magazine interview, but she'd honestly thought she had changed his mind about the "I'm not ready to get serious yet" thing. Obviously not. Roman had been furious about the magazine article, and he'd refused to date her again. A little extreme to her way of thinking, but she figured he would eventually get over it. He had no choice if he was looking for a Washington-bred future wife. As far as she was concerned, Senator Roman Malone was hers, and sooner or later he would realize that and come back to her.

As she left the spa, her cell phone rang. She recognized the ringtone. It was John. She hurriedly clicked on. "Yes, John?"

"I just texted pictures. Senator Malone is living on a yacht while vacationing in Catalina Cove. He usually spends his time fishing every day."

Audria smiled. That didn't surprise her. She knew how much Roman liked to fish. "Anything else?"

"Yes. There is a woman."

Audria nearly missed a step and gripped her phone tighter. "There is?"

"Yes. I've taken pics of them together a few times. She's been on the yacht, and they do spend time together. I take it she's someone he met while in Catalina Cove, because so far, she hasn't spent a night with him on the yacht."

That fact calmed Audria's anger somewhat. At least the woman hadn't been an overnight guest. "I'm headed for my car. I'll look at the pictures then. If I need you for anything else, I will call you."

When she made it to her private car, Sparrow, her chauffeur, was there, ready to open the door for her. She slid onto the rich leather seat, not caring she'd flashed him in the process. Now he knew she hadn't bothered to put back on her panties before leaving the spa.

He leaned in to look at her and, with a knowing grin, asked, "Where to, Ms. Wayfare?"

"To the Lemmon Aire Restaurant. I'm meeting Walter Sims for lunch." She saw the frown on Sparrow's face. He knew of her setup with Walter, who handled her financial affairs. Although Walter was married, fifteen years her senior and the father of two, they got together on occasion to roll between the sheets.

She smiled, thinking Sparrow was probably upset because he knew Walter would be the one getting what he wanted today. One day Sparrow would learn that this was her body and she shared it with whomever she chose. He was lucky he was even on the list.

When he didn't say anything, and just stood there with the door open, she asked in an irritated tone, "Is there a problem, Sparrow?"

He looked at her for a long moment, then replied, "No, ma'am. There's no problem." He closed the door and then walked around the car to get into the driver's seat.

They had ridden a few blocks before she clicked on the phone to see the pictures John had sent her. The first ten were of Roman. He wore the scruffy look well. Unshaven and wearing shorts and a T-shirt, he had a damn sexy look. And just the thought that she used to get some of him had heat settling between her legs.

Then she viewed the rest of the photos. There was a few of him walking with some woman while holding hands. Of all the times they'd gone out, he'd never held her hand. Claimed he wasn't a hand-holding sort of guy. Then her gaze focused on the woman. She looked all right. Not beautiful or gorgeous. Just all right. There were several other pics of Roman and that same woman together, including two photos of them kissing. And the very last one had captured the way he'd looked at the woman after the kiss. That look bothered Audria because she didn't recall him ever looking at her that way.

She honestly didn't see what he saw in the woman. She was wearing a baseball cap, of all things, and her clothes—a pair of jeans and a top—didn't look name-brand. He must have been desperate to show interest in someone who looked so tacky. Audria knew there had never been a time when she'd been in Roman's presence when she hadn't been dressed to the nines or looked dignified and classy. Even when casually dressed, she looked refined. There was nothing sophisticated or classy about this woman at all. However, she couldn't discount the way he looked at her, which meant he was quite taken with her.

She clicked off her pictures and clicked on John's number. "John, this is Audria. I want to know the identity of the woman in the photos with Senator Malone. I want to know everything there is about her."

"I'll get on it right away."

She ended the call, too upset to join Walter for lunch. She sent a text to his private number telling him something had come up and she needed to cancel their date. After sliding her cell phone into her purse, she said to Sparrow, "There's been a change in plans. I won't be joining Mr. Sims for lunch after all."

Without taking his eyes off the road, Sparrow asked, "Where to now, Ms. Wayfare?"

She could tell by the tone of his voice, although it was

respectful, that he was still peeved. Her next words should cheer him up. "Your place."

He met her gaze in the rearview mirror. A smile touched his lips when he said, "Yes, ma'am. My place it is."

CHAPTER THIRTEEN

"GREAT SHOW TODAY, VICTORIA. You gals nailed it as always."

"Thanks, Archie," Victoria said to one of the production managers as she hurriedly made her way to the exit door. She had planned to leave work an hour ago, but had gotten delayed due to her boss's impromptu meeting.

Roman had suggested that he pick her up at her home since they were dining at a place in town instead of near the pier. Shanty's was a popular restaurant in the historic district. She had eaten there when her parents had come to visit and loved everything on their menu. Usually the attire at Shanty's was dressy, but this entire weekend, for the fireworks, they had a more relaxed dress code.

She had finally made it to the adjacent parking lot and stopped walking when she saw Tanner. He had a duffel bag and it looked like he'd been at the gym next door. The television station, Evans's Gym and several other stores shared the same parking lot.

Tanner was built, but she thought Roman's body was just as buff. As if he felt someone watching him, he glanced up and looked over at her. She could tell from the quick expression that had crossed his face that he wasn't happy to see her.

She crossed to where he stood. "Tanner. It's good seeing you again."

"Same here. How have you been, Victoria?"

"Fine. And you?" He definitely wasn't as friendly as he'd been when they'd run in to each other at the bakery. But that was before he'd found out from Blade that he was her intended.

"I'm doing okay. I decided to join this gym today and made a full day of it."

"I see." Was that a coincidence or strategic planning on Mama Laverne's part? But then how would her great-grandmother know of the proximity of the gym to the television station where she worked? But then everybody knew Mama Laverne had ways of finding out even minute details.

"So that's the station where you work?" he asked.

"Yes." It was a shame he hadn't known that, which only meant he hadn't bothered to watch any of her shows. Whereas Roman watched her daily. Even while on the water fishing.

"How are things going with the renovation of the club?" she asked. He appeared a little nervous. Was he hoping she wouldn't mention anything about their pending rain check?

"Great. That's keeping me pretty busy."

She nodded, wondering if that's the reason he hadn't called. She decided to test that theory to see what kind of reaction she would get from him. "I'm busy a lot, too. And I'm dating this wonderful guy."

The huge smile that suddenly broke out on his face was priceless…and basically told her everything. He didn't give a royal flip that she was seeing someone else. In fact, he seemed happy about it. His next words proved that he was.

"Why, that's great, Victoria! Absolutely fantastic! I wish you the best."

He wished her the best? She tried to keep from frowning when she said, "Thanks. He's a real nice guy." What she said was the truth. Roman was a real nice guy. Her next words weren't true, but Tanner didn't have to know that. "It might be turning serious."

"Really? That's good. I'm happy for you. Extremely happy."

Yes, she got that. And if that huge smile on his face was anything to go by, he truly was happy for himself, as well. "Thanks."

He glanced at his watch. "Well, I hate to run, but I have a date tonight."

"Oh, okay. Enjoy your date."

He gave her that bad-boy look when he said, "Trust me, I will."

"See you later, Tanner."

She turned to get in her car at the same time he got into his. She felt nothing at the thought he didn't seem interested in her at all, and that he was obviously still out there sowing his wild oats. Shouldn't she be feeling some kind of emotion, like annoyance or intense anger, jealousy, or… something? She figured the reason she didn't care was because she was enjoying her time with Roman. At least she'd been honest with Tanner by telling him she was dating someone…although she and Roman weren't actually dating. Still, there was no doubt in her mind that Tanner was pleased that she was seeing someone. How crazy was that? That only showed he still wasn't ready for her in his life.

That placed even more meaning on what she'd told Roman. She was free to do whatever she wanted until Tanner placed a ring on her finger. And even then, she wouldn't accept his ring until she knew for certain he was the man she loved.

LATE THAT EVENING Tanner sat in front of the computer in his office at the club. "There you have it, Blade. Hank talked to your electrical team today and they feel confident they'll have the club rewired in two weeks. Simultaneously, two more stalls will be added in that first women's restroom."

"That will push things close, but at least we'll be back on schedule. Why isn't Wyatt on this call?" Blade asked.

Tanner chuckled. "I called him, but he is somewhat indisposed at the moment."

"Indisposed?"

"Yes. I guess when a woman shows up for a booty call, you take care of business. You've been married too long, Blade, if you've forgotten that."

"Whatever."

"Oh, by the way, I ran in to Victoria today," Tanner said.

"I thought you were keeping your distance."

"I am, and it was a coincidence we ran in to each other. There is no way your great-grandmother could have arranged this," Tanner said.

After Lyric had walked out on him, she'd sent someone else to give him a tour and a good workout. The woman was good, but she hadn't been Lyric. If she thought she could dismiss him like that, she was wrong.

"Tanner!"

Hearing Blade almost holler into the phone made him jump. "Damn, man, do you have to yell like that?"

"Well, you hadn't answered my question and I asked you twice."

He had? His mind had definitely been elsewhere. "Sorry about that. I was looking over next week's work order," he lied. There was no way he was telling Blade anything about how a woman had him tied in knots.

"I asked did you get a chance to talk to Victoria, and if so, how is she doing?"

"Yes, we talked, and I was trying my best to keep it

short. She seemed happy and she mentioned she's dating someone."

"Dating someone?"

"Yes, that's what she said. And even said it might be serious."

"Serious?"

"Yes."

"And how do you feel about that?"

Tanner frowned. "And how am I supposed to feel about it? I told her I was happy for her. Wished her the best."

Blade didn't say anything for a minute and then said, "Victoria has to be lying to you, Tanner. There's no way for her to be seriously dating a guy when she knows you're her intended."

"I am *not* her intended, Blade. And why would she be lying about it?"

"To save face. You're supposed to be her guy and she knows that. Since you're not making an effort to do anything about it, like starting a relationship with her, she doesn't want you to think she's somewhere pining for you. A woman has her pride, you know."

Tanner rolled his eyes. "Let me say this again since there is undoubtedly something wrong with your hearing. I am *not* Victoria's guy."

"Trust me, all my brothers and cousins wish like hell that you're not. We know your reputation and we're hoping Mama Laverne made a mistake."

"If she has selected me, then she undoubtedly made a mistake. A big one. But still, need I remind you that you and your cousins all were once womanizers like me, and that some of them still are?"

"Hey, no need to get uptight. We're just concerned," Blade said, clearly enjoying Tanner's discomfort. "You're one of my best friends and I would hate to have to work you over if you broke Victoria's heart."

"I don't plan to fall in love with Victoria, Blade. It's not in my makeup to fall in love with anyone when there are so many good-looking and accommodating women out there."

Blade chuckled. "We all thought the same thing at one time."

"And I'm still thinking that way. I won't ever be ready to settle down with one woman, Blade. I like my freedom too much. Victoria is a nice girl, but there's no way I will ever fall in love with her."

"Not according to Mama Laverne."

"Like I said, she's made a mistake." Tanner looked at his watch. "I spent practically all day at the gym and have a few items to catch up on before calling it a day. I'll talk to you later."

After ending the call with Blade, Tanner leaned back in his chair. Little did Blade know, but Victoria wasn't the woman who'd gotten under his skin. Lyric Evans was.

"I RAN INTO Tanner today."

Roman looked down at the woman by his side. They were standing on the deck of his boat. Like a number of others, they were waiting for the fireworks and laser show to begin. "And how did that go?" he asked, while wondering if this was where she would tell him that Tanner had come to his senses and they'd decided to start seeing each other.

"It went rather well. Almost too well. He's a member of a gym that's next door to the news station."

"That's rather convenient."

"I thought so, too, at first. However, I honestly don't think he knew where I worked. He was as surprised to see me as I was to see him." After pausing a moment, she said,

"It was quite obvious that he was trying to keep the conversation short between us."

Roman just didn't get it. How could her great-grandmother fix her up with someone who sounded so uncaring where Victoria was concerned?

"To see how he would handle the news, I lied and told him that I was dating someone. Even sort of led him to believe it was getting serious," she added.

"And what did he say about that?"

She broke eye contact with him to gaze out at the water. "He said that he was happy for me and he wished me well."

Roman honestly didn't know what to make of that. He wondered how she felt knowing the man she'd been told was supposed to be her soul mate was still fighting it. "Is that what's bothering you tonight, Victoria? The fact that he hasn't come around and isn't even making an effort to do so?" He'd picked up on the fact that she wasn't her usual bubbly self.

She didn't say anything for a moment and then returned her gaze to his. "What concerns me is that it *should* bother me, but it doesn't. I'm okay with the way he's acting because I am not ready for Tanner to be a part of my life. Maybe it's because of the hurt and humiliation I went through with Karl, but I honestly think it's something else."

He lifted an eyebrow. "'Something else,' like what?"

She licked her bottom lip and he got a feeling she was nervous about what she was about to say. "If Tanner was in my life now, then I wouldn't be here with you, Roman. And I have truly enjoyed our time together. I've had more fun with you these last few days than I've had in a long time."

He was glad she felt that way because he honestly felt the same. He'd dated lots of women and none had felt comfortable enough to show him who they really were. They had all gone out of their way to impress him, to show him a side of themselves that he wasn't certain was real or fake. With Victoria, everything felt real. She had a great personality, was warm, kind, friendly—all of that was evident with how she greeted and talked to people. She approached everyone equally; no one was beneath her. Like tonight, for instance, she'd chatted up the busboy who'd cleaned off their table, the waitress who'd served their food and the owner of the restaurant. Everyone was the recipient of her warm smile and pleasing personality.

"In that case, I'm glad things turned out the way they did because I'm enjoying my time with you, too." He reached out to caress the side of her face. "You want to know what I'm hoping, Victoria?"

"What are you hoping?" He could hear the little catch in her voice when his hand moved to stroke her jaw with the tip of his finger.

"That regardless of your great-grandmother's past success in matchmaking, I'm hoping this time she is totally wrong where you and Tanner are concerned."

Their gazes held for the longest time and then she said, "I'm hoping that, too, Roman."

He dropped his hand and eased closer to her. At that moment, he needed to kiss her, taste her like he had last night, like he'd been yearning to do all day. The memories of their one kiss had tortured him through the night, invaded his dreams, made him wish they would kiss at least twice, maybe three more times, before they parted ways.

Then this morning, at Witherspoon Café, that brush across her lips hadn't been satisfying enough. He'd never kissed a woman before in a public place, but the moment he'd seen her walk into the café, he'd wanted to take her into his arms and kiss her senseless. He'd held back then, but he wouldn't hold back now. With that decision made, he lowered his head and slanted his mouth across hers.

CHAPTER FOURTEEN

Victoria was hoping Roman would kiss her again and now she was getting what she wanted. She loved the feel of his mouth connecting with hers. Last night he'd been thorough but gentle. Tonight, he was kissing her with passion and possession.

She wrapped her arms around his neck and kissed him back with equal enthusiasm. This kiss was deep, it was hard and it was what she wanted and needed.

Suddenly, the sound of fireworks infiltrated and they broke off the kiss, but neither moved from the other's arms. They stared at each other while getting their breathing under control. She licked her lips, enjoying the taste of him there.

"The fireworks have started," she said, when neither seemed capable of speech.

He nodded, wrapped his arm around her shoulder and brought her closer to his side, where they stood practically hip-to-hip. She liked being so close to him. It felt right.

She looked up and saw the sky blossom into a bright yellow. The only thing missing was the sun. It was spectacular. The laser show displayed an array of all shades of yellow, then there were flashes across the sky of all things yellow—a yellow rose, a banana, a lemon, a canary, dandelions, a sunflower, a bouquet of daffodils, a stick of butter, corn on the cob and a yellow submarine. The latter brought quite a few chuckles. Then, last but not least, was the yellow cab, which brought out a number of cheers.

Fireworks lit the sky again and music began playing, and those who recognized the song chimed in with the chorus of the '60s song "Mellow Yellow." Victoria laughed, loving it. When the yellow rose had appeared in the sky, both she and Roman had screamed at the top of their lungs, cheering for "The Yellow Rose of Texas."

Once she was sure the show had ended, she turned and said, "Tonight was such fun."

"Yes, it was. Come on and let me get you home."

It was close to midnight when Roman walked Victoria to her door. She glanced up at him as they took the steps to her porch. "Thanks again for picking me up and bringing me home."

"No problem. I enjoy your company."

When they reached her front door, she turned to him. "Would you like to come in for a cup of coffee or something?"

He smiled at her and pushed a lock of hair from her face. "Yes, 'or something.'"

Victoria smiled back at him as she opened the door. "Well, if coffee doesn't suit your fancy, there's beer left from when Corbin came to visit earlier this year."

When they entered her house and Roman closed the door behind them, he took her hand in his. "I'm really not interested in coffee or beer, Victoria. This is what I want."

The moment Roman lowered his mouth to Victoria's, she felt her entire body tremble in pleasure. His tongue tangled so intensely with hers, taking possession of her mouth, that she experienced a degree of arousal the likes of which she'd never felt before. She needed this. She wanted this.

Their other kisses had been off the charts, had left her

over the moon, but this one was one for the pleasure books. Sensations began racing through all parts of her body and desire was taking over her senses. He deepened the kiss and she followed his lead, while yearnings and cravings were encouraging her to take as much as he was willing to give. It was if they were starved for each other. She felt the kiss in every bone of her body as his tongue continued to stroke every inch of her mouth in a way that had her moaning.

The need to breathe had them ending the kiss and she leaned her face against his chest. Victoria was convinced that the air surrounding them was filled with sexual currents, and one move could set off another charge. She stood there, being held in his arms while trying to get her breathing under control.

She finally lifted her head and met the dark, intense gaze staring down at her. Swallowing deeply, she gripped the front of his shirt as if she needed it for support and whispered, "What is happening to us, Roman?"

He reached out and tenderly caressed the side of her face, then said in a low, husky voice, "We have two more weeks to figure things out, Victoria."

Then he leaned down and kissed her again.

PART 2

Only do what your heart tells you.

—Princess Diana

CHAPTER FIFTEEN

WE HAVE TWO more weeks to figure things out, Victoria...
Roman's words kept floating through Victoria's mind
the next morning as she sat at her kitchen table sipping tea
and gazing out the window at the apple grove. Those same
words had kept her up most of the night. To her dismay,
she wasn't sure two more weeks would give them the answers they needed.

She honestly wasn't sure how to proceed at this point.
One thing was certain—she could no longer categorize her
and Roman's relationship as nothing more than "family
friends." Things might have started out that way but somewhere along the line, things had shifted. Although they'd
known of each other for years, she'd never been a part
of Roman's orbit and didn't have the relationship that her
brothers and cousins had shared with him over the years.

Spending so much time with him was an eye-opener
and she was seeing him in a whole new light. Appreciating
Roman as a man had come naturally, especially with him
being so easy on the eyes. She hadn't expected so much
sexual chemistry, such a deep attraction and a kiss that
could stir up so much desire.

As Victoria took another sip of tea, she wondered what
he thought of the text she'd sent him moments ago cancel-
ing their breakfast date, but keeping plans to meet him later

for fireworks. Hopefully, that would give her the time she needed to do some serious thinking.

ROMAN REREAD THE text he'd received earlier from Victoria.

Bailing out on breakfast. Sorry. Doing household chores that need my attention. See you at five for dinner and fireworks.

He couldn't help wondering if she really had household chores that needed her attention or if their kiss last night had her putting space between them. At least he would be seeing her for dinner. If she felt that she really needed space then she could certainly take it. However, he couldn't see the attraction between them lessening anytime soon. In fact, he had a feeling that things were just really heating up.

Roman slid his phone into his jeans pocket and sipped his coffee. Standing on the deck of the yacht, he took in the gorgeous view of the water. Nice sight. He had to admit that for the last week he'd been appreciating another gorgeous view—Victoria. He was convinced there was more going on between them than either expected, or possibly even wanted or was ready for.

Last night he'd told her that the next two weeks would tell the story. What if the story was one neither of them wanted to read? He shook his head knowing he would want to read any story involving Victoria. How could he not when he was so taken with her?

And he *was* taken with her. Roman rubbed his hand down his face. Damn, who was he fooling? He was more than quite taken with Victoria Madaris. He had fallen in love with her. He didn't need another two weeks to figure that out. What he had to figure out was how to convince her that her future should be with him and not that Jamison guy.

Another obstacle he faced was her dislike of politicians and the paparazzi. One was who he was, and the other he had no control over, especially if they thought there was a story to broadcast. He needed to take things one at a time. Over the last week, she had gotten to know him, Roman Malone Jr., the man and not the politician. He had to make sure she continued to do so over the next two weeks.

It would be up to him to make sure she did.

"WILL YOU DANCE with me, Victoria?"

They'd dined at the Cove Side, a popular restaurant known for its food and live music. Now that dinner was over, the band was starting up. They still had plenty of time to spare before the fireworks started at nine.

She glanced at him. "Yes, I'll dance with you, Roman."

He stood to offer her his hand and the moment they touched, he was aware of her in every single pore in his body. And from the look in her eyes, she was aware of him, as well. When they reached the dance floor, he pulled her into his arms. With his arms around her waist, he drew her closer, making him aware of her pressed against his length.

"Did you get everything done that you needed to do?"

She looked up at him. "What things?"

He met her gaze. "Whatever those household chores that needed your immediate attention earlier today."

It was obvious from the look in her eyes that she hadn't expected his question. "Oh, yes, I finished everything."

"Good."

The band was playing a slow number and he appreciated it because he needed this. He needed her hands resting on his shoulders, her nearness and the scent of her. He wished that right now, he could lean more in to her, whisper into her ear that she was making him feel emotions that he hadn't ever felt before. And then tell her why. Specifically, that he had fallen in love with her.

There was something about her that had gotten beneath his skin, deep down to his very nerve endings, from the first. More than anything he wanted what they'd started here in Catalina Cove to continue when he returned to DC. But knowing how she felt about politicians and potentially being thrust into the limelight, would she agree to it?

Now would be a good time to start an open dialogue with her about the obstacles that could keep them apart. "Did anyone ever tell you why my father turned down the chance to run for governor?"

If she found his question odd, she didn't say so. "No, I never heard anyone say."

"It wasn't that he didn't think he could do the job or didn't have the support. Mom would have backed whatever decision he made." He paused a moment and then continued, "Dad had known that being a senator in the state of Texas had its own demands and knew just what being governor meant. He refused to subject his family to any more scrutiny and lack of privacy."

"Oh, I see," she said. "But you don't have a problem with the scrutiny or lack or privacy?"

"I think anyone would, Victoria. But my desire to be a public servant outweighs all of that." He was who he was. He did what he did. Certain things came with the territory he'd decided to be in. More than anything, he wanted her to one day share his life. That meant he needed her in that territory with him.

And that was his plan. He loved Victoria and was claiming her here and now, regardless of her belief that she was to one day belong to someone else. All was fair in love and war and he would declare war if he had to.

The music came to an end and he reluctantly released her. "Thanks for dancing with me."

"Don't thank me. I enjoyed our dance, Roman. I think we move well together."

He smiled as he led her back to the table. "I think so, too."

WE DO MOVE well together, Victoria thought again hours later as she stood beside Roman on the top deck of his yacht waiting for the fireworks to start. Tonight's color was red, which happened to be her favorite color. She wondered if the sky would appear like it was on fire or something. She couldn't wait to find out. Anything to take her mind off the man standing close to her.

"Would you have breakfast with me tomorrow?"

She was surprised he was asking since she had backed out on him today. And now she regretted doing so. She enjoyed spending time with him, yet for a moment, emotions she hadn't been used to feeling had made her run scared. She'd done more than taken a pause. She'd taken a seat and the unknown had nearly made her too afraid to stand up again.

All it had taken was to have a serious talk with herself and remember what she'd decided. She did not have a ring on her finger. She had not promised herself to Tanner and he had certainly not promised himself to her. He was going on with his life as if she didn't exist. And there was no reason for her not to do the same. When the time came, there was no doubt in her mind that whatever was meant to be between her and Tanner would be. Until then...

She figured because of her skittishness after their last

kiss, Roman would leave it up to her to make the first move, and she had no reason not to make it. Not when she'd made up her mind about a few things. The main one that headed the list was that she wanted Roman Malone.

At that moment she intentionally leaned her body closer to his side. The moment she did, it seemed as if a jolt of pure energy passed between them. The connection made her acutely aware of his strength and male power. She'd never, ever indulged in an affair with a man. For her it had been only Karl, and after he'd shown his true colors, she hadn't wanted to risk her heart again. She wasn't risking it now. With Roman she didn't have to worry about him taking advantage of her for his benefit, or using her for any sort of financial gain. He was his own man, successful in his own right, and she liked that about him.

Without saying anything, he placed his arm around her and drew her closer to him. They stood that way for a minute while drinking their wine. When he noticed she'd finished hers, he then offered her some of his. Looking into his eyes, she took a sip from the same place on the glass where his mouth had been.

"Thanks," she whispered, barely able to get the word past her throat.

Instead of replying, he took the glass from her hand and set aside both glasses. Then he turned her in his arms as he lowered his mouth to hers.

Victoria hadn't expected this—a kiss that was more electrifying than the ones they'd shared last night. And more passionate, as bone-melting fire began spreading through her veins. She welcomed the greedy demand of his mouth. His tongue seemed to have a mind of its own and was staking a claim with toe-curling determination.

She began moving her tongue in response to his. His

low growl of approval seemed to vibrate right into her. Although she'd never slept with any man other than Karl, she had shared kisses on dates. She could definitely say that no man had ever kissed her with this much tongue-stroking abandonment.

When he finally broke off the kiss, she moaned beneath his breath, resenting he'd ended the kiss and wishing it could have gone on for a while longer. Evidently, he was wishing the same thing, because he gently kissed her forehead before his mouth traveled downward to the tip of her nose and then to her lips. That's where he paused, drew in a ragged breath and asked, "Do you want to continue this below?"

She knew why he'd asked. They had an audience. Although they were standing on his boat, there were a number of other boats docked at the pier waiting for the fireworks to start. She would like to think that none of them were paying any attention to an amorous couple. But then there were always those who preferred tending to someone else's business.

Victoria also knew if they went below, one kiss would lead to another and then another, and pretty soon, kissing wouldn't be enough. Was she ready for what was beyond kissing? She moaned again when he began nibbling at her mouth, then proceeded to place soft, wet bites along her neck.

"Roman…" She could barely get his name past her lips.

"Hmm?"

Deciding that she was ready, she said, "Yes. Let's go below."

He kissed her again, then asked in a breathy voice, "Are you sure, Victoria?"

Unable to speak, to tell him she hadn't been surer of anything in her life, she simply nodded.

That form of communication was enough for him. He took her hand and led her down the stairs.

THE MOMENT THEY were down below and away from prying eyes, Roman drew Victoria into his arms to kiss her again. He thought he would never tire of kissing her and had no problem with it going on and on. It would be up to her how long it lasted and how far they would take it. He would make sure whatever they did from now on was her choice.

But he had no problem with using a little persuasion.

Shivers were rushing through her body—he could actually feel them. His arms around her waist tightened to hold her steady while he deepened the kiss. He loved the way she was kissing him back and loved hearing her moans of pleasure even more. He had been hungry for more of the taste of her since their first kiss. The ones that followed had only increased his appetite. Now he intended to get his fill. Without saying a word, he was letting her know just what he wanted and how he wanted it, and that he intended to make sure she wanted it just as much.

Suddenly, she broke off the kiss, dropped her head to his chest and let out several ragged breaths. He stroked the center of her back while trying to get his own breathing under control. Victoria was doing things to him. Making him want things he hadn't before.

She finally lifted her head to stare into his eyes at the same time she slid her hands beneath his T-shirt to gently caress his chest. "Roman..."

"Yes, sweetheart?" he responded, pressing his lips between the curve of her neck and shoulder.

"I—I... I..."

He lifted his head to stare at her again. "What do you want? Tell me and I will give it to you."

She leaned close and breathed the words against his lips. "You, Roman. I want you."

Her words made him crush his mouth to hers and sweep her into his arms to carry her to the bed. He was taking possession of her mouth the same way he intended to take possession of her body. After tonight she would belong to him and there was nothing anyone would be able to do about it because he intended to keep her. She had his heart. She was his heart. And tonight was the start of their forever.

CHAPTER SIXTEEN

VICTORIA COULDN'T HELP but surrender to the sensations Roman's kiss was making her feel. It seemed every inch of her was being sparked to life, and the moment he placed her on the bed, her body began throbbing in areas she'd never known a body could throb.

Her chest rose and fell as she tried controlling her breathing. When he backed away from the bed, his gaze locked on her. Her body warmed under his regard. There was just something about the way he was standing there, looking at her, that sent sensual shivers all through her. His eyes darkened and his nostrils flared as he continued to stare at her. Her body was reacting to his bold perusal on many levels. She was still wearing clothes. How would he react if he was to see her naked? Would she be able to handle the intensity of the heat?

"Time to remove clothes, don't you think?" he asked in his rich baritone.

"Yes, I think so" was all she could say while thinking how attuned she was to Roman and how comfortable he'd made her feel with him…even with seeing the huge, swollen bulge at his crotch. If there had ever been any doubt of his desire for her before, there certainly wasn't any now. At this moment, a longing unlike anything she'd ever felt or imagined, consumed her, and she knew that tonight, no matter what she and Roman did, no matter what they shared, it was right.

"Let's undress each other," he suggested, returning to the bed with a confident swagger she'd come to admire.

When he reached the bed, she lifted up her arms and he tugged her blouse over her head, the cool air causing goose bumps to form on her skin. "I need to hurry and cover you," he said when he had removed all her clothing except her bra and panties.

She always liked sexy underthings even when there hadn't been a man in her life to appreciate them. But from the look in his eyes when his gaze roamed all over her, he let her know that he liked her matching bra-and-panties set of blush pink. "You look so damn beautiful, Victoria," he said in a voice that sounded raw with desire.

"Thank you."

She then leaned up to tug his shirt over his head and loved the broad expanse of chest she exposed. Because of her cousins and brothers, she'd seen plenty of male chests in her day; however, she was convinced that Roman's chest was a work of art. It was muscular, solid, hair-roughened and well-defined.

She just *had* to touch it, so she reached out and did just that, loving the way her fingers felt trickling through the hair on his chest. Then, wanting to get closer, she snuggled against his chest, burying her face in it. She licked her tongue across and around one rock-hard masculine nipple to the other and felt a tingling sensation on her tongue.

"Victoria…"

She leaned back to look up at him while gliding her hands up his sexy, sculpted chest. "Yes?"

"I need you."

Hearing him say those words caused a distinct warmth

to flood the area between her legs. "Your jeans," she said, deciding to let him remove them as she watched.

"What about your underthings?" he asked, taking a step back from the bed to remove his jeans.

"I'll save that for last."

He held her gaze as he lowered his jeans and slid out of them. When he stood completely naked before her, she roamed her gaze over every inch of him, fully appreciating and desiring everything she saw. *What a man. What a mighty big man.*

"Now I want to enjoy my view of you," he said as he moved back to the bed. Reaching out, he unsnapped her bra and moaned when her breasts were set free, spilling out for him to see. He cupped them in his hands and began gently massaging and kneading them in a way that made heat stir between her legs. No man had ever paid homage to her breasts like he was doing.

He lowered his hand to her waist, then in one smooth tug, he was easing her panties down her legs. When they were completely removed and he'd tossed them aside, he glanced back at her and smiled and said in a deep, husky voice, "I'm about to give you a night you will never forget, Victoria."

Then he bent his head and captured her mouth like he was about to devour her.

ROMAN WASN'T SURE how long he could last kissing her. Intense heat was firing his insides, making it hard for him to stay in control. Other women had garnered his interest before, but none had made him fall in love with them. This was the woman he was convinced was his perfect other half. The woman he wanted to spend the rest of his life with. The woman he knew he loved.

He broke off the kiss and drew in a ragged breath, trying to slow down a little. Easing himself down, he lay beside her. Facing each other, the sexual chemistry between them was the strongest it had ever been. Needing to taste her, he decided he would start at the top and work his way down south. He wanted her more than he'd ever wanted a woman.

Leaning in, he began licking along her jaw, then moved lower to trail openmouthed kisses along the curve of her neck. He loved the feel of her hands skimming across his shoulders, and speaking of shoulders, his mouth moved to one of hers. The skin there felt like satin beneath his lips.

He leaned back a little to take a look at her chest, and thought her breasts were perfect, and was convinced her nipples were made for his mouth. To prove his point, he leaned in and eased one stiff bud between his lips, then began sucking hard.

"Roman…"

He was too busy feasting off her to answer. He'd never considered himself a breast man, until now. He couldn't seem to get enough, so he moved his mouth to the other nipple and began sucking, and then massaging, the nipple with his tongue.

Her hands had moved from his shoulders to the sides of his cheeks, as if she wanted to pull his mouth free of her. Instead, she was holding his mouth in place while he greedily devoured her breasts. Each time he sucked on a nipple, even more desire clawed at him.

Knowing it was time to move on, he released the plump pebble to shift downward to her flat stomach, and he began trailing wet kisses all around her navel. He loved the feel of his tongue gliding across her smooth skin. Simultaneously, his hand kneaded her hip bone… He loved touching her there.

Moments later, he moved his mouth lower to the area between her legs, ready to delve into her womanly core. He began kissing the warm folds between a pair of luscious thighs before inserting his tongue inside of her.

"Roman!"

At first contact her hips thrust upward, and in doing so, pressed against his mouth. He took the opportunity to lock his mouth to her, delving his greedy tongue deeper, obsessed for more of the warm taste of her. He lapped her up with a hunger he'd never had before for a woman, causing her hips to buck upward again. But then he knew Victoria wasn't just any woman. She was *the* woman. The one he wanted to give his name, share his life, bear his babies...

His hands clamped down on her hips to keep her in place as his tongue lapped, licked, penetrated and pillaged. There wasn't a part of her he didn't want to know and taste, and he was enjoying the experience thoroughly. From the sound of her moaning out his name, she was enjoying it, as well.

Suddenly her moans turned into a scream and she tightened her hold on his head. Her body seemed to ignite against his lips. He kept his mouth locked to her as she continued her orgasmic meltdown. And he was loving every single moment of her experience.

Satisfied that he had gotten his fill of her taste for now, he raised his head and met her pleasure-filled gaze. His chest swelled knowing that he, and he alone, had put that look there.

Easing off the bed, he moved to grab his jeans off the floor to pull out a condom packet. He was very much aware that Victoria was watching what he was doing as he sheathed himself. He glanced back to where she was lying, totally naked in one sexy pose with her legs still open. He smiled.

Just looking at her there made his shaft throb even more. Yet as he moved back toward the bed, he again wanted her to be certain she was ready for this, because making love to her would definitely change the nature of their relationship. "You still sure about this?" he asked her.

"Yes, I am sure, Roman. No matter what lies in my future, right now you are my present."

It was on the tip of his tongue to tell her that no matter what her grandmother might have predicted, he was her present and intended to be a part of her future. When she reached out her arms to him, hot desire burned away all thoughts, other than that he wanted to be intimately joined with her.

Unhesitant, he went into her open arms, drawing close as he settled between her legs. He kissed her, loving the warm and delicious taste of her mouth as he straddled his body in place over hers. When he stared down at her, a semblance of wild, raw need passed between them.

He loved her, needed her and wanted her. It would be up to him to show her just how much, because from now on, he knew his body, mind and soul would all be in sync with hers.

When he began easing inside of her, he felt how hot, slick and tight she was. As he moved deeper, stretching her flesh in the process, their gazes held, and he saw the sultry "come on in" smile on her lips. Her sheer acceptance of him, of this, overwhelmed him, and more than anything he wanted to give her a night she would never forget.

Unable to take things slow any longer, he thrust the rest of the way in, going so deep that he was convinced he was inside her womb. The thought made him go still and he loved the way her womanly muscles were holding him in their tight grip. The feel set fire to him, aroused him even more. He began thrusting into her over and over again, loving the sound of her moans and the way she was chanting his name.

He set the pace and she eagerly followed the movements, lifting her hips to meet his every thrust. Raw, primitive need escalated within him, began totally consuming him. His mind went blank of everything except the way being inside of her made him feel. At times, her inner muscles would clench him, lock him to her and make it difficult to pull out, only to thrust hard back in again.

Suddenly, she screamed his name and he felt her body jerk hard, then her legs tightened around his waist and her nails dug deeper into his shoulders. Her orgasm triggered his own. He felt his balls tighten and the need to explode built within him, causing him to throw his head back as a gut-wrenching sound of pleasure escaped from between gritted teeth.

It seemed he kept coming and her body was in tune to keep receiving. She was pure energy in his arms and when one orgasm ended, before either of them could catch their breath, another one began. Nothing like this had ever happened to him before and he was experiencing sensation after sensation that seemed nearly endless.

Roman was convinced at this moment there was not another woman with this much sensuality who walked the face of this earth. Would there always be this much of an orgasmic overload whenever they made love? A feeling so powerful it could literally short-circuit his brain? And cause a desire in him to want to make love to her all day and all night...nonstop?

When he felt their bodies begin winding down in exhaustion and draining of strength, he leaned down and dropped small kisses on her face and throat while shifting his body off hers. Feeling more content than he'd ever felt after making love to a woman, he pulled her close, cradling her body against his. He was convinced she could hear the raggedness of his breathing, as well as feel the racing of his heartbeat. He suspected she had no idea that those beats were a declaration of his love for her.

The last thing he thought when sleep consumed them both was just how perfect she felt in his arms.

VICTORIA COULD NOT help waking up with a smile on her face, and the feel of her body nestled in strong, warm arms made her smile even more. Last night had been everything she'd dreamed it would be and more. All through the night, Roman had stoked her fire, had explored her with his tongue to the point that she was certain her clit had his name all over it.

The only time they had taken a semblance of a break was when they'd heard the sound of the fireworks. They had paused to look out the porthole in time to see frissons of red light up the sky, giving it a fiery effect. Similar to how they'd been feeling. The sight had been beautiful and the fireworks truly magnificent.

She then thought of the care Roman had given to her last night. After their first time, he had gone into the bathroom, returned with a warm washcloth and gently wiped her body down. The gesture had been personal yet thoughtful. When she mentioned she hadn't done this since Karl in college, he had warned her that today her body might be a little sore. When she shifted in bed, she saw he was right.

"What are you thinking, sweetheart?"

His term of endearment warmed her from head to toe and she rolled onto her back to gaze up into eyes. "How long have you been awake?"

He reached out and caressed her cheek, and his touch stirred her insides. "Since sunrise."

She then remembered that he told her the highlight of his day was being on deck to see it every morning. "Sorry you missed seeing it."

"I didn't. I could see it through there," he said, indicating the porthole that was across from the bed. The same one they'd seen the fireworks through last night. "But I hate that you missed it," he said. "I didn't want to wake you. But we'll see it together tomorrow morning."

Her heart thudded in her chest. Was that his way of saying he intended for her to be here again tomorrow morning? In his bed? Should such an assumption from him bother her? It didn't. In fact, his words bolstered her thinking that he wanted to share the rest of his time in Catalina Cove with her as much as she wanted to spend those days with him.

"I'm holding you to that, Roman."

As if satisfied with her answer, he leaned in and gave her a kiss. If it was meant to be a "good morning" kiss, it took a turn and quickly became a "fire up your hormones" kind of kiss. One she totally enjoyed and appreciated. She groaned a protest when he ended it.

"Now tell me what you were thinking about."

Her heart continued to thud as she asked, "What makes you think I was thinking of anything?"

He smiled down at her. "Because you had been awake for a while."

There was no way she would tell him what she'd been thinking, so she asked, "And how do you know when I woke up?"

"Your breathing pattern changed."

She nodded. He must have been paying close attention

to her to notice that. "Then why didn't you let me know you were awake?"

His smile widened as he gathered her naked body against him, and she settled comfortably in his embrace. "Because I was fighting the urge to be a greedy ass and make love to you again."

A chuckle escaped her lips. "I would not have thought you to be a greedy ass."

He leaned in and placed a tender kiss on her lips. "Trust me, I would have been. You, Victoria Madaris, bring out the lustiness in me."

The thought that she could arouse him thrilled her. "Then maybe I need to learn how to tame your lusty nature."

"You can certainly try, but my lustiness is something you don't have to worry about this morning. You're sore. After last night, there's no way you're not."

"Okay, I admit that I am a little."

He nodded. "The best thing to do is walk it off. How about going for a walk along the pier this morning? Since today is Sunday, it shouldn't be crowded. Then we can go to Witherspoon Café for brunch."

Both sounded good to her. "Only if you take me home after our walk to shower and change clothes."

"That's a deal." And then he leaned in and kissed her.

CHAPTER SEVENTEEN

TANNER ENTERED EVANS'S GYM on Sunday. He'd read through the gym's pamphlet to know they didn't open until noon today. It had been his intention to show up yesterday, but he'd changed his mind at the last minute, deciding not to appear too eager to see Lyric again, although the naked truth was that he was very eager to see her.

Lyric's mother was not working the front desk. Instead, there was a smiling teenaged girl who looked to be sixteen or seventeen. Her name tag read *Liza Evans*. Obviously, another family member. A sister, perhaps?

"Good morning," she greeted.

"Good morning," he said. Now that he was standing closer, he was certain she was probably Lyric's sister. She looked like a younger version of Lyric. He wondered if he ever saw Lyric smile if it would be a replica of this one. "I need to sign in."

"Sure," she said, handing him the sign-in sheet.

When he handed the clipboard back to her, she glanced at his name and her smile widened. "So you're Tanner Jamison?"

Obviously, she recognized his name from somewhere. "Yes, I'm Tanner Jamison, and you are…?"

"Liza. Really, it's Elizabeth, but I prefer being called Liza."

He extended his hand out to her. "Glad to meet you, Liza. You're Lyric's sister?"

"Yes, Lyric's sister and my parents' 'oops' baby. They didn't see me coming, and needless to say, I was quite a surprise to everyone."

He chuckled. "I bet." He saw that she had a pleasing, bubbly and friendly personality, and thought she should share all three qualities with her sister.

"I'll handle Mr. Jamison, Liza," a sharp voice said behind him. He glanced over his shoulder and was not surprised to see Lyric. He blinked. *Wow!* If he thought she looked beautiful the other times he'd seen her, today she looked totally gorgeous. Sexy, as well. He could blame it on her outfit, which was different from the loose-fitting jogging attire she'd worn Friday. Today she wore a yoga outfit with a sleeveless crop top that showed enough skin to have his heart pounding, and a pair of matching leggings that clearly revealed a small waist and every luscious curve on her body. Unlike the previous time, instead of a ponytail, her curly hair flowed to her shoulders.

He watched her walk toward him with a sexy sway. A model on a runway could not have done it any better. She came to a stop in front of him and he had to fight hard not to slide his gaze from her face to her chest.

"Mr. Jamison."

"Ms. Evans."

"If you want to get started, just go through those doors there."

He nodded. "Do I get to work with you today? To make up for what I didn't get Friday?" When he saw her frown, he knew being reminded of that day hadn't made her happy.

Her eyes narrowed. "Lucky for you my two o'clock appointment canceled, so yes, I can give you your hour of training."

"No, Ms. Evans, it's lucky for you."

Her gaze narrowed even more. "Mr. Jamison, I—"

"Remember what Mom said, Lyric," Liza said, reminding them that they were not alone. He wondered what their mother had said. Obviously, it had been something about him.

He watched Lyric look at her sister and smile. "I'm trying to remember, Liza." Lyric Evans was actually smiling. He wished he could have snapped a photo of it.

The smile was short-lived. When she looked back at him, her frown was in place again. "You can go ahead and get started on treadmill number eight. By then I'll have a list of all the other equipment for you to work on today."

"Thanks, Ms. Evans." He then walked off. She might not be smiling, but he certainly was.

LYRIC THOUGHT SHE was losing her mind, or at least evading her grip on reality, and all because of one man. Tanner Jamison. Although she was currently working with a client, she couldn't help noticing him out the corner of her eye. To say he had the attention of every woman in the gym would be an understatement.

She'd told her parents over dinner Friday night that they needed to rescind his membership because he would be trouble. It was obvious to her that he was a staunch womanizer. A man who thought he could have any woman he wanted.

Unfortunately, her parents were too kind. They said there was no way they would rescind his membership when he hadn't done anything. In fact, both her parents had met him Friday and thought he was a nice man. Her mother even accused her of being paranoid because of what Westley had done to her, and stressed to her to be nice to Tanner Jamison.

From the moment he'd strolled into where the treadmills were, everyone's focus had been on Tanner. And the sad thing was, everyone's attention was still on him after he'd done an hour on the treadmill at top speed like it was nothing. He'd barely broken a sweat. He had moved from the treadmill to the stair-climber and still no sweat. Now he was at the weight bench. Seeing his firm thighs and bare chest while working out on the bench was enough to send any female's thoughts into overdrive. Even hers.

"So, who is the hottie?"

Lyric glanced over at one of the gym's regular members, Hattie Grover. "He just signed up."

"Umm, I would love trying some of him."

The woman's bold declaration was not surprising. Hattie was attractive. At least Lyric knew a lot of the men who frequented the gym thought so. She also knew Hattie was looking for hookups. After a nasty divorce, she was against a serious involvement and had confided in Lyric plenty of times she just wanted to enjoy great sex. A part of Lyric wished she could have that same attitude when it came to men. Then she wouldn't have to worry about another heartbreak.

"I'll chat with you later, Lyric."

Then as Lyric watched, Hattie strutted over to use the exercise bike—the one that happened to be across from the weight bench Tanner was using. Refusing to give either Hattie or Tanner any more of her attention, she decided to go relieve Liza at the front desk for a while.

"Ms. Evans?"

Lyric turned from where she had been wiping down

some of the equipment to find Tanner Jamison dressed and ready to leave. He had gone through every piece of equipment on the list she'd given him, not once but twice. He was leaving in good time since the gym would be closing in less than thirty minutes. It was hard to believe he had stayed the entire time. She knew the moment Hattie had given up on him when it became apparent that he obviously wasn't interested in the hookup the woman wanted.

"Yes?"

"I'm leaving and was wondering if you'll be here tomorrow?"

She wondered why he would be interested. "No one will be here tomorrow. Evans's Gym will be closed for Labor Day."

"You have plans?"

She wondered what business of it was his if she did? She crossed her arms over her chest, then wished she hadn't when she noticed his gaze followed the movement and seemed to be zeroed in on her breasts. She was convinced that was why she suddenly felt her nipples harden. "Why would you want to know that, Mr. Jamison?"

A smile curved his lips and she wished it hadn't. It seemed the air shimmered around that smile. "First of all, I prefer you call me by my first name. I'm Tanner. And I hope I can call you Lyric, which is a pretty name, by the way."

She had no problem with calling him Tanner and him calling her Lyric since she was on a first-name basis with most of those who came to the gym. "Fine. Now why would you want to know about my plans for tomorrow, Tanner?"

"Because I'd like you to spend Labor Day with me. Call me if you can."

His statement surprised her and before she could recover

from what he'd said, he had placed a business card in her
hand, turned and walked out of the gym.

TANNER ENTERED HIS condo and tossed his duffel bag on
the chair. He had gotten a good workout at the gym. Sunday was usually his day to unwind and watch a preseason
football game on the tube. However, teaching Lyric Evans
a lesson was more important.

Why?

He shrugged off that question as he headed for the
kitchen to grab a beer from the refrigerator. Why, of all
the thousands of women he'd met in his lifetime, did she
get under his skin? At least he had convinced her to call
him by his first name and stop sounding so damn formal
when she addressed him. He had liked how it sounded
when she had said it.

He frowned as he took a slug of his beer, thinking his
ever-observant mind suspected something was going on
with Lyric Evans. Not only had he seen wariness in her
eyes, but he'd also seen mistrust and pain. Had some man
hurt her before?

He usually didn't have many dealings with women who
carried around baggage. But for some reason, he would
take on hers if it meant having her in his bed. Replacing
the hurt that shadowed her eyes with pleasure was something he wanted to do. He knew he'd been bold by asking
her to spend tomorrow with him. All she had to do was
say yes or no. But, honestly, he hadn't given her time to
say either before he'd placed his business card in her hand
and walked out.

Would she toss the card in the trash or would she be
tempted to call him? He had the rest of the evening to find
out. He was certain Lyric knew just what a day spent with

him would entail. There was no way she didn't know what he wanted from her. Now the question was, did she want the same thing from him?

LYRIC WALKED INTO her condo and collapsed on her sofa after placing the bag of goodies from her godmother's bakery on the coffee table. It wasn't that she was physically tired as much as she was mentally drained. Why had Tanner Jamison decided to spend the day at the gym again? He had hung around all day Friday and now again today. And why had he propositioned her to do the very thing she'd contemplated doing with a man? Have a no-strings affair.

She was convinced that such a thing is what she needed. It had been close to a year now and her battery-operated sex toy had been doing a good job. Until now. Until she'd seen all those muscles on Tanner Jamison's body. Those hard thighs. The size of his crotch whenever he did certain exercises. The strength of his legs whenever he walked around. Those massive shoulders…and she could only imagine how they would feel beneath her fingertips.

Drawing in a deep breath, she knew she needed a tall, cold glass of water. Maybe a cold shower would be better. She stood and pulled out the card she'd slid into the pocket of her top. Tanner's business card, with his cell phone number scribbled on the back. Should she toss it in the garbage or put it to good use?

Maybe it was time to prove to herself that men weren't the only ones who could engage in a meaningless affair and walk away. Expect nothing out of it but pleasure. And Lord knows she definitely needed pleasure and truly believed he could deliver. She would admit Westley hadn't done anything for her, and most of the time she'd been faking it. Just the thought of spending time with Tanner Jamison was firing up her blood. She tossed the card on the table. She needed to think about whether she wanted to take on a man like him. But if not him, who? He'd been the only man who could make temptation rock through her veins whenever she came within a few feet of him.

After eating dinner and pacing her living room floor for over an hour, Lyric had made her decision. After picking up the business card and her cell phone off the table, she quickly placed a call to Tanner.

"Hello."

She swallowed. Why did his voice have to sound so good, just like she figured the rest of him would be? "This is Lyric."

There was a pause, and then… "Yes, Lyric?"

She swallowed again. "I've decided to spend Labor Day with you. Just tell me where to meet you."

"I'd rather pick you up."

If he thought she would provide him with her address, he was wrong. "I'd rather we meet somewhere." Then she quickly said, "You can pick me up in the gym's parking lot."

He didn't say anything, and it was as if he was tossing around her suggestion in his mind. Then he said, "Okay. I will pick you up at ten. And dress comfortably."

"Where are we going?" she asked him.

"It will be a surprise."

She frowned. "And what if I don't like surprises?"

"Trust me, Lyric. You're going to like this one."

CHAPTER EIGHTEEN

SUNDAY AFTERNOON, ROMAN and Victoria walked into the Witherspoon Café for brunch. Several of Victoria's friends were sitting at a huge table and beckoned them over to join them.

Roman looked forward to getting to know Sawyer and Vashti, Ray and Ashley, and Isaac and Donna. He trusted Victoria's judgment when it came to a person's character and he'd determined her friends were good people to get to know. Especially Sawyer, who was the town's sheriff.

Isaac and Donna were expecting their baby by Thanksgiving and were happy about it. Ray and Ashley's two-year-old twins were sitting in high chairs and looked adorable. Roman turned to Sawyer, who was sitting next to him. He recalled that, in addition to two daughters in college, he and Vashti had two kids under the age of four, so he asked, "And where are your littles ones?"

Sawyer grinned. "Our daughters arrived in town from college yesterday for the Labor Day weekend. That means our little ones are at home being spoiled by their older sisters."

When a waitress came to take his and Victoria's orders, another couple joined them—Nina Murray and Arnett Staples. Nina was best friend to Donna Elloren. Nina and Arnett, who had gotten married a couple of weeks ago and had just returned from their honeymoon in Paris, had grown up in Catalina Cove but now lived in California. They owned a home in the cove, which gave them a reason to return to town often.

"The two of you are going to Kaegan and Bryce's cook-out tonight, right?" Ray asked Roman and Victoria.

Victoria smiled brightly. "Yes, that's our plan."

"Then you don't want to eat a lot now. Kaegan and Bryce will have food aplenty. All the seafood you can eat," Ashley added.

An hour or so later Roman and Victoria had returned to her home. The moment they walked inside, he pulled her into his arms. "I thought that was a nice group at the café."

"Yes, they are nice. I usually join them for dinner at the café after church on Sundays."

Roman nodded. "I have an idea. Since we're going to the cookout later, how about you pack an overnight bag to spend the night with me on the boat? That way we can get up in the morning, go to breakfast and then enjoy all the Labor Day activities planned for tomorrow."

She wrapped her arms around his neck. "I think that's a wonderful idea."

Roman was glad she thought so. He had less than two weeks left in Catalina Cove and wanted to spend as much time with her as he could.

"I need to go pack," Victoria said, about to take a step back.

Roman tightened his arms around her waist, and said, "Later."

He then lowered his mouth to hers.

THE NEXT MORNING as the sun shone through the porthole of the yacht, Roman thought it was a total turn-on watching Victoria sleep. He loved the peaceful look on her face, the way her hand rested beneath her ear and the way her lips slackened. He especially liked the slow rise and fall of her chest, as if there was nothing weighing it down.

He glanced over at the clock. It was close to nine. More than once he'd been tempted to wake her and make love to her all over again, as if the many times they'd done so last night after returning from the cookout hadn't been enough. In a way it hadn't been, at least not for him. He'd never considered himself a greedy ass where sex was concerned, but Victoria could spark a hot reaction from him without much effort. He'd discovered that with her he'd acquired an appetite that astounded him, a stamina he didn't know he had and a need that only she could feed.

He drew in a deep breath, knowing that at some point today, tomorrow, or one day this week, they needed to talk. He would be leaving soon to return to Washington, and he wasn't ready for things to end between them. In fact, he never wanted them to end.

Roman felt it was time to let her know just how much the time they had spent together had meant to him. Not only that, but he also wanted her to know that he wanted more. He wanted to continue to see her, to build a solid foundation with her. He wanted her to get used to his life as a politician. Not just get used to it, but be willing to share it with him.

He didn't want to rush her into anything. He would give her the time she needed to consider an exclusive relationship with him. She needed to fully understand what that meant if and when Tanner Jamison showed up after deciding he was ready to settle down.

Roman needed to make sure she wouldn't break his heart by choosing Jamison over him just because her great-grandmother had declared he was the man for her. The thought of that happening bothered him the most.

"Why did you let me oversleep?"

Victoria's question had him staring into a beautiful pair of sleepy eyes. Leaning over, he placed a kiss on her lips. Then decided that wasn't enough and deepened the kiss. When he heard her moan, he pulled back.

"It's Labor Day, and you can never oversleep on a holiday. Besides, had I awakened you, you wouldn't have gotten the rest you needed. We had a rather active night."

A knowing grin touched her lips. "Yes, we did, didn't we?"

Snuggling her closer into his arms, his chin rested on the crown of her head. "Yes, we did."

"Did you enjoy Kaegan and Bryce's party?"

"Yes. I still can't believe all that food—shrimp, crabs, oysters, lobsters, fish and ribs. And they were the perfect hosts."

"Yes, they were."

"And I learned a lot about living on the bayou. I'm glad I got to go with you."

"I'm glad, too." Victoria stretched and then asked, "So what's for breakfast?"

"How about we get dressed and go over to Witherspoon Café. I got a taste for their blueberry muffins," he suggested.

Victoria pulled away from him, laughing. "See! I warned you that you'd get hooked. How will you manage when you leave Catalina Cove?"

Her question gave him pause. He wasn't all that concerned about leaving behind the blueberry muffins—he was concerned about leaving *her* behind. "Don't worry, I'll manage. I think breakfast at the café is a great idea. Besides, I need to talk to you about something, anyway."

She lifted an eyebrow. "Oh? What?" she asked, shifting to her back to look up at him.

"We'll talk later. For now…"

He leaned in close to her mouth. "I want you, Victoria," he said, easing into a straddled position over her. He then rubbed the length of his huge erection against the folds of her womanhood. Damn, that felt good. What felt even better was that he wasn't wearing a condom. A decision they'd made last night. Although she hadn't been sexually active for a while, she was still on the pill. He wondered if she realized just what an important decision that had been for them to make.

"I want you, too," she whispered close to his lips. "Soar me to the next universe, will you, Roman?"

Her words made him thrust hard, burying his shaft deep within her and loving the feel of her inner muscles clenching him tight. "Gladly."

Closing his eyes, he began thrusting hard inside of her, and she was taking his every stroke. He loved this. He loved her and he was convinced nothing in life was better than making love to her this way, or any way.

Their orgasms came fast and furious, ripping into them and making them cry out in ecstasy together. They were soaring to the next universe and beyond, and he groaned out her name over and over again. Then he leaned in and captured her mouth with his again.

She didn't know it yet, but she was his and would always be his. And he intended to make damn sure of that.

CHAPTER NINETEEN

TANNER WAS WAITING on Lyric when she arrived at exactly ten the next morning. When he saw her outfit, he felt his heart rate increase. Her curvaceous body was wearing a pair of yellow shorty shorts and a black top tied at the shoulders. She had sunglasses on and a cross-body purse across her shoulder. The open-toe, heel-style sandals on her feet did something to her legs. Made them look even more shapely and gorgeous. Overall, Lyric Evans was presenting a very scrumptious picture.

Be still my heart... He frowned, quickly thinking that his heart had nothing to do with this. Just the area below his waist did. What other reason would he be missing out on his family's annual Labor Day cookout in Houston today? He had planned to fly home last night but instead he was here. As he leaned against his car and stared at the woman walking toward him, he had to admit that she was worth not eating any of his father's prized barbecue ribs today.

"Good morning, Tanner," she greeted when she came to a stop in front of him. Not only did she look good, but she also smelled good. And he wasn't imagining things. She was smiling, so did that mean she was in a good mood? If so, that would be the first time around him.

"Good morning, Lyric. Happy Labor Day. And you look beautiful." That was no lie.

"Happy Labor Day to you, too. And thanks." She removed her sunglasses, gave him a once-over and said, "You don't look so bad yourself."

He chuckled and glanced down at his jeans and shirt before gazing back into her eyes. He had needed to break the eye contact with her. For a minute it seemed as if he'd been drowning in the depths of her dark eyes. "Glad you think so. Ready?"

"Not quite," she said, sliding the sunglasses back on her eyes. "There are a couple of things I need to know before I go anywhere with you."

"And what are those things?"

"First off, I need to make sure you aren't seriously involved with someone else. I have a problem with two-timing men. A woman deserves better."

He wondered, had some man two-timed her? "I date women, not commit to them, Lyric."

She lifted an eyebrow. "You have a problem with commitment?"

"No, I don't have a problem with it, commitment just isn't me." Deciding to be totally up-front with her so there wouldn't be any room for misunderstanding later, he said, "I'm a man who enjoys women. Practically live for casual hookups. Totally into pleasure sex. Now what is your next question?"

He was keeping things honest. If she was looking for more today than pleasure sex and wanted to be more than a casual hookup, then she could just get back in her car and drive off because that's all he was offering. No need to dwell on how many women had tried changing his way of thinking and failed.

"My next question is where are you taking me? I won't leave here without knowing my destination."

"You won't let me surprise you?"

"No. I don't know you that well."

He nodded, seeing her point. "I'm taking you on a picnic to my place on the Bolivar Peninsula, near Galveston. Crystal Beach. Ever been there?"

"No, but I heard it's a beautiful place."

"It is."

"You're talking about Texas. And just how are we supposed to get there?"

He smiled again. "In my plane. I'm also a pilot. And I promise to have you safely back home before midnight."

She didn't say anything. Instead she stared at him and for a moment he wondered if she could read his mind and suspected the list of activities he had planned for them today. "So, Lyric Evans, are you going to spend your day with me?"

Lyric didn't say anything for a minute, then looked up at him and said, "I know the only thing you want from me, Tanner. Just so you know that's the only thing I want from you, as well."

She removed her sunglasses, as if she wanted him to see her eyes to know just how serious she was when she said her next words. "Today for us will be one and done. No repeats. Understood?"

He nodded and grudgingly pushed back the thought that those were the words he would normally say. This was the first time any woman had ever said them to him. "Yes, understood."

"NICE PLANE, TANNER," Lyric said, snapping on her seat belt. She glanced around the cockpit. This was her first time in one.

"Thanks."

"How long have you had your pilot's license?"

"I got it six years ago. This Cessna is jointly owned by me and my business partners, Blade Madaris and Wyatt Bannister," he said, looking at the controls.

Lyric glanced over at him and thought he looked good in his jeans and shirt, and the aviator glasses he was wearing made him look rather sexy, not that he hadn't before. She saw him studying the controls and, in a way, was glad that gave her time to study him. He definitely smelled good.

He looked at her. "You ever flown in a small plane before?"

"No. This is my first time. For me the bigger the plane, the better. But I have ridden in a helicopter before. Does that count?"

"It will be a totally different experience. I think you'll like it."

She hoped so. Flying never bothered her, but like she'd told him, she'd never ridden in a plane this size before. "At least the weather is nice."

"Yes, it's a nice day for flying," he said, glancing over at her before turning his attention back to some documents on a clipboard. "We'll be there at Crystal Beach in no time. In a little less than an hour."

Lyric watched him and thought this wasn't the first time her attention had been drawn to his hands. She'd noticed them yesterday at the gym. They were big and powerful-looking. At least she'd thought the latter while noticing how he'd gripped and lifted those barbells. He'd made a usually hard task look easy. Last night while sleeping, she'd anticipated today and dreamed of those same hands gripping her in certain places.

"Ready?"

She switched her gaze from his hands to his face and

saw him smile. Had he noticed how she'd been staring at his hands? "Ready?"

"Yes. For takeoff?"

"Yes, I'm ready."

Lyric watched how smoothly he moved the plane down the runway and then how expertly he geared it toward blue skies. She didn't say anything, figuring he needed total concentration. Pretty soon, the plane leveled off.

"You can stop holding your breath now, Lyric."

She glanced over at him and chuckled. "How did you know I was holding my breath?"

"I could tell."

She decided not to ask how, when his attention hadn't been on her—at least she'd thought so since he hadn't been looking at her. What she decided to do was find out more information about him. It didn't matter that today would be one and done—she still wanted to know him. "Tell me about you, Tanner."

Glancing at her, her asked, "What is it you want to know?"

"Anything you want to tell me."

Tanner didn't say anything for a moment, and she wondered if he would tell her that there wasn't anything about him that she needed to know. Instead, he began talking and said, "The Jamison family is a large one. My parents have been married for over forty years and are from Dallas. I have two older brothers and two older sisters."

"So you're the youngest?"

"Yes, and they like to remind me of it." He smiled. "They think I had it made growing up, a lot more freedom than they had. My great-grandfather started a funeral business over sixty years ago. I'm the only Jamison not taking an active role in the company."

"Why?"

"I decided before I left for college I would major in finance and not in handling dead bodies. I convinced my family I would be better at growing the family fortune. They took a chance on me and haven't regretted it now." He glanced over at her. "What about you? I met your younger sister, Liza. Any others?"

"Yes. I have an older brother. Liam is five years older and operates an Evans's Gym on the west coast in San Diego. The one we have in New Orleans is small beans compared to the huge facility Liam and his wife, Paula, operate."

There was no need to tell him that she'd learned all the secrets of single men from Liam, who'd once been a devout bachelor. She knew the pickup lines men used and what asses some guys could be. Liam had shared a lot with her because, as he put it, he didn't want her to ever get tangled up with some smooth-talking, no-good dude. Too bad he hadn't been around to spare her from Westley.

"Do you have any hobbies?" she asked him.

Tanner shot her a look that gave her an idea of what she figured one of his favorite hobbies would be. "Besides chasing women."

He smiled. "Umm, let me think. Believe it or not, I'm active in a number of community causes."

She stared at him, wondering if he was pulling her leg. "Community causes like what?"

"I volunteer at the homeless shelter. I'm also big brother to a number of boys, and on the board of Habitat for Humanity." He paused a moment and then said, "My partners and I also build and donate a house to a single mother at Christmas every year." He then added, "And I participate in the cancer walk each year."

"You actually find time to volunteer for all of that?"

He chuckled. "Yes, they are things I enjoy doing, so I make time. The cancer walk has a lot of meaning for the Jamison family."

"Why?"

"The walk is named for my grandfather, who died of cancer ten years ago. He was well known in the city and involved in a number of charities."

Lyric didn't say anything because she also was involved in a number of community causes. Although she spent a lot of her time helping out at her family's gym, she still worked at the soup kitchen every other Wednesday after work. On the first Tuesday of every month, she taught fire prevention to senior community centers and the Boys and Girls Clubs of America. Then every Thursday night she went to the children's hospital to read bedtime stories to the kids.

What he'd shared with her had definitely given her another perspective of him, one she not only hadn't expected, but also hadn't been ready for. It was kind of enlightening to discover there was more to Tanner Jamison than his philandering ways.

"A car will be waiting for us at the Galveston airport when we land. The drive to Crystal River is less than thirty minutes," he said, looking over at her. "I've told you some things about me, now tell me something about you that I don't know."

There was no need to tell him about all her community involvements, so she told him something she figured he would never guess about her. "While in high school and college, I used to compete in the national jigsaw-puzzle tournament each year."

"You did?"

"Yes. I was state champ twice but never made national.

Most of the puzzles were five hundred pieces and my time was usually less than hour."

"I'm impressed."

"Thanks."

As if deciding they'd shared enough personal information, they then kept the topics of conversation general. The weather, politics, entertainment, the economy. They even talked about foods they liked to eat, and he claimed that he was pretty good in the kitchen.

"Get ready. We're about to land."

Time had gone by fast and she was glad their conversation had taken her mind off the flight. She looked out the window and felt the butterflies going off in her stomach at the thought of what today had in store.

Moments later, when he'd landed the plane, she looked over at him and said, "That was a nice flight, Tanner. I enjoyed it."

He reached out and caressed her cheek. "And I intend for you to enjoy today, as well, Lyric Evans."

"YOUR BEACH HOUSE is beautiful, Tanner," Lyric said the moment he opened the door to his home on Crystal Beach and she walked inside.

"I'm glad you like the place," he said, walking through and opening the window blinds to reveal a beautiful view of the Gulf. The sand appeared a crystal white and the water a shimmering blue.

She'd been impressed the moment she'd seen the marker indicating they had arrived at Crystal Beach. And when he continued driving to a section of town where beach cottages were located, she'd been even more impressed. His home and the two others in the private cul-de-sac were two-story Mediterranean style.

"My partners, Blade and Wyatt, own the other two houses on this street."

"That's what I call picking your neighbors," she said, grinning.

"Yes, that's true. Come on and let me give you a tour," he said, taking her hand. Lyric thought that this wasn't the first time he'd done that. He'd also held her hand when they'd walked off the tarmac from his plane. Each time they touched, it seemed her body's most primal reaction kicked in with a vengeance.

This house had three bedrooms, two bathrooms, an eat-in kitchen and a dining room downstairs, with a bonus room that he said that he used as a game and theater room on the top floor. Also, the second floor had a guest bedroom with a bathroom and balcony.

As they walked back down the stairs, he said, "I've already ordered lunch. I just need to call to let them know to deliver it."

"All right."

He placed the call and when he put his phone back in his pocket, he took hold of her hand again. "Let me show you the spot where we will have our picnic."

Tanner led her through the kitchen to an outside patio overlooking the beach. He pointed to an area that reminded her of a tropical paradise. "Blade, Wyatt and I tossed coins to see who would get this house because that lagoon came with it. Isn't it beautiful?"

"Yes, it most certainly is." And she agreed that it would be the perfect spot for a picnic.

"By the time we gather everything we need, lunch will be here."

She followed him back inside, where he pulled a little red

wagon from one of the closets. "It will be easier to transport everything out in this."

Tanner and Lyric moved around the kitchen gathering plates, eating utensils, napkins, wineglasses and a bottle of wine. Then they went to a linen closet and Tanner pulled out a blanket. It was a nice day outside and because the beach was private except for the three houses on the cul-de-sac, this section was empty.

"Your friends won't be using their places today?"

"No. Blade and his wife, Samari, are visiting her parents in New York this weekend, and there's no telling where Wyatt is. His folks live in San Antonio, so he might be spending the holiday with them. That means we have this entire beach to ourselves."

Lovely, she thought, not sure that was such a good idea. Too late to start having second thoughts about being here alone with him. Last night she'd been certain that engaging in casual sex would be no big deal and worth all the pleasure she could derive from it. Now she was having misgivings.

She jumped when fingers snapped in her face. She glanced over and saw Tanner smiling. "You zoned out on me for a minute," he said.

"Sorry, I was thinking about something."

He chuckled. "Must have been deep. You seemed miles away."

At that moment the doorbell sounded. "That's probably our lunch."

Tanner headed for the door.

CHAPTER TWENTY

"Did you enjoy brunch?"

Victoria leaned back in her chair and smiled across the table at Roman. After making love, it had been too late for breakfast so they'd settled for brunch. "Yes, everything was delicious, as usual. I see this place is packed with locals and a lot of tourists in town for today's Labor Day festivities."

Later today there would be a boat parade. Several vendors had set up along the pier selling all sorts of items, from seafood dinners to T-shirts. Roman had promised that when they left here, they would stop by the ice cream shop the Ellorans owned for a bowl of ice cream.

She looked over at him. "You said we needed to talk about something," she said, recalling when he had said it there had been an intense look on his face. She had an idea what he wanted to discuss with her and decided to make things easy for him.

"I think I know what you're going to say, Roman."

He lifted an eyebrow. "Do you?"

She nodded. "Yes. You have a little more than a week left in Catalina Cove and you're concerned I've gotten clingy and won't know how to let go when the time comes."

She saw the surprise in his eyes. Had she thought wrong, or was he surprised she had guessed correctly? He leaned back in his chair and then said, "No, just the opposite. My time with you has been special, Victoria, and more than anything I want to continue to see you after I leave here."

His words gave her pause. The thought that he wanted them to continue seeing each other after he left Catalina Cove was something she hadn't even considered.

"My time has been special with you, as well, Roman. But I'm not sure continuing what we started here is a good idea."

"Why? Because of your involvement with Tanner Jamison?"

"Tanner? What does he have to do with anything?"

"You're promised to him, so the way I see it, he has a lot to do with everything."

She rolled her eyes. "Well, he doesn't. I've already shared my reasons with you. Nothing has changed. Spending time with you here was one thing, being seen together where I become part of your world is another. I know I wouldn't like it."

"How do you know if you've never tried it?"

Although she didn't want to admit it, he'd raised a good question. In fact, she was unable to provide him with an answer. Before she could think of one, he pressed on and said, "You know I could have thought the same thing about your profession. I don't like the media most of the time, either, and you're a part of it."

She lifted her chin. "Yes, but I'm not a part of the media that you need to be concerned with, Roman, and it would not have been fair to group me with those who annoy you."

"I feel the same way, Victoria. It's not fair of you to group me with all politicians. Namely the corrupt ones. I believe I have strong ethics and outstanding integrity."

Although she hadn't had a reason to keep up with his career in the senate, she supported his views on a lot of things. Besides that, her uncle Jake supported him a 100 percent and was one of Roman's biggest contributors. That fundraiser Jake and Diamond held last year was proof of that. And when it came to people, her uncle Jake was a good judge of character.

"I know you do, Roman, and I'm sorry if I made you feel that you don't." She reached across the table to touch his hand. "I honestly believe that you are one of the good guys, and I see the point you're trying to make and concur it's a valid one. However, there's the other issue that will bother me. You're always on some reporter's radar and any woman you're involved with will be, as well."

He nodded. "Yes, I know of your fear of being in the limelight."

"I don't fear it. I'd just prefer avoiding it."

He didn't say anything for a minute and then said, "So you mean to tell me that if your boss came to you and said there's a television station in New York that wanted you as part of their team, and taking the job could make you a household name, you would turn it down?"

She frowned. "Of course not. I would be crazy not to grab that opportunity."

"Even if, subsequently, you'd become the next Oprah and be cast in the limelight?"

She didn't say anything for a minute because she didn't have to. He had cornered her into admitting that she was capable of being flexible about things when it suited her.

"I've told you what I want regarding our relationship, Victoria. But you have to want the same thing. I believe we owe it to each other to see what, if anything, can become of us. Things might have started off between us as mere friends, but I believe it's more than that now."

She had to agree with him. "Yes, it's more than that,"

she said, although she refused to define just what their relationship was. The one thing she did know was that she didn't sleep with her friends.

"So will you at least think about it?"

Sighing deeply, she nodded. "Yes, I will think about it."

"Thanks. Another thing I'd like you to think about is your involvement with Tanner Jamison. If we agree to continue to see each other after I leave here, I can't help but wonder what will happen if Tanner gets his act together and wants to claim you as his."

Victoria drew in a deep breath knowing there was a possibility that might happen since Mama Laverne hadn't failed in matching up couples yet.

Even if her great-grandmother was certain Tanner was the person for her, Victoria wasn't convinced. He didn't love her, she didn't love him and she refused to sit around and wait for him to make a move. She might have thought she was capable of playing the waiting game for Tanner, but that was before Roman. Before spending time with him, sleeping in his arms and making love with him.

Drawing in another deep breath, she said, "You're right. I have a lot to think about."

"Will you give me your answer before I leave here?"

She nibbled on her bottom lip for a moment and then said, "Yes."

Her response brought a smile to his lips. "And another thing. If we decide to continue to see each other, there's a ball at the Kennedy Center next month. I'd love to invite you as my date."

"Whoa," she said, holding up her hands. "Not sure I'd be ready for something like that so soon, Roman."

"I hope you will, Victoria. I have no problem being seen with you and hope you don't have a problem being seen with me. Things have been pretty low-key here, but I think the best way to deal with everything once I leave here is to be transparent. Once people see we're nothing more than a couple dating, the media will eventually leave us alone."

She wondered if he really believed that. "I wish I could be as certain about that as you are."

"Have faith." He glanced at his watch. "Do you still want to make a pit stop at the ice-cream shop?"

She shook her head. "No. I want to go back to the boat with you."

She needed him to hold her and make love to her. Including today they had eleven days left to be together in Catalina Cove. That would be all they had if she decided not to agree to continue to see him after he left.

He stood and held his hand out to her. "Then let's return to the boat."

ROMAN AND VICTORIA walked out of the café not aware they were being watched. The man who'd been seated at the table across from theirs pulled his cell phone from his shirt pocket and clicked in a number. A huge smile was on his face. "It's me. I'm sending over a lot more pictures. There's also something else that might interest you. It seems the senator and the woman are having a secret affair. I didn't clearly hear all of their conversation, but enough to know she's already involved with someone else, might even be engaged to someone named Tanner Jamison. Sounds like the senator might be involved in a love triangle with this woman. I think that's definitely news the tabloids would love getting their hands on."

AUDRIA ENDED THE call with her private investigator, a smile spreading across her lips. Now she didn't feel as hopeless as she had when she'd received that packet on Friday revealing the woman's identity. She wasn't the nobody Audria had assumed she was. Victoria Madaris was part of the wealthy Madaris family and would have been strong competition since the Madarises and Malones had family ties that went back years. On top of that, additional pictures had shown that Victoria Madaris could clean up nicely—too nicely. But still, Audria felt Victoria had a long way to go to best her. The woman looked okay, but she had no refined features, which she would need one day to be a president's wife. Her hair coloring was awful, and she definitely needed a new stylist. She looked like a girl next door instead of one rolling in dough. What a waste of wealth. Why was she even working with the last name of Madaris?

Over the weekend, Audria had racked her brain to find something—anything—that she could use as ammunition against both the woman and Roman. Now, thanks to her trusted PI, she'd been given some. From the reports she'd read last week, Victoria Madaris had an aversion to politicians and had even said so in an interview she'd given a year or so ago. She also had an aversion to being in the limelight, although she herself was a television personality on a talk show. Lucky for her, her television show was in a local market and not on a national scale.

Well, Audria was about to make sure she was thrust into the limelight, and she knew just the tabloid to do it. She knew Buddy Fields at *The Tattler* and he was just the person who could spin a story that would cause a scandal big enough to ruin a person's reputation.

She didn't want Roman's reputation totally ruined—she just wanted it shredded to the point where he would decide distancing himself from Victoria Madaris would be the smart thing to do. Then he would have to seek out Audria to be by his side as the only way to shine with the Washington elites again. Of course, when Roman realized just how much he needed her, she would make demands of her own...like him placing a ring on her finger.

He had dangled her around long enough. And when they got married, they would have the most elegant wedding the nation's capital had ever seen. And it would be a beautiful June wedding.

Audria moved around her bedroom doing a happy dance. Yes! That was her plan and she was more than certain it would work. Roman might be fascinated with this woman now, but that wouldn't last because Audria, of all people, knew that nothing meant more to Roman than his political career. And now that the powers that be in DC had let him know he could be a top contender for the highest job in the land, there was no way he would choose Victoria Madaris over his political aspirations. No way.

CHAPTER TWENTY-ONE

TANNER SPREAD THE huge blanket on the sand. Together he and Lyric took the picnic basket out of their lunch wagon, followed by a bottle of wine and wineglasses. There was another smaller basket that contained napkins, utensils, hand sanitizer and other miscellaneous items.

Dropping down on the blanket, he reached out his hand to her. "Come join me," he invited. She took it and eased down beside him.

He poured them both glasses of wine and looked out at the water. "I love it here," he said after a brief pause. It had taken a minute to get his libido in check. All kinds of sensations had swamped him when she'd placed her hand in his. Then, when'd she dropped down beside him, their thighs had innocently brushed, and he'd actually felt something akin to an electrical current spear through him.

On top of that, he was trying to figure out why on the plane ride here, he had shared a lot about himself with her. More of himself than he typically would with a woman he intended to have a brief fling with. He had told her about his family and the things he liked doing. It was as if he was trying to convey he had other passions besides those in the bedroom. Why would it matter to him for her *not* to think he only had a one-track mind, when he *should* want her to think that? He needed to focus on the reason she was here with him. The only reason.

"Do you come here often, Tanner?"

He glanced over to see her looking at him. "Not nearly enough. It's hard to get away sometimes. I'm a very busy man." He smiled. "But not too busy to spend time with a very beautiful woman today."

She chuckled and said, "Maybe now is when I should tell you about my brother."

He raised an eyebrow. "Your brother?"

"Yes."

"What about him?" he asked, taking a sip of wine. Her fragrance was getting to him and he wasn't sure how it was overriding the scent of the Gulf.

"He used to be New Orleans's number-one bachelor. He was a real womanizer and because of him I know all the codes men use to categorize women. I also know the lines men drop to reel women in."

He tilted his head to look at her. He needed to get her out of his system, and it wouldn't go any further after that. "You think I just gave you a line?"

"Yes."

"Why would you think that when you are beautiful?" Surely, she had to know that. There was nothing plain about her at all. Every part of her that he'd seen was gorgeous and she had a great-looking body. And sitting so close to her on the blanket was making him aware of her in every pore of his body. Her nearness, the scent of her and that rare sexual aura that she seemed to emit were all making it hard to remember that he had pegged her as a one and done—an OD.

"How is the club coming along?"

She would interrupt his thoughts to ask him about the club when she hadn't answered his question. But then, he had given her what most would consider a line; however, in this case it had been the truth. "No thanks to you, we are running two weeks behind, but our goal is still to open by New Year's Eve."

She didn't seem bothered by the slight irritation in his voice. "I had a job to do and I did it, Tanner. One day you'll thank me for keeping those who patronize your establishment safe. And as far as opening on time, you will. I have a feeling you can do anything you put your mind to doing."

"And what if told you that right now my mind is on doing you, Lyric?"

Lyric took a sip of wine, definitely not ready to answer that, so she didn't. "Let's table that question for later. Like I told you before coming here, I'm well aware of your game plan." Why did men think they were the only ones with agendas? "I didn't eat breakfast and I'm starving. What's in the basket?"

He gave her a look that clearly stated he wasn't sure what to make of her, then said, "Take a look and see."

She did. There was a box of fried chicken, a container of potato salad, bags of chips, a container of coleslaw and slices of pound cake. "Everything looks good, Tanner." *He* looked good.

Nearly too good, she thought, as she put food on both their plates. What she'd told him was true. She was hungry and sitting beside him wasn't making things better. Now she had to deal with two different types of hunger. One for food and the other for a man. She'd never had problems with the latter before, but now something was happening to her that she didn't quite understand.

Why was just being near Tanner causing her to feel all sorts of sensations she'd never felt before? There was the reaction she felt anytime they touched…like what just happened with their fingers when she'd handed him a plate. Then there was that giddiness she felt in the pit of her stomach every time their gazes connected. More than once his eyes had lowered to her chest. Could he see how her nipples had hardened just from sharing a spread with him?

She bit into her chicken, determined not to let being around him unnerve her.

"You like it?"

"Huh?" she asked, taking time to chew and swallow her food. She then licked her lips.

He smiled. "Umm, I got my answer. Lip-licking good, apparently."

She licked her lips again and smiled. "Yes, it's delicious."

"I know the owner. He's a friend of mine and I'll tell him you liked it."

A short while later, she figured Tanner could tell his friend that everything had been delicious. The wine was great, too. His idea of a picnic on the beach had been a swell one and she was glad she had accepted his invitation. Had she stayed home she would have spent the day dusting and vacuuming.

"Since you served our food, I'll gather up our trash," he said.

"Okay."

She watched him and when his hand innocently brushed against her thigh, her heart skipped a beat. It had been innocent, right? He hadn't given her any indication that it hadn't been, but this man was experienced when it came to women. Thanks to Liam, she knew something about how womanizers operated, but what she lacked was experience. That had to be the reason her nerves were dancing, and her stomach was doing somersaults. Whatever he had planned for her today, she was ready. Anticipation had her brain racing.

How could she want a man with this much intensity when knowing all he wanted was to get one thing from her, and one thing only? He'd even told her that his mind was on "doing" her. You couldn't state things more plainly than that. At least he was keeping it honest.

She'd never been a casual kind of girl when it came to sex, but curiosity was egging her on to try it, just this once. Was Tanner the one man who would give her the sexual pleasure she'd never found in another man's arms? And what if he did? What would happen when she saw him again at the gym? Could they act like nothing had happened?

"What are you thinking about, Lyric?"

She glanced over at him, saw how he was looking at her, waiting for her answer. She studied his features. Why did he have to look so darn handsome? There wasn't anything about him that she wasn't aware of. And then there were his delectable-looking lips. Just staring at them was causing a surge of yearning to erupt inside of her.

"Lyric?"

His deep, warm voice saying her name brought her back to the present. "I was just wondering."

"About what?"

"If your lips taste as good as they look." Feeling bold, she leaned in and captured his mouth with hers.

TANNER DEFINITELY HADN'T expected this. He'd figured he would be the one making the first move, and now she was taking charge. He'd kissed plenty of women in his day and could immediately tell that although she was initiating, she didn't have much confidence in what she was doing. However, the passion was there. And at that moment, it was the passion that had him moaning out his pleasure as she took hold of his tongue and began sucking on it…hard.

If she thought he was disciplined enough to stay still like a statue while she played around with his mouth, then she was wrong. Fire was spreading through all parts of him and he couldn't stay motionless, so he began roaming his hands all over her. Especially toward her chest. He needed to touch her breasts before taking them into his mouth and sucking on them. He had dreamed of her hardened nipples sliding in his mouth during countless dreams and today he intended to make it a reality.

When her tongue began twirling around with his, he knew he was at the point where he needed to take over or else he would be climaxing before she did and that was something he didn't do. He always made sure the woman got her pleasure before he got his, and that was under all circumstances.

He fought for control but when she pressed her hand to the back of his neck to place pressure to their mouths, he couldn't help but moan again. Her delicious taste was making him feel crazed. Suddenly she pulled her mouth away and drew in a deep breath. Her eyes opened and she stared into his as her lips creased into a smile, giving him the impression that she was pretty damn pleased with herself. He smiled back, glad she felt that way.

"Now can I take over?" he asked against her moist lips.

She stiffened for a moment as if surprised he'd spoken, then she relaxed before nodding. It was then that he slanted his open mouth over hers, deciding he was about to show her his version of a mind-blowing kiss. Over the years he'd earned the reputation of being a master in the bedroom when it came to women and kissing was one of his specialties.

Without wasting any time, he began eating up her mouth like his survival depended on it, moving his head from side to side with their lips locked tightly together. She evidently liked what he was doing because she tightened her arms around his neck and tried imitating his tongue. Her attempt was refreshing but not needed. He had this.

And to show her just how much he had this, he deepened the kiss to take it to the next level while sliding his hands beneath her shirt. He found the front clasp to her bra and with an easy twist of the wrist, he had her bra undone and felt the exact moment her freed breasts sprang into his hands. She knew, too, and when she almost pulled her mouth from his, he locked down deeper and his tongue moved in a way that quickly made her regain her concentration. A warmth spread in his chest as he cupped her breasts. Damn, they felt good, and when he rubbed the pad of his thumb across one of the swollen nipples, he heard her moan deep in her throat.

Tanner wasn't sure what her sexual experience was, but he intended to make this time the best she'd ever had. He was arrogant enough to believe that he could. Why he was so intent on doing such a thing with a woman he'd slotted as an OD, he wasn't sure, since he didn't plan to have any more contact with her after today. He would chalk up the three-month gym membership as money well spent for an opportunity to do this.

But then, hadn't she made it clear that he was an OD, as well? Why did that bother him? He should be elated she felt that way. He would dismiss his annoyance for now, and her moans were helping him do so. Things couldn't get better than this—making out with a beautiful woman on a blanket at the beach with the scent of seawater flowing through his nostrils and the breeze floating across his skin.

Suddenly, her moans became deep groans, and when she tightened her arms around his neck and her body began shivering, he knew what was happening to her. Apparently, some knot of desire she'd been tied up in for a while had started to unravel. Now her tongue was trying to counter the increasingly intense movement of his own, driving him to a level of want and desire that was almost unbearable.

He felt like a sex-starved teenager about to make a score with the most beautiful girl at school. Her response to him was overwhelming and was making every cell in his body sizzle.

Their tongues were mingling in a dance so intense and sensual that he could feel a drugging rush of desire hit him below the waist. He was aroused beyond reason, hard as a rock, and his shaft was twitching in all kinds of ways, pressing against his zipper. Bone-melting fire was quickly spreading through him. Lord knows he was trying to stay in control of the situation, but he was discovering he was losing the fight.

Suddenly, she snatched her mouth from his when her body began convulsing in one hell of an orgasm. But he wanted it to be the one she would remember and decided to add the topping on the cake by tasting her in yet another way.

His mouth replaced his hands on her breasts. Her body jolted again, practically shoving her breast down his throat. He loved it. He loved her breasts and all but began making a meal of them. They were firm, plump and perfect. Now his hands were touching her, moving past her panties. His fingers sought her center and found it drenched.

He released her breast from his mouth and returned to her lips, nipping around them while his fingers began making circular motions around her body. She began moaning his name. "Tell me what you want me to do, baby."

The eyes staring at him were glazed, the result of two orgasms, and it wouldn't surprise him if her body wasn't gearing up for a third. For some reason he felt she needed a third and he wanted to give it to her. "Tell me what you want," he repeated.

"I want your mouth there," she whispered against his lips. "No man's mouth has ever been there and I need to know how it feels."

He blinked. Had she just confessed that no man had ever gone down on her before? This beautiful, curvaceous, sensuous woman. What kind of inept men had she been dating in her lifetime? He quickly decided he would take care of that oversight right now.

As he eased her back on the blanket, her legs seemed to automatically open. He slid down her shorts and her panties right along with them. When he revealed her womanhood, which looked so damn perfect, he had to bite back a groan. And just to think no other man's mouth had touched this. He felt like one lucky bastard.

He licked his lips and when she moaned his name, he shifted his gaze to her face. At that moment, he felt a deep kick in the chest, close to his heart. He went still, glad the moment had passed, but he knew it had left something behind. A tenderness he'd never felt for a woman before. He wondered where the hell that had come from and why. But he didn't have time to ponder that perplexing question. Right now, his tongue was anxious to get inside of her and he couldn't wait a minute longer.

Reaching out, he began fingering her between her legs and found her wetter than before. He watched her raise her hips as a bolt of desire shot through every part of him.

He placed his hands on each side of her hips and began tracing her own wetness across her thighs. He then eased his hands under her bottom and whispered, "I'm going to place your legs on my shoulders, baby." This would give him easier access to the part of her that he wanted, that his mouth was watering for.

"I want to make this good for you, Lyric." He doubted she knew just how much he meant that. "Just close your eyes and enjoy."

He leaned in and buried his head between her legs. He'd never known his tongue to be this ravenous, penetrate so deeply, lap so greedily. It was as if her taste was one he'd been waiting his entire life to sample and now that it was here he couldn't get enough. When she began moving against his mouth for deeper penetration, he began sucking hard and nibbling her clit with his teeth. If there was any way he could mark this, he would. Even if such a thing wasn't possible, he intended to leave her with the reminder that as her first, he had been worth waiting for.

He could feel her body jerk against his mouth and his tongue released her clit to begin doing his special kind of twirling motion inside of her. When her legs tightened around his neck, he recognized her impending orgasm and was ready for it.

He gripped her hips tighter and his tongue went deeper and began eating away at her like it was his last meal. The scream that erupted from her lips might have scared off the birds, and might have even carried far enough to have disturbed the creatures of the sea. What it did for him was nearly push him over the edge to do something in his pants he hadn't done since his teen years.

He fought to hold back his own release to make sure— absolutely sure, doubly sure—that she got hers. Her second scream and the trembling of her thighs and hips were clear indications that she had. She began moaning and the sound made his heart pound and the lower part of him ache, but he refused to remove his mouth from her until the last spasm had left her body.

Moments later, when it had, he leaned back on his haunches and stared down at her. She was naked except for her bra, which he hadn't clasped back in place. Her body had gone still, and her eyes were closed. As he continued to stare down at her, her eyes slowly opened and met his gaze, and her lips eased into a smile. A smile he'd put there.

Right now, an emotion he'd never felt before seemed to take control of him and he tried fighting it off. He didn't understand it and didn't want to deal with anything he didn't understand. Instead, he swooped her into his arms to carry her into his home.

CHAPTER TWENTY-TWO

EVEN AFTER TANNER placed her on his bed, Lyric felt as if she was still floating in the air and her body was refusing to come in for a landing. It seemed every single cell in her body had gotten pulverized into one sensuous ball of fire.

She felt like she was in another world, but wasn't *too* far out in the universe not to notice Tanner was stripping off his clothes to reveal a body she'd only seen a hint of in his workout attire.

Now she was getting a total, unobstructed view, and what she was seeing was arousing her all over again. His body was magnificent. Not for the first time she thought the man and his body should be on the cover of a fitness magazine.

She bit down on her bottom lip thinking she could probably have an orgasm just from looking at him. She'd gotten three already. Or had it been four? Maybe even five? She had lost count. Her first ever without the use of her battery-operated toy. That was pathetic, but the truth.

Totally naked, Tanner headed toward the bed and intense heat throbbed between her legs with every step he took.

Her gaze moved all over him. The amount of hair on his chest was sparse, but created a trail that led all the way down to his groin. And speaking of that area…

Lyric sat up in bed, estimating that she would have to wrap both hands around what he was packing. *Oh, my.*

Just looking at him while he rolled on a condom was getting her wired to the point that she just might blow a fuse. How could any man be so perfectly built? She needed to get an eyeful and sear it into memory because she was well aware after today he would walk away and not look back.

He placed his knee on the mattress and reached out, then after sliding her bra off her shoulders and tossing it aside, he drew her to him to rest his forehead against hers. "Your scent is powerful, Lyric. It reached out to me all the way across the room, letting me know you wanted me again."

She pulled away from him and knew she had a baffled look on her face. "What?"

He smiled. "It doesn't matter. But you want me again, right?"

Oh, yeah, he was definitely right. "Yes."

His smile widened. "No reservations?"

How could he ask her that after she'd shared her first oral sex experience of any kind with him. "None."

"Good." When he looked at her breasts fully uncovered, he actually licked his lips, sending a rush of blood through her veins.

"Before we leave here today, I plan to make another meal out of you."

She swallowed knowing that was his way of letting her know they would be engaging in oral sex again. "I'd like that." No need to lie about it when she'd liked the feel of his tongue inside of her. And since this would be their only time together, the memories would help sustain her.

"You tasted good. Real good."

She wasn't sure what she should say to that, but since she took it as a compliment, she said, "Thank you."

"And," he said, humming close to her ear, "I plan to suck your breasts again. Your nipples taste good, too."

His words caused a sensual pull in the area between her legs. He was totally different from Westley and any other guy she'd had sex with. They never told her what they planned to do. They just did it and expected her to keep up.

Tanner was making her feel like a sensuous woman for the first time...ever. She liked the thought that she was embarking on doing some things she'd never done before with him. Sure, this wasn't her first rodeo with intercourse, but she had a feeling Tanner was about to take her on the wildest ride of her life and what she'd done in the past wouldn't compare.

Tanner leaned in and kissed her. Soon she was purring in his mouth from the intensity of the kiss. Closing her eyes, she was swept away in a sea of earth-shattering sensations as he deepened the kiss, with long, intense strokes of his tongue. When she felt her back touch the mattress, he released her mouth. She opened her eyes to see him straddling her body.

"Tanner..."

She wasn't exactly sure why she said his name at that very moment. Maybe it was because his kiss had stirred a desire in her that she knew only he could take care of. There was an ache between her legs and she was convinced he was the only one who could take it away.

"Tell me what you want, Lyric."

Why did he want her to do that when he knew what she wanted? Hadn't he told her that her scent had already told him? "You know."

"But I want you to tell me, anyway. I want to hear you say it."

No guy had ever asked for her input before. "Do whatever you want."

He shook his head. "No, I want to do whatever you want."

Lyric had never known a man so generous and accommodating in the bedroom. She decided to be honest with him. "I don't know what to tell you."

A gentle, understanding smile touch his lips. "Maybe this will help."

He leaned in and went for a breast, easing a nipple between his lips, and began sucking. Did he not know what doing that did to her? How it drove her hot with desire. How it increased that pull between her legs.

He moved to her other breast and she noticed his fingers had slipped down between her legs and were now drawing circular motions around her clit. This was too much and she closed her eyes and groaned.

"Now can you tell me what you want, Lyric?" a deep, throaty voice asked.

Oh, yeah, she could tell him all right. Opening her eyes and meeting his gaze, she said, "I want you to take me, Tanner. Hard. Over and over again. Deep."

"It will be my pleasure…and yours."

And then he thrust hard into her. He was huge and her body stretched to accommodate him as he went deep and even deeper still. It seemed she heard a click somewhere as if their bodies had locked. He went still and stared at her as if he'd heard that click, as well. Or maybe she'd imagined it and he'd gone still for another reason.

She was about to ask if anything was wrong when he began moving again, thrusting in and out of her, moving his hips in perfect rhythm. Every time he thrust, her body rose up to meet his and their gazes would connect. With each thrust, he drove her closer to the edge, making her moan. When he began moving at a rapid pace, like a jackhammer, she knew she'd never experienced this degree of pleasure before in her life.

She wouldn't last much longer and when her body began splintering, she screamed out his name. He kept pounding into her, pushing her to the edge.

"Explode again for me, baby."

As if her body had been programmed to react to his command, sensations began swamping her and she felt an explosion of pleasure take over her. She was pushed over the edge, and as if the detonation of her body was what he needed to complete his own, she felt his body nearly buck them off the bed just seconds before he threw back his head and a guttural sound, which included her name, exploded from his mouth.

She'd never experienced anything like this before. Where had all this sexual energy come from? Would she be able to walk out of here on her own, or would he have to carry her out? At that moment, it didn't matter. Nothing mattered except all the sexual pleasure she was feeling.

She was convinced nothing could compare to this, and she was experiencing it all thanks to him.

TANNER AWOKE AND glanced over at the clock. It was close to six in the evening. At some point they needed to get dressed and leave to return to New Orleans. Earlier, while Lyric slept, he had slipped into his jeans and gone to the beach where they'd had their picnic to gather the items they'd left behind, including pieces of her clothing. Luckily, because there hadn't been a high tide, nothing had been swept out to sea.

The items had gotten sandy, which prompted him to wash her things. It was the first time he'd ever done anything so intimate for a woman, but he'd felt comfortable tossing her shorts and panties into the washer and dryer. In fact, he thought her panties were a cute pair and thought it was sexy that it matched the bra he'd taken off her earlier.

Once he had taken care of that, there had been no reason not to wake her for them to head back to New Orleans. He had gotten what he'd set out to get from her, and he definitely had no reason to feel guilty about that since he'd done her a favor and had introduced her to oral sex. And he could tell from the number of orgasms she'd experienced that she had liked it. However, seeing her in his bed had made him groan in raw appreciation, and the next thing he knew, he'd removed his jeans and gotten back in bed with her to hold her while she slept. Eventually, he had fallen back to sleep, as well.

"Thanks for today, Tanner."

He looked over at Lyric. She was awake. At the sound of her voice, his shaft sprang to life, hard as a rock, and he was back to being greedy as hell.

"You're welcome, Lyric."

He knew she had thanked him for more than just the picnic on the beach. That made him want to press for answers to something that bothered him. "There is something I need to know, though."

"What?" she asked.

"How long were you with your last boyfriend?"

She had to be wondering why he was bringing the man up. "Why do you want to know?"

"Curious."

She held his gaze for a moment and then said, "Almost a year."

He nodded. "And during all that time he never…?"

She evidently knew where he was going with his line of questioning and quickly said, "No, he never."

He rolled his eyes. "What an idiot."

That made her smile and she laughed, agreeing with him. "Yes, what an idiot."

They suddenly burst out laughing and it felt so damn good. Then he asked, "Why did you waste your time with him?"

She broke eye contact to look at an abstract picture on the wall behind him. For a moment he wasn't sure she would answer, then she looked at him and said, "I really liked him initially, and he was fun to be around. He made me feel special."

"Except in the bedroom."

She released a deep sigh. "I honestly didn't think anything was wrong in the bedroom, Tanner. At least not at first. It wasn't until I would overhear women whispering at the gym, comparing notes of their bedroom experiences, that I realized some of what they were saying were things I had never felt to the degree they had, or stuff I had never done with Westley. Oral sex was one of them."

"Didn't you ask him about it?"

She shrugged. "At first I honestly didn't feel comfortable discussing it with him because I didn't want to come across as being unsatisfied with what we were doing in the bedroom."

She paused a moment and then said, "When I finally felt the need to ask him about it, he said oral sex wasn't a big deal, was really overrated and that I wouldn't like it. And as for why my orgasms weren't as powerful as his, he said it was due to our sexual experience levels."

Then, as if deciding she might have shared too much with him, she said, "It doesn't matter anymore because I know better now."

He nodded. "Moving forward you will know what to expect," he said, although the thought of her letting another man go down on her like he had was annoying as hell.

"You're right, I'll know what to expect." She made a move to ease off the bed, but he reached out and touched her arm. Lyric glanced over her shoulder at him.

He suddenly realized that there was something about Lyric that had made him let down his guard. Somehow during the course of the day it had slipped, and it was time to take control of the situation again. He had to remember that she was an OD—one and done. Anything else would spell trouble for him. She was the kind of a woman who could get under a man's skin—if he let her—and there was no way Tanner would let that happen.

"Let's get dressed," he said. Then he added, "And just so you know, I won't be coming back to the gym after today."

"I knew you wouldn't, Tanner, and I think it would be for the best if you didn't, anyway. I told you that before leaving New Orleans."

Yes, she had, so he should be feeling great. So why did the thought of never seeing her again begin to bother him in a way that it shouldn't have?

PART 3

When in doubt, follow your heart and be led down
the path of true love.
—Felicia Laverne Madaris I (Mama Laverne)

CHAPTER TWENTY-THREE

ROMAN HEARD THE sound of Victoria's footsteps when she entered her kitchen. Turning, he smiled and leaned against the counter to look at her. She looked gorgeous dressed in an eggplant-colored pencil skirt and cream-colored blouse. It was a look that was both professional and sexy.

"Good morning, Roman."

He pushed away from the counter and leaned in to place a kiss on her lips. "Good morning to you, too."

He thought the last three days had been pretty damn awesome. They had joined the festivities in the town's square after the fireworks Labor Day night to celebrate the close of Catalina Cove's five-day celebration.

Because she had to work Tuesday, he had taken her home before midnight and ended up spending the night. He had liked being with her in the morning, making love to her and watching her get ready for work before she left. That had pretty much set the stage for the days that followed, with them spending every night together, either at his place or hers.

He was determined to spend as much time with her as he could before he returned to DC. She hadn't yet given him her decision as to whether not they would continue things after he left. He was desperately hoping that she would because he wasn't ready to give her up and knew there was no way he ever could.

"I've decided to take tomorrow off," she said.

He lifted an eyebrow. "You have?"

"Yes. They will be preempting our show to cover the New Orleans Marathon. With tomorrow being Friday, that means I get another long weekend. What do you think about that?"

He thought it was great if she intended to spend that extra time with him. "I got an idea."

She smiled up at him. "And what idea is that?"

"That we take the yacht out, set anchor and spend the weekend in the middle of the Gulf. Just the two of us." They had taken the boat out for fishing but had never stayed out overnight.

She tilted her head as if she was giving his idea some serious thought, then her smile deepened when she said, "Great! Let's do it!"

He pulled her into his arms and captured her mouth with his. He felt an overwhelming sensation within and knew he would never tire of holding her in his arms and kissing her.

And loving her.

He wished he could tell her how he felt, but couldn't. He didn't want to place any pressure on her about whatever decision she made about their future. When they pulled back for breath, he gazed at her perfect face, framed by her beautiful mass of dark brown hair, and looked into those gorgeous brown eyes.

"I'll file the necessary float plan and we can leave early tomorrow," he said, studying her mouth and feeling tempted to kiss her again.

"Okay. Now I need to leave to attend this morning's meeting."

He took a step back. "I figured you would be running

late so I prepared an egg sandwich and coffee to take with you."

She closed the distance and leaned up to kiss his cheek. "You take good care of me."

"Always."

"And you will be here when I get home, right?" she asked him.

"Yes. I'll be right here."

He wrapped his arms around her for what probably was the longest goodbye kiss he'd ever given a woman.

VICTORIA WAS CLEARING OFF her desk to call it a day when her cell phone rang. From the ringtone she knew it was Christy. She pulled her phone from her purse and said, "Hey, Christy."

"Hey. Everyone thought you'd come home for Labor Day to attend Jake and Diamond's cookout."

Victoria leaned back in her chair. "I thought about coming since I needed to talk to Mama Laverne. However, I wanted to spend the weekend with Roman. He's returning to Washington next week."

"Sounds like things have heated up between the two of you."

Victoria thought that was an understatement when her mind recalled how they'd spent the last few days. "They have, Christy. He even wants us to continue seeing each other after he returns to Washington."

"How do you feel about that?" Christy asked.

"Not sure. I'll give him my answer soon."

"What about Tanner?"

That was the same thing Roman had wanted to know. "Tanner is the reason I need to talk to Mama Laverne. Roman leaves next Friday morning and I'm flying to Whispering Pines to see her on Saturday. I don't understand how things can be developing between me and Roman when I'm promised to Tanner."

"You won't be able to talk to Mama Laverne next weekend. She left this morning with Uncle Milton and Aunt Dora on a twenty-day cruise."

Victoria threw her head back and sighed. She'd forgotten about that cruise her great-grandmother took with her oldest son and daughter-in-law about this time every year. "Twenty days?"

"Yes."

"Then I need to talk to her when she returns."

Christy didn't say anything and then she asked, "How do you feel about Roman, Victoria?"

She decided to be honest. "I'm falling in love with him, Christy. I know that I am. That could only mean one thing."

"What?"

"Somehow Mama Laverne made a mistake in pairing me with Tanner."

"SWEET THING, I GOT the photographs you sent over and read your PI's report. Sounds like your senator has been busy."

Audria leaned back against the seat of her car. She hated when he called her "sweet thing" and would usually correct him. But not this time. She needed Buddy's help. "So when will you run the story?" There was no need to tell him that she'd doctored John's report to make things look worse than they really were. People didn't read *The Tattler* for the truth, anyway.

"The Monday after he returns. My sources tell me the senator will be back in DC sometime that Friday. I want to think of it as 'The Monday Surprise' and prefer using my capital reporters to question him. They are known to be aggressive. And I have a reporter in place in New Orleans, as well, for Ms. Madaris. It's best to handle them separately. On top of that, we also plan to question Tanner Jamison to see if he had any idea just what his girlfriend has been doing behind his back."

She could hear a shuffling of papers, then Buddy said, "Only thing, we can't find any articles or news reports of a romantic relationship between Jamison and Victoria Madaris or an announcement of an engagement. The only thing we could find is the mention of him opening some nightclub in New Orleans."

"Not sure why their engagement hasn't been public, unless they are keeping it a secret for some reason. I figure the reason he's opening the club in New Orleans is to keep an eye on her. I think deep down, Tanner Jamison knows she can't be trusted," she theorized as she glanced out the car window, knowing what she was saying was all lies, but Buddy wouldn't question it. More than anything, she needed him to run that article.

"You're probably right and that's the angle we're going for. We're going to paint Jamison as the victim in all this, with the senator and Victoria Madaris having an affair behind his back. In other words, we will implicate the senator in a love triangle with the Madaris woman. Even if they deny it, it will throw shade on both of their reputations because we have all those photos to back up our claim."

Audria's smile widened. That's what she wanted. Roman would seek her out to help clean up his image. "And I happen to think that angle is a good one."

"You owe me, sweet thing, and I intend to collect. Be at my place tonight at nine and don't be late."

Audria frowned at the sound of the phone clicking in her ear.

CHAPTER TWENTY-FOUR

TANNER TOSSED THE report he'd been trying to read for the past half hour on his desk. He rubbed the bridge of his nose, feeling a tension headache coming on. He never got headaches of any kind. What was going on with his body…other than the obvious signs of sexual withdrawal?

He stood and shoved his hands into his pockets as he walked over to the window to look out. The workers had left for lunch and he was in the building alone. Hank had popped into his office more than once to report the renovations of the bathrooms were finished and the workers had started on the walls and floors. Then there had been the sounds of men at work, voices, the sound of a hammer against wood and the hum of a drill. Now everything was quiet…except for the sound of his heart beating in his chest.

What in the hell was wrong with him? Why did Lyric Evans still have him tied in knots? After all they'd shared on Monday, she should be out of his system by now. Yet here it was Thursday and she was even more deeply embedded in there. He thought about her every waking moment and when he went to bed at night, he dreamed about her, reliving every single thing they did together. Every touch, every kiss, and the feel of him sinking deep into her body and hearing her scream his name as their bodies exploded together.

He rubbed his hand down his face. He'd had sex with

many different women, and the experiences had all been good. But what he'd shared with Lyric had been exceptional, totally extraordinary and over the f-ing top. He honestly didn't know how to deal with it and why it had affected him so intensely. He should have moved on by now. She should have been three women ago, but he hadn't had another woman since her. He didn't want another woman. Somehow, she'd infiltrated every part of his body whether he wanted it or not. None of it made any sense to him.

He turned when the cell phone on his desk rang. Recognizing the ringtone, he quickly moved across the room to pick it up. "Yes, Blade?"

"Hey, man, just wanted to verify all the kitchen equipment has been ordered. You should have gotten the paperwork today."

"I did. First thing this morning. The courier was waiting for me to sign on the dotted line when I arrived."

"Good. How are things going?"

"On schedule."

Blade didn't say anything for a minute and then asked, "You okay? You don't sound like yourself."

Tanner figured no, he didn't. And because Blade used to have a players' card like him, maybe he could answer a question for him. "Why is it that after a man nearly screws a woman's brains out, he still can't get her out of his system?"

Blade, Tanner noted, had gone quiet. Then his friend said, "You got some damn nerve telling me what you've been doing to my cousin Tanner."

Tanner blinked. "Your cousin?"

"Yes. Was the woman Victoria?"

"Victoria! Hell, no! I haven't seen Victoria in weeks. I told you about the last time I saw her and she told me she was seeing some dude, and I said I was happy for her and meant it. No matter what Ms. Laverne got you all believing, I am not the man for Victoria. Damn, man, how many times do I have to say that? I'm into someone else, Blade. Someone that should be an OD but refuses to be."

"She's stalking you?"

He wished. "No. In fact, she's probably gone her merry-ass little way and I haven't even crossed her mind. I'm the one with issues."

"And why do you have issues? Sounds like you just need another night with her. It works that way with some ODs. They become TDs, two and done. It happens even when you don't want it to. Better yet, why not make her a CH? Then, as a casual hookup, you won't have that problem."

"I can't."

"Why not?"

"Because there's something about her that tells me I can't put my guard down. She's different."

"Umm, funny you should say that," Blade said.

Tanner lifted an eyebrow. "Why?"

"Because that's one of the first things I thought about Sam, that she was different from the other women I'd messed around with."

Tanner frowned. "I didn't say she was different from the others. I said she was different."

Blade laughed. "I'm going to let you go, Tanner, because you're not making much sense and being difficult. In fact, your entire attitude is concerning."

Tanner slid into the chair at his desk. "Concerning in what way?"

"If some woman got you tied in knots and she's not Victoria, then that's concerning. Why aren't you interested in my cousin?"

Tanner rolled his eyes. "Oh, now you want me to be interested in her?"

"No. I'm just concerned that you're not. This scenario is not playing out the way it should. Not how my great-grandmother's matchmaking plan usually works. It usually kicks off with a rough start, but then it runs smoothly, and the couple eventually falls in love."

"I'm not falling in love with anyone. Your cousin or any woman, Blade."

"I hate to tell you this, but you won't be able to stop it, and from the sound of things, if the woman isn't Victoria, that could only mean one thing."

"What?"

"Mama Laverne made a mistake in picking you for Victoria. You should have caved in by now and be all into Victoria. It took me less than thirty days to get all into Sam, and about the same amount of time for Lee and Nolan to get into Carly and Ivy. You're not acting normal."

"I *am* acting normal. The only thing we agree on is that your great-grandmother made a mistake if her plan was to hook me up with Victoria. I like Victoria, but I can't see myself falling in love with her. She and I don't share anything in common."

"But you and this woman who put an itch in your crotch do have something in common?" Blade asked.

"Yes. In fact, Lyric and I have several things in common," he said, not denying the itch was definitely there. But deep down he knew it was more than just an itch. It was an intense yearning the likes of which he'd never felt before. He'd discovered she was someone who was easy to talk to and he'd shared things about all the charities he was involved in. On the flight from Crystal Beach, she had mentioned she was involved in similar charities here in New Orleans. Even with her long work hours every day and assisting her parents at the gym on the weekends, she still found time to help in the soup kitchen, to read bedtime stories to the kids at the children's hospital and assist the vet at the animal shelter on occasion.

"Sounds like there's more to this woman than her being a bed partner for you, Tanner. That makes my concern for Victoria increase."

"Why?"

"Because unlike the rest of us, Victoria had no problem letting Mama Laverne select a man for her, which means she expects you to one day get in line and fall in love with her."

"That won't be happening," Tanner said, getting tired of repeating himself.

"Then I can see Victoria getting hurt."

"I can't see her getting hurt. Like I told you, the last time I saw her she looked happy and even told me she was seriously involved with someone."

Bladed snorted. "That's bullshit. Victoria is not seriously involved with any man. And I told you that she probably just told you that to save face and not have you think she was pining for you, waiting for you to get your shit together about her. If you aren't the man meant for her then either Mama Laverne made a mistake, or you're too much of a stubborn ass to accept your fate."

"I don't know how many times I have to tell you that your cousin is not my fate."

"Then somebody needs to talk to Mama Laverne before Victoria's heart gets broken."

"Then maybe your family needs to intervene and have a talk with your great-grandmother."

"She's on a cruise."

"Then I suggest you talk to Victoria."

"That won't do any good since she thinks Mama Laverne's word is the gospel, and usually it is. The best person to talk to is Mama Laverne, and my cousins and I will have a talk with her when she gets back from her cruise."

"YOU SURE YOU'RE OKAY, honey?"

Lyric looked up into her godmother's warm eyes, which seemed full of concern. Granted, she hadn't been as talkative today as she normally was. But that wasn't cause for any alarm. "I'm fine, Goddie. I just have a lot on my mind."

She wasn't surprised when Susan LeBlanc slid into the chair across from her. Lyric had stopped by the bakery to sample a few beignets before heading over to the children's hospital for story hour. She was one of the volunteers who read to the young patients.

Westley always complained about the amount of time she devoted to her charities instead of to him, trying to make her feel guilty. She was so glad it hadn't worked. Now she was seeing just what a selfish bastard he'd been.

And why was she still constantly thinking about Tanner to the degree she'd barely thought of much else? Tomorrow was Friday and she would be working at the gym. She didn't expect a lot of people since most were participating in the New Orleans Marathon. Even her parents would be running in the race. Tanner was to have been her eight o'clock appointment in the morning, but she knew not to expect him since he would not be returning to the gym. In fact, when he'd dropped her off to get her car on Monday evening, he'd again reiterated his position and—not to be outdone—she'd firmly reiterated hers. They wouldn't be seeing other again. It was a mutual decision.

"Lyric?"

She'd forgotten her godmother had joined her at the table. "Yes?" The last thing she wanted her godmother to do was worry about her. She'd done enough of that after her breakup with Westley and discovering his betrayal with Wendy.

She and her godmother always had that kind of relationship. Susan was someone she'd always been able to confide in. Of course, she didn't tell her everything that went on in her life, but over the years she had shared a lot with her. Susan was sixty and her mother, Yvonne, had been Lyric's grandmother Isabelle's best friend since grade school. Susan had promised Isabelle Evans that if anything ever happened to her that she would be there for her three grandchildren. When Isabelle died three years ago, Susan had kept her promise.

"I was just wondering," Lyric murmured.

"About what?"

"How can a woman meet a guy and not like him at first, but after spending a day with him, she can't think of anyone else?"

Susan lifted an eyebrow. "I would say that person made an impression on her. Something he hadn't done when they initially met."

Her godmother was right. Her initial impression of Tanner had been that he was arrogant and conceited. He was probably still those things, but she had to hand it to him, he deserved to have an ego after what all he'd done to her and had given her. He'd been the most gracious, giving and considerate lover any woman could have. And then the fact that he had washed her clothes for her. That had been thoughtful of him. She hadn't expected any of those things of him.

"You're dating again?"

Lyric shook her head. "No. It was just one date." No need to tell her godmother what all they'd done on that one date.

"Why just one date?"

"We didn't connect like I thought we would," she said quickly.

Susan LeBlanc tilted her head and gave her a curious look. "Obviously, the two of you connected in some way better than you expected. Otherwise you wouldn't be thinking about him so much."

Before Lyric could think of a response to that, her godmother stood when a customer came into the bakery.

TANNER WALKED INTO his apartment thinking how different it looked. Since he wasn't a fan of clutter, he had taken the time to finally unpack and put stuff away. Doing so had kept him busy and he had needed that. Otherwise, he would have spent his time thinking about Lyric, and remembering their time together and wondering what she was doing now...and with whom.

She was constantly intruding on his thoughts, disrupting his concentration. It was so out of character for him. Never had a woman filled him with such desire and longing that he was certain her scent was still on him, even after taking countless showers. All it took was for him to remember her taste. Damn, he wondered if what some guys said was true. The one woman whose taste you couldn't do without was the one who could either be your downfall or your salvation. He didn't want Lyric Evans to be either.

Moving to his kitchen, he grabbed a beer out of the refrigerator, uncapped the bottle and took swig. What he did want was to move on with his life, pick up his normal routine. He had a little black book full of names, yet he hadn't had the desire or the inclination to call one of them, even when he desperately felt the need to get laid.

He threw back his head in frustration as he leaned against the kitchen counter. What the hell was happening to him? Why was he behaving like a man possessed? A man on the verge of losing his control, his mind...and his heart.

His heart—the possibility totally freaked him out. Surely, it had to take more than one day in bed to feel something like that. He must be dealing with a case of intense lust and nothing more—is this what was called being p-whipped?

Damn. He knew his problem was more serious than Blade thought. He seriously doubted making her a TD, two and done, would be a fix. If anything, it might push him completely over the edge. Little did Lyric know, but his day with her had blown his mind in several ways. Hell, now he even liked her as a person.

On the flight back to New Orleans she had even told him about her ex-boyfriend and discovering that he was sleeping with a woman she'd considered a friend. A woman who'd frequented the gym that she'd befriended.

Now he understood why she needed to make sure he wasn't already involved with someone before agreeing to spend Labor Day with him. Tanner figured she'd been candid with him because she knew it would be the only time they would spend together.

Tanner took another swig of his beer and then drew in a deep breath. He pulled out the little black book he kept in the pocket of his jacket to see who he would call tonight. He'd gone without female company too long. Tomorrow was Friday and it was time he made plans to kick-start his weekend.

Moments later, he tossed the book on the counter, not

believing he still couldn't do it. The thought of making love to a woman other than Lyric did something to him. It was crazy that the one woman he craved was the one he was determined to keep his distance from.

Feeling frustrated as hell, he finished off the beer and decided to shower and hit bed early.

CHAPTER TWENTY-FIVE

"IF YOU DON'T wake up now, sweetheart, you're going to miss the sunrise. It's a beautiful view through the porthole."

Victoria lifted one eyelid and then another. She figured the sunrise wasn't the only thing she would be missing out on if she didn't open her eyes, if Roman's erection poking into her backside was anything to go by.

Smiling, she slowly flipped over to gaze up into a gorgeous pair of dark eyes and delectable lips nearly covered in a beard. "Will you be shaving when you return to DC?"

She could tell her question surprised him. "Why? Is my beard bothering you?"

She knew why he was asking. He had to apply cream to a few beard burns between her legs more than once. "No. I've gotten used to it and like it."

He chuckled. "Thanks, but yes, it will be off before I land in DC. It will no longer be needed."

He had mentioned last night how glad he was that the paparazzi had left him alone since he'd been in Catalina Cove. She was glad, too. Shifting to her side, she glanced out the porthole. The sun was about to come up. "You're right. It's beautiful."

"Beautiful just like you."

She thought that he could say some of the nicest things. And do some pretty nice things, as well. When she had arrived home from work yesterday, he had been waiting for her with soup from the Green Fig, one of the new restaurants in town. Victoria had previously met the owner, Sierra Crane, and her beautiful little girl.

Sierra had grown up in the cove and like so many others, had not returned after college. She had landed a high-powered corporate job in Chicago. Now divorced, she was back in Catalina Cove to raise her daughter. Victoria was glad because the woman was using her late grandmother's soup recipes at the Green Fig and they were delicious. The takeout soup container was a cute miniature keg that kept the transported soup hot.

The minute Victoria had walked into her house, the aroma of the soup had gotten to her, as well as the sight of Roman standing in the middle of the living room. She'd done something she'd never done before. She began stripping off her clothes right then and there. Needless to say, they had made love before eating dinner.

"Did I thank you for dinner yesterday?"

He chuckled as he nibbled around her mouth. "Several times, but you can always do it again."

"Thank you, Roman." She wrapped her arms around his neck and pulled his mouth to hers. He had such a beautiful mouth. A mouth she loved kissing, and he had shown her how to do so in so many ways. She tightened her arms around his neck as they continued kissing. It was as if the privilege to do this again would be taken away from them and they were making it last.

Suddenly, he pulled away and when she opened her eyes it was to see a pair of sexy brown eyes staring at her. The intensity in his gaze made her feel hot and she released a slow, deep breath.

"Let's watch the sunrise, baby," he said in a deep, husky voice.

She nodded. Pulling herself up, she snuggled next to him as they looked out the porthole to see the beauty of the sun coming up, seemingly out of the water, and moving slowly into the sky. Starting today, they would spend the weekend in the middle of the Gulf. After breakfast they would head toward the area where the Mississippi River flowed into the Gulf of Mexico. It was reputed to have the best fishing spots anywhere.

Roman's chin rested on the crown of her head, and Victoria appreciated being able to share this moment with him. She had shared a lot of memorable moments with him, some that would be etched in her mind forever.

Forever.

Why was she thinking about forever with him? Maybe because that's where her heart was. Was it? She turned her head to find his delectable mouth right there, and at that moment she needed to kiss him again. As if he read her thoughts, he whispered, "It's yours to take. Not just my mouth, sweetheart, but all of me."

All of him...

Why did the thought of taking all of him sound like something she definitely wanted? With him she could be naughty or nice, she could take what she wanted. Is that why she felt empowered? In Roman's arms, she had become a responsive woman in ways she hadn't thought possible. He'd taught her how to tell him what she wanted and then went out of his way to deliver. And he always did.

She could feel his hard, solid erection pressing against her and it felt good. Deciding it would feel even better inside of her, she began rubbing her backside against him in invitation.

"Is that your way of letting me know what you want, baby?" he asked while sliding his hand between her legs.

She closed her eyes, thinking just how good his hands felt, and when a finger slid inside of her, she moaned his name.

He leaned in and she felt the warmth of his bare chest on her naked back. He licked the side of her face. "You taste good."

Roman whispered exactly how he wanted to take her this time, and she moaned at the image that came into her mind—her, on her knees with him behind her.

As soon as they got in position, he ran his fingers through her hair to tilt her face back to him. "The rest of our days spent here together I intend to make things so wonderful for you with me, that when I leave, coming to me in DC won't be a choice for you, Victoria. It will be a necessity. Either you will come to me or I will come back here to you. I won't give you up."

He gripped her hips and entered her, thrusting hard and deep, then went still. She loved the feel of him embedded deep within her like this, opening her wide. She heard the sound of his heavy breathing and knew he was trying to regain control, as well as savor how he felt inside of her. The same thing she was doing.

Suddenly he began moving, thrusting into her, pounding his flesh against hers, the sound increasing her desire. He began chanting her name with every stroke and she, in turn, groaned his, over and over. She thought they fit perfectly together as he brought her close to the edge, only to snatch her back again and again. Was he deliberately trying to drive her crazy? If so, he was definitely doing a good job at it. The pleasure she felt from the top of her head to her toes was overwhelming.

"Come for me, baby," he said, leaning over to lick the

side of her ear again. "You come. I come. Let's do it together."

As if his words had pushed a button, she felt her body begin exploding and knew the moment his did, too—they were in sync. She felt him release inside of her and knew there was more to come because they had this thing for multiple orgasms.

They both came again. And then, as if he still couldn't get enough, he helped roll her to her back and entered her again after placing her knees on his shoulders.

"I want to look at you," he growled.

Their gazes met and she saw him clearly and knew at that moment that he was the man she loved.

I won't give you up...

His words floated through her mind. She got it now. He was claiming her. Roman was claiming her.

This time when her body exploded, she let out a loud scream, and he quickly covered her mouth as he continued to make love to her. When he finally released her mouth, she let out a guttural groan. Moments later, he collapsed beside her, gathered her limp body into his arms and kissed her face all over.

"You all right?" he asked her softly.

Unable to speak, she just nodded slowly. The last thing she remembered before closing her eyes to sleep was the feel of his arms wrapped securely around her.

"I TAKE IT you were pretty hungry," Roman said, watching Victoria scarf down the soup and sandwiches he'd brought along. After making love earlier, he had left her sleeping in bed while he raised the anchor to head out toward the Gulf. Having missed breakfast, they were on the top deck eating lunch and enjoying being out in the middle of the water with no other boat in sight.

While at the Green Fig yesterday, he'd also bought a keg of several kinds of soup, including chili, and several types of sandwiches for their sea voyage.

Victoria glanced at him and smiled. "Weren't you hungry, as well?"

He chuckled. "Yes. You can say that I was."

She stood to throw away her trash and he couldn't help but stare at her, thinking Tanner Jamison's loss was certainly his gain. But would it really be Jamison's loss if there was some doubt in her mind about which man she would one day truly belong to? The one who was desperately trying to show her with action how much he loved her, or the one currently missing in action, but chosen for her by someone she loved and whose opinion she trusted?

"Isn't it beautiful, Roman?"

He followed her gaze, and as far as the eye could see, the view was of the beautiful blue, rippling waters of the Gulf. The smell of the sea filled his nostrils and a light breeze ruffled the air. He then turned his gaze to Victoria and saw how that same light breeze was fanning her hair around her face, giving her a stunning look. "Yes, it's beautiful. You're beautiful, too, and I want you."

Needing to make love to her again, he swept her into his arms and carried her below. He didn't want to think about the lonely days without her, but when they came, he would have this. The memories.

A SHORT WHILE later Roman and Victoria were back up top. He was at the wheel, maneuvering the yacht through the Gulf waters, and she was there by his side. Not surprisingly, she knew how to operate the boat, as well. But for now, she was enjoying the scenery while he had the wheel.

It amazed him that he'd found a woman who enjoyed doing some of the same things he did. Not only did she like to fish, but she also liked to hunt and camp outdoors. Then there was the other side of her that he appreciated, the side that was compassionate. Last night he'd told her about an education bill he planned to introduce in the next session. She'd told him how much she supported such a bill and was glad someone finally, as she put it, "had the balls to do it," and hoped it passed. Just knowing he had her backing meant everything.

Regardless of what she thought, she would make a great politician's spouse. But first he had to convince her to consider becoming a politician's girlfriend. He would be leaving the cove in a week and hoped she would give him her answer before he left.

"It's 'tell me something I want to know' time," she said, getting his attention.

He smiled. This was a game they'd started playing the first day they went fishing together to get to know each other better. They were free to ask any question to get an answer to anything they wanted to know about that person. It was fun and had revealed a lot about her to him; he hoped she'd also learned a lot about him. "Okay, what's your question?" he asked.

"Have you ever had a crush on anyone? And please don't tell me that, like all my brothers and cousins, Aunt Diamond was your fantasy girl while growing up."

Roman chuckled. "I could see Diamond being that. She was a very popular actress who was, and still is, beautiful. But no, I didn't have a crush on Diamond. But I did on Syneda."

"What! Clayton's Syneda?"

He laughed. "Yes. But remember I knew Syneda long before Clayton did, since my aunt Nora and my uncle Paul were foster parents to both Syneda and Lorren."

Lorren was married to her cousin, and Roman's oldest godbrother, Justin. While growing up, Victoria had thought it was simply wonderful that two childhood best friends, Lorren and Syneda, had married the Madaris brothers, Justin and Clayton. "That's right. I had forgotten about that. So how long did the crush on Syneda last?"

"All through my teen years. I think it was the golden bronze hair and green eyes that did it for me."

Victoria grinned. "I think that's what did it for Clayton, as well. Small world."

"Yes. I got over her once I went off to college. Imagine how I felt when I came home my sophomore year to discover my godbrother Clayton was going to marry my dream girl. I thought Clayton was the luckiest man in the world."

"I think he thought so, too. He still does. There's never a dull moment around those two. I like Syneda a lot. She's a lot of fun. In fact, I think all my male cousins hit the jackpot with the women they married. And I adore my sister-in-law Ivy, as well. She is just what Nolan needs."

He nodded. "Now what about you? Have you ever had a crush on anyone? And please don't say it was movie actor Sterling Hamilton. He was Spring and Summer's crush for years."

She shook her head. "No, it was a boy in my fifth-grade class named Thomas Bellamy. I thought he was so cute. But then his family moved away, and I never saw him again."

She paused and then said, "This time next week you'll be back in Washington."

He nodded. "Yes, I will be." He wanted to ask if she'd

made a decision yet about them, but didn't. He didn't want to rush her, but more than anything he hoped she would agree for them to continue what they'd begun in Catalina Cove.

CHAPTER TWENTY-SIX

TANNER WISHED HE could call himself all kinds of fool as he crossed the parking lot to Evans's Gym, but he couldn't. He could no longer let his obsession with Lyric get the best of him. He didn't give a damn that his fixation on her was so out of character for him. The only thing that concerned him now was his sanity. There still were a lot of things that weren't clear in his mind, but the one thing he desperately understood was that had to see Lyric again. And he had to see her today.

It had taken several mind-twisting and gut-wrenching days to accept that his attraction to her wasn't normal; to accept it was too intense, too time-consuming and taxing on his brain to be ignored. This thing with Lyric was totally different and he needed to know why. And the only way he could figure it out was to see her again.

It was Sunday and the gym didn't open until noon. It was only ten. He had been prepared to sit in the parking lot and wait those two hours for her to arrive. When he'd seen her car, that meant she was already inside, and he was grateful for that.

The entry to the gym was locked. He peered through the glass door and didn't see anyone at the counter, and the lights were off. So he rang the doorbell then shoved his hands in the pockets of his jeans and stared down at his feet while wishing so many questions weren't flowing through his mind. What if she wasn't inside, but was at one of the nearby shops? Then, what if she saw him and wouldn't let him in? What if—?

"Tanner? What are you doing here?"

He jerked his head up and there she stood. Lyric had opened the door and for a moment he couldn't speak. All he could do was stand there and look at her, taking in the beauty that had become a permanent fixture in his mind.

"Tanner?"

He tried to retain control of his mind. "I need to talk to you, Lyric."

She raised an eyebrow. "What about?"

"I'd rather not discuss it out here. May I come in?"

She seemed to give his request some thought, then said, "Yes, come in." Stepping aside, she beckoned him to enter and then locked the door behind him.

"I took a chance in coming here," he explained. "I hadn't expected you to arrive this early."

"I worked serving breakfast at the homeless shelter this morning until nine. It made more sense for me to just come here instead of driving all the way back home. I just made a pot of coffee, you want a cup?"

"Yes. Thanks."

She didn't bother turning on the lights, and he followed her through the door where the exercise equipment was and then down a hall to a small office that had her name on the door. He tried not to notice just how good she looked in her gym clothes, but did so, anyway.

"This is my little cubbyhole, so to speak," she said, gesturing at the small room. "It's where I take care of miscellaneous things."

She went behind her desk and sat down. "So what do you want to talk to me about, Tanner?"

He didn't know where to start since he'd never done anything like this before. He closed the door and leaned against it. "I needed to see you again."

Her brow furrowed. "Why? I think you made it absolutely clear I was an OD." At what had to be his surprised expression, she said, "I told you about my brother and that I know all the codes you players use to categorize women."

Yes, she had said that.

"Why this need to see me again? And if I recall, I made it pretty clear you were an OD to me, as well."

He didn't like her reminding him of that.

"So what's the problem, Tanner? You want to upgrade my status or something? If so, I'm not interested."

He frowned. "Could we dispense with the talk of codes and statuses, please?"

"Then I don't know what you want from me," she said, glaring at him. "You can't just waltz in here when we've both made it pretty damn clear it was just that one day for us. That's all I wanted and all I was prepared for."

He hoped she didn't mean that. Especially when he knew he wanted more, although he hadn't been prepared for it, either. The moment she had opened the door and he'd seen her, he'd known. She was the woman who had gotten under his skin so deep that he doubted anything could get her out now.

"Monday was a game changer for me, Lyric. After having you, I figured my desire for you would disappear. But it didn't. I've been thinking of you a lot. Day and night. Breakfast, lunch and dinner. Memories of our time together are constantly on my mind. I remember all of it, not just the sex."

He paused a moment to rub a hand down his face. "I keep thinking about the flight over to Crystal Beach and back, our conversations, the picnic. I had no idea you could become an ache I can't get rid of. I've never had these feelings for a woman before. Nothing even close."

There was no need to admit to calling his oldest brother, Mason, not once but twice. Hell, he'd even talked to Blade again. He'd been trying to get some perspective on what the hell was happening. He hadn't liked it, and figured he could fight it, ignore it, or just not give a damn about it, but found none of those options worked. Unless he wanted to become a drinking man, he had to eventually face the fact he'd been p-whipped by a woman who hadn't even been trying.

Of course, his brother and Blade thought they had it all figured out and felt it was more serious than that. They thought he'd fallen in love. He'd tried to assure them that such a word wasn't even in his vocabulary. They'd laughed and said it hadn't been in theirs, either, and they'd been unexpectedly tackled by love pretty much the same way.

"I haven't wanted another woman since having you," he said. "The thought of sharing another woman's bed no longer has any appeal. The very fact that I'm even admitting all this to you is crazy. But I can't help it. I need you to know where I'm coming from and why, Lyric. What's been happening to me since Monday is some really weird shit. Normally I like women, but now the only woman I want is you."

Damn, he'd said a mouthful and all of it had come from his heart. His heart… Could he really be in love with her? Hell, if he was, then it made sense now. What other reason could there be for this madness?

She crossed her arms over her chest. "It's a phase."

"A phase?" Is that what she thought after all he'd just said? *News flash.* He didn't go through phases.

"Yes, and there's no doubt in my mind that you'll eventually get over it."

No, he wouldn't be getting over it. "When it happened to your brother, did he get over it?" he asked her.

She didn't say anything for a minute. Then she asked, "What do you want of me, Tanner? Why did you come here? For more sex? To let me know I've been promoted to CH, your casual hookup list?"

Her words sent sharp anger through him. If only she knew how vulnerable he felt right now, and it was something he'd never had to deal with before. "I told you, Lyric, I don't desire any other woman."

"And did you not hear what I said about it being just a phase? You'll get over it."

He pushed off from the door. "I honestly don't think that I will. I want all of you, Lyric. Not just the sex. You're different."

"How so? I fell into your bed quick enough like all the others."

"But you *are* different. You're not a one and done, or even a casual hookup."

"Really? Then what am I?"

He took another step closer to her. "You're the kind of woman that a man would want to be in a relationship with for the long haul." He chuckled in surprise. "You're the kind I would usually stay damn clear of. You're a keeper, Lyric."

LYRIC STARED AT TANNER, thinking he had it all wrong. She was definitely not a keeper for anyone. Westley had effectively proven that. She hadn't permanently written off having a serious relationship. Just not anytime in the near future. She had trust issues she had to deal with before giving her time and attention to any man, and she didn't even want to think of her heart.

She knew people could change, even die-hard womanizers. Her brother was a prime example of that.

"I'm going to ask you again, Tanner. What do you want of me?"

He took another couple of steps and now stood directly in front of her desk. "A chance for you to get to know me and for me to get to know you. I shared some of myself with you, but not all. I want you to get to know the real Tanner Jamison."

She nibbled on her bottom lip. "What good would that do?"

"We won't know until we do it. It's not about sex, it's about us. As much as I want you, Lyric, I will be operating on a hands-off policy until you give the word."

She stared at him. "And if I never give the word?"

"I feel certain that you will one day. I believe by getting to know me you will see that I would never hurt you and that I'm ready for a change in my life."

Lyric wished she could believe him, because although she was deliberately acting standoffish, resisting every point he was making and trying not to succumb to the desires she was feeling, she had thought of him every day and every night, too. At work, at play and even when she was helping out at her favorite charities. Should she even waste her time with him? He wasn't giving her any guarantees of anything, other than what sounded like an exclusive relationship for the time being. Is that what she wanted again? She'd shared one with Westley and look what had happened.

However, he had said she would be in control. A hands-off, "get to know you" period was an interesting idea. They knew they had amazing chemistry and it would give them a chance to figure out whether or not they even liked each other. But how long would they last without sex? He'd said he'd let her decide when she was ready to engage, but just having him stand in front of her desk was wreaking havoc on her mind and body. The temptation to give in to desire would be very strong.

"How often do you want us to see each other?"

"Every day."

Surprised, she echoed, "Every day?"

"Yes. I want us to spend time together doing something constructive every day this week. I'm flying out early Friday morning to Texas for an aunt's birthday party and won't be back until Sunday night. I want to spend as much time as possible with you before I leave. You can, of course, come with me."

"No, thank you. I don't want to travel anywhere with you again. And what will we be doing every day we spend together? What's the meaning of *constructive* in your book?"

"Whatever the meaning is in yours. I want you to decide how we spend our time together. You work ten-hour days so you might not want to do anything but sit around and watch a show on television with me, meet up for dessert and wine, or enjoy dinner somewhere. You have to eat sometime, right?" He paused a moment, then added, "I want to prove to you, Lyric, that you are a keeper."

Lyric gazed into the depths of his dark eyes and saw something she hadn't seen before in the time she'd known him. A plea. A desperate plea. He actually wanted this, although she wasn't sure what he thought he would be getting out of it when she would be calling the shots. *A keeper? Her? Puhleez*. But just the thought he somehow believed it broke a barrier within her. One she'd erected after her breakup with Westley, who hadn't treated her like anything other than a convenience.

"Okay, fine, Tanner. We can try this for two weeks and that's it."

A smile spread across his face and he said, "You won't regret it, Lyric."

She sure hoped she wouldn't. She broke eye contact with him and studied the floor. She didn't bother looking up when she saw the toes of his shoes, indicating he'd come around the desk and was standing by her chair. She looked up at him and when he offered her his hand, she took it.

Immediately, just his touch sent sensations spiraling through her. And from the way he was looking at her, she knew he'd felt them, as well.

He gently pulled her to her feet. His face was close to hers, right there, nearly lip to lip. She could feel the heat of his breath on her mouth.

"May I kiss you to seal our agreement?"

She honestly didn't think that was necessary, but with his mouth so close to hers, he had her remembering his taste and how delicious it was. She licked her bottom lip at the memory. Their lips were a breath apart and she said, "Yes."

"You don't know how much I needed to hear you say that, Lyric." He took her mouth in a ravishing kiss.

Like he had on Monday, he was kissing her thoroughly and deeply. Tanner was kissing her in a way that lit up every part of her body. Over the next few weeks, they would not make love. When he saw that he wouldn't be scoring with her again, he would move on to someone else.

In the meantime…she'd begun throbbing down there, as well. A little at first, but now it was as if she was being stroked between her thighs with the same pace and rhythm his tongue was moving in her mouth.

She could actually feel herself getting wet and moaned his name. It was then that she remembered his kiss alone had the ability to make her come. How had she forgotten that? Snatching her mouth away, she drew in a sharp breath and took a step back. Tanner had her at a disadvantage. She was putty anytime his tongue, that gloriously experienced tongue, went inside her mouth.

"I have some things I need to do before I open up the gym," she said, breathless.

"Mind if I hang around?"

Her eyebrows shot up. "Why?"

"I need a good workout and promise not to get underfoot. Then I'd like to take you to dinner later. That is if you don't mind sharing a meal with me."

She tilted her head and looked at him. "I thought you were going to let me decide how we spent our time together."

He nodded. "Okay, you're right. Dinner was just a suggestion."

"One I accept."

He smiled. "Thanks. And you don't have a problem with me hanging around for a while?"

A part of her wanted to say yes, she had a problem with it, because she knew she'd be ogling him every chance she got. But instead, she said, "No. I honestly don't expect we'll be too busy today. We weren't yesterday. Most of our regulars participated in Friday's marathon and are giving their bodies a break."

He nodded again. "Okay. I'll go to the car to grab my gym bag. I'll be back in a second."

Lyric watched him leave, hoping her decision to spend time with him was one she would not regret making.

CHAPTER TWENTY-SEVEN

"I CAN'T BELIEVE how lucky I've been today," Roman said, glancing over at Victoria.

"Speak for yourself."

He shook his head, grinning. He had caught several types of fish. His pail was full, practically brimming over. Unfortunately, except for a red bass, and a small one at that, the fish weren't biting Victoria's hook. "Be careful. You're sounding like a jealous fisherman."

She rolled her eyes. "Who cares? Just because you're having a good day doesn't—"

He lifted his eyebrows. "A good day?"

"Okay, okay. You're having an *exceedingly* good day. That's no reason to brag."

Roman threw back his head and laughed. "So says the woman who's been bragging on all our other fishing adventures. The woman who took a picture of her huge catch and texted it to all her family to see. The woman who—"

"Okay, Roman. I get the reminder. Please don't rub it in," she grumbled.

"Sure, sweetheart. I'll save my rubbing for later, at a more opportune and pleasurable time."

Their gazes held for a moment and he knew his words had had the intended effect. He only hoped the more time they spent together, the more she would want to continue seeing him after he left Catalina Cove.

One of the things on his agenda was a meeting with Bryce Witherspoon-Chambray. He had contacted her a couple of days ago regarding waterfront property to purchase. Although he had enjoyed sailing on the yacht, he wanted to build a home—a summer home in the cove so he could return whenever he wanted.

"Are you ready to go back to work tomorrow?" They had left Catalina Cove on Friday and were headed back now. It was a beautiful Sunday afternoon and several boaters were out. Luckily, they had claimed this particular spot right before sunrise, and he was glad. The fish were biting. At least for him.

"No, I am not ready. I needed Friday off and this weekend with you. However, my family was a little upset that I didn't come home for Labor Day. As usual they had a huge cookout at Whispering Pines. I haven't been home in a while."

He nodded. "How long is a while?"

"Not since the Fourth of July. I talked to Mom and she said Lindsay was brave and brought a guy home."

Although it had been years since he'd seen her, Roman knew Lindsay, Victoria's sister, was five years younger and attending law school at Harvard. "How did your brothers and cousins handle that?"

"They were their usual troublesome selves. The interrogators. But Mom said the guy held his own and didn't seem the least bothered by their inquisition."

"Are things serious between Lindsay and the guy?"

Victoria shook her head. "I talked to Lindsay yesterday and according to her, they're just friends. But I'm not sure the family is buying it. For years Reese and Kenna were 'just friends' and we all saw how that turned out."

He wondered if she'd given any thought that their relationship had evolved the same way. They'd started out as friends who'd wanted to share each other's company and... they'd gotten to know each other, both physically and emotionally. He definitely liked both. No, he definitely *loved* both.

"I wish we didn't have to go back to Catalina Cove."

Her words prompted him to glance over at her. The midday sun slanted across her features, making her look even more beautiful. "Any other place you rather be?"

"I could stay right here, in this same spot in the Gulf with you forever."

Forever...

Whether she knew it or not, that one word packed a lot of promise. Was that a hint of what her answer would be? That she didn't want things to end any more than he did?

At that moment, he wanted to put aside his fishing rod and go to her, hold her, kiss her and then take her down below and make love to her. He felt whole whenever their bodies were connected in a way that he hadn't thought he was capable of feeling.

They had gone to bed last night making love and had awakened this morning making love. By no means did he want her to assume the physical part of their relationship was what he enjoyed the most—although he had to admit the physical part was good, *damn* good. He'd also fallen in love with her—the woman she was—and he was convinced his life wouldn't be the best it could be without her in it.

He met her gaze and held it when he said, "I could stay right here, in this same spot in the water with you forever, too, Victoria." She had no idea how much he'd meant it.

"Prove it," she said.

He would have taken her words a whole different way if he hadn't seen the sparkle of mischief in her eyes. That sparkle meant she was up to no good. "And how do you want me to prove it?"

She smiled sweetly. "By changing positions with me. I want to fish on that side of the boat for a while. Seems the fish are jumping more over there."

He burst out laughing. "What am I going to do with you, Victoria Madaris?"

"I have a lot of ideas tucked away for later, Roman."

He winked. "I'm counting on it, sweetheart. I am definitely counting on it."

LYRIC ENTERED HER apartment and released a deep breath as she closed the door behind her. Good to his word, Tanner had spent the entire day at the gym. Like she'd told him, very few people had come in, so he basically had had all the equipment to himself.

She'd tried not to notice his powerfully built shoulders, his well-defined deltoids, pectorals and biceps, along with his broad chest. Every time he moved a muscle, it seemed her body moved a muscle, as well, in all the sensuous places. Then there were his hands—hands she'd remembered so well. They had touched her, gripped her hips to thrust hard inside of her. His fingers had brought her to an orgasm several times on that memorable Monday. She had studied those same hands today and had remembered their touches, their caresses, their ability to make her feel things she hadn't experienced with any other man. All in one day. Monday had definitely been Labor Day because he had labored to make her feel pleasure in the extreme.

When it was close to dinnertime and she still had paperwork to do, instead of waiting to go out to eat, Tanner had left the gym to get takeout for them. He had returned with a big container of seafood jambalaya, cornbread and a huge salad from a restaurant. They'd shared the meal in her office.

Over dinner, she'd established a schedule for the week. Dinner again tomorrow. A movie on Tuesday. A jazz concert on Wednesday. He'd even agreed to go with her to the children's hospital on Thursday for story time. Then he was flying out Friday to attend an aunt's birthday party and wouldn't be back until Sunday. She figured she would need that time-out period to recover from his presence. Just being around him today still had certain parts of her body tingling.

He had hung around the gym, waiting until she had locked up, and walked her to her car. He'd held her hand during that short walk. When they reached her car, he'd turned her into his arms and kissed her goodbye. There was no doubt in Lyric's mind that the coming week ought to be interesting.

CHAPTER TWENTY-EIGHT

"To what has been a wonderful time spent with you in Catalina Cove," Roman said, lifting his wineglass in a toast. "And I will forever cherish the memories."

"And it will be the same with me," Victoria said, before they clinked their glasses together.

It was hard to believe his three weeks in Catalina Cove was coming to an end and he would be leaving tomorrow. For their last night together, they were dining at the Lighthouse. The cove's lighthouse-turned-restaurant was *the* place to dine.

Roman noticed Victoria hadn't said much during dinner and he hoped that wasn't a sign she would be giving him bad news, that she'd decided it would be best for them not to continue what they'd started. He loved going to sleep with her in his arms and waking up with her the same way. It was going to be hard to adjust to not having her with him when he returned to Washington.

A short while later they were heading back toward the marina to spend their last night together on his yacht. He thought she looked absolutely gorgeous in her red pantsuit, and walking beside her and holding her hand felt like this was the way it should be. The night air off the Gulf was cool, but it didn't do anything to counteract the heat flowing within him from touching her. Being with her. Feeling a need for her.

When they reached the marina, they walked hand and hand along the pier, neither of them saying anything. He wondered what she was thinking and more than once was tempted to ask, but always changed his mind.

Once on the yacht he asked, "Would you like another glass of wine, Victoria?" They'd each had a glass during dinner.

"No, but thanks for asking," she said, kicking off her heels. Then, as he watched, she smiled and crossed the floor to him. "Aren't you going to ask me what I've decided, Roman?"

He drew in a deep breath. "No. I felt when you were ready to tell me, you would."

She nodded. "Thanks, and I appreciate it. I needed time to think through a lot of things." She paused. "My answer is yes, Roman. I want to continue what we started here in the cove."

Roman was totally elated and pulled her into his arms. "You have made me a very happy man, Victoria. So very happy." Still holding her around the waist, and with a huge smile on his face, he moved back to look down at her. "Does that mean you'll be my date at the Capital Ball next month?"

She smiled up at him. "Yes. However, I do have a request."

"And what is that, sweetheart?"

"I want to tell my family about us first. I want them to hear it from me that we've started seeing each other. Christy already knows, but it will be quite a surprise to everyone else. I'm sure word has gotten around that Tanner is the man Mama Laverne has chosen for me and some might think I'm rebelling against her interference, when that's not it at all. I just don't agree with her choice for me. I believe she made an honest mistake."

He didn't say anything for a minute, then asked, "How do you think she's going to feel about it?"

She shrugged. "I'm not sure. I'll find out when she comes back from her cruise and have a chance to talk with her. But it won't change anything. My mind is made up. I want to continue to be with you, and I honestly don't see Tanner in my future."

Roman drew in a deep breath as he drew her closer to him. "I want you to see yourself in mine, Victoria, and more than anything I want you to see me in yours. I wasn't going to tell you this until you made your decision. I didn't want what I said to influence you in any way."

She tilted her head to look at him. "What?"

"I've fallen in love with you. That might not have been the plan when we began hanging together, but after getting to know you, spending time with you, making love to you, there was no way you could not wiggle your way into my heart. You have and it doesn't matter if you love me back or not. I love you. I want forever with you. I couldn't leave here with you thinking all we shared was a meaningless affair, because every minute I shared with you meant something special, Victoria."

"Oh, Roman." She dropped her head to his chest. He became concerned when he heard her crying.

He lifted her chin to look up at him and saw the tears in her eyes. "I'm sorry I've made you cry, sweetheart, but I couldn't hold my love back a single day without letting you know."

She swiped at her tears. "I'm crying because I'm happy. I've fallen in love with you, as well. And because I love you, I want to be with you. I want forever with you, too."

"Oh, baby." At that moment he felt on top of the world. The woman he loved just admitted to loving him in return.

Roman swept her up into his arms to carry her down below. Tonight's lovemaking would have new meaning. They had declared their love for each other, and he believed in his heart that upon doing so, no one could come between them. No one.

PART 4

Nothing is impossible when you follow your heart.

—Anonymous

CHAPTER TWENTY-NINE

ROMAN DROVE THROUGH the streets of the nation's capital to meet Mint for breakfast. It was a beautiful Monday morning and he couldn't wait to give him the name of the woman who would be his date to the ball at the Kennedy Center. The woman he loved.

After making love on the yacht, he had taken Victoria home and then made love to her again, ending up spending the night. He had hated leaving her before daybreak Thursday morning but the sight of her lying in her bed with a satisfied smile on her face would forever be etched in his mind. Her plans were to visit her family in Houston this coming weekend to break the news about them.

Plans were made for him to fly to Houston and join her after she met with them on Saturday, and then the two of them would go to his ranch in Austin to decide on the best way to officially come out as a couple.

He resumed driving when the traffic light changed and turned into the parking lot of Bristol's, one of his favorite places for breakfast in DC. Victoria had introduced him to the Witherspoon Café while he'd been in Catalina Cove, and he couldn't wait to take her to Bristol's. Hell, he couldn't wait to see her again on Saturday. It didn't matter that he'd just seen her Thursday. It had only been four days, but he still missed her something awful.

As usual, he pulled up to the restaurant's valet-parking

stand, then stopped the car and got out. The moment he closed his car door, seemingly out of nowhere, he was surrounded by reporters with microphones and flashing cameras.

"Senator, what do you have to say about the article appearing in this morning's paper?" Several microphones were shoved in his face.

"What the hell? I have no idea what you're talking about," he said.

"Are you saying that for the past month you have not been having an illicit affair with a woman engaged to marry someone else?" one reporter asked loudly.

"Or that you're not involved in a lover's triangle with Victoria Madaris, niece of wealthy rancher Jake Madaris, and a man by the name of Tanner Jamison?" another reporter asked.

Hearing Victoria's name from a reporter's mouth made Roman go still. Before he could say anything, Mint suddenly appeared at his side with an angry look on his face. "The senator is not answering any questions," he barked. "He will have a press conference later and you can ask your questions then."

Mint turned to Roman and said in a low voice, "Get back in the car and I'll follow you back to your place. It's secure and they can't get through the gates."

For several seconds Roman just stood there, his gaze locked with Mint's as he tried to get an understanding of what the hell was happening and how Victoria was involved and why.

"Roman, get back in the car and let's go," Mint said.

Roman blinked, opened the door and climbed back into his car, then drove off, knowing Mint was not far behind. He wasn't surprised when he got to his condo to find even more reporters waiting outside the gate. He was glad they were unable to get in. When they saw his car, several ran toward him, but he kept driving through the entrance, pausing only to enter his security code. He glanced in his rearview mirror to see Mint was directly behind him.

Once inside his home, he waited for Mint to enter.

"What the hell is going on, Mint?" he demanded.

"I tried to reach you the moment I saw this," Mint said, tossing a tabloid on the table in front of him.

Roman picked it up. On the cover was a photo of him and Victoria standing on the deck of the yacht kissing. The headline read, "Senator Roman Malone Involved in Love Triangle."

"There are more photographs inside," Mint said.

Roman turned the page and then cursed when he saw the spread. There were pages and pages of photos of him and Victoria in each other's arms, kissing, holding hands, her sitting in his lap. Even one of the night he'd swept her off her feet to carry her below. She was wearing that red pantsuit, which meant the photo had been taken as recent as last Wednesday night. The photographs clearly showed a couple into each other.

He tossed aside the tabloid and looked up at Mint. "I want to know who took those photos. I'm a single man and Victoria is a single woman. What we do is nobody's business."

"That's not what the article is saying, Roman. It said the two of you were overheard discussing the man she is engaged to marry, a guy named Tanner Jamison, and how you and Ms. Madaris were carrying on an affair behind his back."

"That's not true," Roman snapped, pulling his phone out his jacket. "I need to call Victoria."

He paced the floor as her phone continued to ring. Then he recalled that she mentioned when they talked last night that she had an early morning meeting at the station and probably had her phone off. "Damn!"

"So, Ms. Madaris is not engaged to marry someone else?" Mint asked.

Roman glared at him. "No, and I want to know who put that lie out there."

Mint rubbed the top of his head. "Right now, we need to deny those allegations, Roman. Is there any way we can fly Ms. Madaris here to—"

"No! I will not ask Victoria to come to Washington for this BS. She didn't want to get involved with a politician because of shit like this."

"But you know for a fact she is not involved with Tanner Jamison?"

"I'm positive. You and I know *The Tattler* doesn't care about the truth. All they do is spread lies to sell papers. In the meantime, both Victoria's and my reputations are taking a beating. I don't give a damn about mine, but I won't let anyone slander hers."

Mint didn't say anything for a moment, clearly deciding to let Roman calm down before asking another question. He watched as Roman tried calling Victoria's phone number again with no luck.

"Calm down, Roman," Mint finally said. "When she turns her phone back on, she will see all the missed calls and return yours."

Roman looked at him and, as if what he said made sense, Roman sat down on the sofa, holding the phone in his hand.

Mint drew in a deep breath. "I need to handle damage control, Roman, but first I need to know an answer to a very important question. What does Victoria Madaris mean to you?"

Roman looked Mint straight in the eye and said, "Victoria is the woman I love and intend to marry one day."

"EXCUSE ME, I NEED to take this," Mr. Richards said to Victoria when a phone call interrupted their meeting.

She glanced out the window and saw the clouds forming, and was glad she'd listened to the weather report and brought her umbrella. She smiled when she remembered her phone conversation with Roman last night. He had arrived in Washington Friday and they'd talked every day since. But talking on the phone in no way replaced him being with her in the flesh. She was missing him like crazy and couldn't wait to see him this coming weekend.

"Victoria?"

She looked up at her boss. "Yes, Mr. Richards?"

"Are you engaged to be married?"

She lifted an eyebrow, wondering why he would ask her such a thing when she wasn't wearing a ring on her finger. "No, of course not."

"So a man by the name of Tanner Jamison is not your intended?"

"My intended?"

"Yes."

"If you're asking if I'm engaged to Tanner, then no. He's a friend of the Madaris family."

"What about you and Senator Roman Malone. Are the two of you involved?"

Victoria's frown deepened. "Mr. Richards, what is this about? Why are you asking me these questions?"

"I'm asking you these questions because of this," he said, turning his laptop toward her. "I just got a call that this article came across our wire service. It's headline news in this morning's *The Tattler*, that Capitol Hill tabloid nearly everyone in Washington reads. Even those who swear they don't."

Victoria looked at the computer screen and her eyes widened. There on the front page was a huge photograph of her in Roman's arms and they were kissing. He had a beard, but the person who took the picture identified them both.

"There are more photographs where those came from," Mr. Richards said.

Swallowing, she nodded and flipped through several screens all containing pictures of her and Roman. All showing them hugging and kissing, and some appeared pretty darn steamy. She went back to the first page and read the headline. "This is crazy and all lies. I am not involved with anyone but Roman."

"So you deny also being involved with Tanner Jamison?"

"Yes. Tanner and I don't have that kind of relationship."

Mr. Richards nodded. "Then someone deliberately wanted to make it look like you did. And something else you need to know."

"What?"

"I also just learned that there are reporters camped outside. We refused to let them in here, but the moment you leave they will swarm on you with questions about the alleged love triangle. Are you ready to deal with them?"

Victoria drew in a deep breath, shook her head and said, "No, I'm not ready to deal with them."

Mr. Richards nodded. "Then let me handle it."

TANNER LEANED BACK in his chair and glanced out his office window. It was Monday morning and he was glad to be back in New Orleans. He had arrived late last night, too late to call Lyric, and he was looking forward to their date this evening.

Although he had enjoyed spending time with his family over the weekend, he had been anxious to return here to be with her. Last week had been wonderful. He had taken her out somewhere every night, and he had gotten to know more about her, and she him. As they discovered more about each other, they were surprised to see all they had in common. It wasn't just their charity work and community involvement, but their taste in food, political affiliations, what they enjoyed doing in their spare time and the hobbies they liked.

He honestly didn't mind taking things slow because he was building a relationship with her that wasn't based on sex. They hadn't made love again since Labor Day. He wanted her and would end their date each night with a kiss that left him panting, fully aroused and desiring her even more. And he knew from their good-night kisses that she desired him just as much. However, he wanted them not to rush things while she built trust in him and faith in their relationship.

One promising thing was that she had invited him to dinner at her parents' home this coming Friday night and he felt good about that. He wanted to believe that in time she would fall in love with him as hard and deeply as he knew he loved her.

He glanced up when there was a knock on his office door. "Come in."

"Mr. Jamison, we have a problem."

That was the last thing Tanner wanted to hear. "What is it, Hank? Is something wrong with this morning's delivery?"

"No. It's reporters. They're outside. Swarming all over

the place. We won't let them in, but they want to talk to you."

Tanner lifted an eyebrow. "Reporters? Talk to me about what?"

"They told me to give you this in case you hadn't seen it yet." Hank handed him a newspaper, more precisely a tabloid.

Tanner frowned when he saw the picture and read the headline. His frown deepened when he began reading the article. "What the hell! Who authorized this paper to print these lies?" He and Victoria weren't engaged, nor had they ever been involved. This was an unflattering article about Victoria, meant to defame her character. The Madaris family was not going to like this one damn bit and heads were going to roll.

"So what do you want me to do about those reporters? They're a pesky bunch," Hank said.

"I'll take care of them after I make a few calls."

Tanner tried calling Victoria. When he couldn't reach her, he called Blade. "Have you seen the headlines in *The Tattler*?"

"Yes. Mom called. She saw it in the grocery store."

"Where is Victoria? I tried calling her," Tanner said.

"I just talked to Uncle Jake. Thanks to Victoria's boss, he made sure she got out of the television station by a side door to bypass those reporters. Victoria heard from her friends in Catalina Cove that reporters were there waiting for her to come home. Her boss gave her two weeks off and she decided to go to Texas instead. Uncle Jake's jet is on its way to New Orleans get her now."

Tanner nodded. "Reporters are here, as well, but I haven't spoken to them. I don't know where they got their story, but it's all lies. Victoria and I were never involved and she's free to date anyone she wants."

"Yes, but obviously the intent was to damage her and RJ's reputations. Uncle Jake got a call from Alex. He's mad as hell and is going to trace the story."

"Good. If anyone can find out who fabricated this lie, Alex can." Alex Maxwell was married to their cousin Christy and was tenacious as a private investigator. One of the best. He was also a former FBI agent with a skill for finding out anything he wanted to know.

Tanner checked his watch and knew he had to call Lyric. He could just imagine what she would think if she read the article. Mainly, that he was involved with another woman while pursuing her. Damn!

"I need to call Lyric, Blade. I don't want her to see this garbage and think any of it's true. Lyric and I decided to begin seeing each other exclusively, and I don't want anything to mess things up with us."

"Exclusively? Are you now admitting that you're falling for her?"

Tanner sighed deeply. "I've already fallen. Hard."

After clicking off the phone, he tried calling Lyric and his call went to voice mail so he left a message. "Lyric, this is Tanner. I need to talk to you. Please call me back when you get this message."

ROMAN SNATCHED HIS phone off the table the moment it rang. "Victoria?"

"Yes, Roman, it's me."

"Where are you, sweetheart?"

"I'm on my way to the airport. Uncle Jake is sending his jet for me. My boss managed to get me out of the station without any reporters seeing me. He also gave me a couple of weeks off. Hopefully things will calm down by then."

Roman doubted it. When *The Tattler* got ahold of a story they thought was hot, they would run it to death. "I'm sorry about this, and I promise to find out who put out all these lies. Not only that, our privacy was violated by the cameraman stalking us and taking photos without our consent."

"It doesn't matter, Roman. This is the very thing I was trying to avoid. This is why I can't become involved with you."

He felt a sudden pain in his heart. "No, Victoria, you said you loved me. Was that not true?"

"Yes, I love you, but it doesn't matter."

"Sweetheart, love always matters. Please don't let them win. You deserve to live your life whatever way you want to live it and with whomever you want. That tabloid printed nothing but lies."

"But they lied about *me*, Roman. They slandered my character. Made it seem like I am a loose woman with no morals."

"And we know that isn't true, baby. Don't let them get to you." He drew in a deep breath, knowing they had gotten to her. He could hear the hurt in her voice and wished he was there with her. To hold her and make her believe that everything would be all right. "Have you heard from Tanner?" he asked.

"No, but I see he tried calling me. I wanted to return your call first and to tell you that I think it's best for us not to communicate for a while. The article also implied that I'm a bad influence on you. The last thing I want is to cause harm to your reputation."

"I don't give a damn about my reputation, Victoria, and I refuse to let that damn tabloid come between us with lies."

"Things happened just like I was afraid they would," she said sobbing. "I never wanted to be in the limelight, so I am ending things between us, Roman."

The sound of her crying tore at him, made his heart ache. "No! Please don't do that."

"There is no other way."

"What about me, Victoria? Are you willing to turn your back on me?"

"I'm trying to save you from a scandal, Roman. People who read that article won't care about the truth. They love the lies and sensationalism. Forget about me. Be with someone who can tolerate the sort of life you live. I can't. Goodbye, Roman."

She then clicked off the phone.

CHAPTER THIRTY

JAKE MADARIS PEEKED over at his grand-niece sitting across from him in the cabin of his jet. He'd originally planned to just send his plane for her, but then decided he needed to see for himself that she was okay. She wasn't.

She hadn't said much since boarding and he'd decided to let her be. Diamond would know what to say and do when they got to Whispering Pines. Understandably, that damn tabloid had upset her. Lies, especially twisted ones, were hard to take. The media could be brutal sometimes. He, of all people, should know.

For years they'd assumed Diamond and actor Sterling Hamilton were having an affair, not knowing Jake and Diamond were secretly married. Nor had the media known that Sterling was one of Jake's best friends and that Sterling was the one who'd gotten them together.

When Jake heard a soft whimper, he looked over and saw she was crying. After unsnapping his seat belt, he went over to her, unsnapped her seat belt and then gathered her into his arms and then sat her in his lap. He recalled years ago when he had done the same thing when she'd been a preteen and the horse that he'd given her years earlier as a pony had gotten sick and died. He had been the one to break the news to her, and that night she had cried while he'd held her.

"I gather Tanner is not the man you love, Victoria."

She looked up and he saw the tears glistening in her eyes. She shook her head. "No. I don't know how Mama Laverne thought me and Tanner could be a perfect match. Tanner is not ready to settle down, Uncle Jake. He is all wrong for me and I'm all wrong for him."

Jake nodded. "I can believe Mom got this one wrong. She's not perfect, you know."

"She's got a hundred-percent track record. I'd hate to disappoint her," she said on a sob. "But my heart belongs to Roman."

"Then follow your heart." He paused a moment and then said, "When I met Diamond, I didn't think I was ready for love but soon discovered she was everything I needed and wanted."

Victoria didn't say anything for a minute. "I love Roman, Uncle Jake," she said. "But I can't handle being in the lime-light. He's a politician and with him, that comes with the job. Everything I do or say will be dissected. People will find fault and think I'm not good enough to be a politician's wife. I wouldn't be able to stand the heat." She buried her face in his chest.

"Then I have to question if you truly love him, Victoria."

She yanked her head up and looked at him. "Why would you think that?"

"Because I know that with love come sacrifices and compromises." He handed her a handkerchief from his jacket pocket and said, "I was a rancher who loved being a loner. I had my family, Whispering Pines and an occasional hookup when I felt the need. I was happy. Content. Then I met Diamond and fell in love. As an actress, her life was about being in the spotlight. That was something I detested and definitely hadn't planned for. However, once I fell in love with her, I knew I would gladly become part of her world, even if it included being cast in the limelight with her. I would accept it as one of the costs of loving her. She was worth it. I put up with the tabloid reporters' lies, which they still sometimes print, by the way. Bottom line, falling in love with someone means falling in love with who they are, what they are and whatever problems and issues that come with them."

He chuckled softly. "Last I read, Diamond and I are getting a divorce, but then according to the tabloids, we've been getting that same divorce now for close to twelve years. It doesn't faze us anymore and we're preparing and educating the kids, so it won't faze them when they grow up," he said of his son and daughter, ages eleven and eight.

Jake then said, "Roman is a well-liked and popular senator who is going places. What you have to decide is whether you want to be by his side. He will need a woman who loves him as much as he loves her. A strong woman who can take the heat. So I guess the main question is, if Roman being a politician in the limelight, and loving him the way you say you do, is worth it to you?"

TANNER GLIMPSED AT his watch. It was past noon and Lyric hadn't called him back, and that had him worried. What if she'd already seen the article, believed what she read and now refused to talk to him? Hank had been right—there were a number of reporters camped outside the club waiting for him when he walked out. After giving them a terse statement of "no comment," he had gotten into his car and left. His destination was the NOFD where Lyric worked. He didn't know if she was there or out in the field somewhere doing inspections, but at least finding that out was better than doing nothing.

A short while later he walked into the building to find that same chatty blonde whom he'd spoken to the last time he was there. The same one who'd given him Lyric's work schedule. He hoped that she was just as chatty today. He felt a semblance of hope when she smiled when she saw him. "You're back."

"Yes, I'm back. I have a question about the original inspector's report. A Lyric Evans. Is she here? I need to talk to her."

Still smiling, the woman said, "Lyric was here earlier but I think she got sick because she went home unexpectedly. Would you like to speak to someone else here who can help you?"

"No," Tanner said, as he headed for the door. "There's no one else."

When he got into his car, his phone began ringing. He didn't recognize the caller. If some reporter had somehow gotten his personal number, the person would regret it. "Who is this?"

There was a pause. "Tanner, this is Roman Malone. I got your number from Blade Madaris. I hope we can talk."

Tanner nodded. "Yes, we can talk."

"I guess by now you've seen the article."

Tanner rubbed the bridge of his nose. "Yes, I've read it. And it's all lies. Victoria and I are not engaged to be married. We never even dated."

"I know. I spoke to Jake Madaris earlier and he said Alex Maxwell is on the case."

Tanner nodded again. "That's what I've been told, as well. I'm certain Alex will find out who started those lies."

"I am certain he will, as well. In the meantime, this is my plan..."

A SHORT WHILE later Tanner was knocking on Lyric's door. At first, when she didn't open, he was beginning to think that maybe she'd gone to the gym instead of coming home, when her door suddenly swung open. One look at the anger on her face and he knew she'd seen the article.

"If you let me in, Lyric, I can explain."

She glared at him. "What is there to explain? I asked if you were involved with anyone and you said you weren't. That paper says otherwise."

"And you want to believe a tabloid known to print lies over me? Will you not give me a chance to tell you the truth?"

He watched her nibble on her bottom lip, then she said, "Fine. Come in. You have exactly five minutes." She moved aside to let him enter.

When she closed the door behind him, he turned around and shoved his hands into his trouser pockets. "First of all, Victoria and I were never engaged. She and I never even dated. She happens to be the sister and cousin to several friends of mine. That is all."

Lyric crossed her arms over her chest. "Then why would your name be linked to hers? Why is that paper claiming otherwise?"

Tanner rubbed the back of his neck. "Because Victoria's great-grandmother, who loves playing matchmaker, got it in her head that Victoria and I are well-suited and should one day marry."

"What?"

"Yeah, I know it sounds crazy, but it's true. She's been doing it for years and with good results, I might add. However, she made a major mistake if she thought Victoria and I should be together. The last time I saw Victoria was a few weeks ago when I was leaving the gym, which is right by the television station where she works. She was leaving, too, and told me that she was seriously dating someone, and I told her I was happy for her."

"But what if she was lying and just told you that to make you jealous? What if—?"

"I refuse to believe that, Lyric. If you read that article, then you know it makes both me and Senator Malone seem like innocent pawns in some game Victoria is playing, and that isn't true. I talked to Senator Malone on the drive over here and we both agreed that someone is deliberately trying to smear Victoria's name and ruin her reputation."

The thought of that angered Tanner because he knew what a nice person she was. "Senator Malone loves Victoria and will be holding a press conference in Washington today to address the allegations."

He drew in a deep breath. "I've also contacted the press here, who are presently camped outside my club, to let them know I will be doing the same thing. What they are doing to Victoria is unfair and a slander to her character. And knowing the Madaris family like I do, they won't stand for it. Nobody messes with Jake Madaris's family and gets away with it."

When Lyric still didn't say anything, he took another deep breath. "I enjoyed the time I spent with you last week, Lyric," he said. "It only confirmed what I'd suspected all along. I've fallen in love with you. You might not want to believe it, but it's true. That's why I wanted to prove to you that you were a keeper. My keeper."

He paused a moment then continued. "If what they'd printed in the paper was true, then I wouldn't be here. The old Tanner Jamison wouldn't give a damn what you thought of him because all you would have been was another lay. But you're way more than that to me. I love you, and I wanted to give you the chance to know me and hopefully reciprocate those feelings."

When she still didn't say anything, he tilted his head back and rotated his neck to work out the tension there. He returned his gaze to her. "Maybe this is a tryout for us and your trust for me is being tested. Hell, I don't know. All I know is how I feel about you and if you decide you can one day love me back, then you know where to find me."

He then turned and walked out the door.

HOPING IT WAS VICTORIA, Roman grabbed his phone before checking to see who was calling. "Hello?"

"Roman, this is Audria. I just read that article in the paper. How awful that someone is trying to ruin your reputation."

He rubbed his hand down his face as he continued his pacing. "Don't worry about it. I got this. I have a press conference scheduled for later."

"That's what Dad said, and he suggested I call to offer my services."

Roman stopped his pacing. "What services?"

"I want to be there and stand by your side when you deny those allegations. When you admit there is nothing serious between you and Victoria Madaris. I figure when they see me at that press conference with you, giving you my full support, they'll know all you shared with that woman was a meaningless fling and that you and I are back together. That should dispel the talk and salvage your reputation."

Roman shook his head, knowing Audria had it all wrong if she thought for one minute that all Victoria had meant to him was a meaningless fling, or that he needed her by his side for anything. But whether she knew it or not, her words had made him suspicious of something. Namely her. "Like I said, Audria. I got this. Goodbye."

VICTORIA WASN'T SURPRISED upon reaching Whispering Pines to find her brothers, cousins, aunts and uncles, grand-uncles and grand-aunts, there in the yard waiting for her. Nearly the entire Madaris clan. Although she appreciated the support, she figured they would be worse than the press with all their questions.

Uncle Jake reached over and touched her hand. "You don't have to tell anyone anything you don't want to. I think they're mainly surprised that you and Roman are involved. They assumed the guy you would fall in love with was Tanner."

She nodded. "I thought so, too, but evidently that's not the case. I talked to Tanner after we landed while you were getting the car. He's also met someone and fallen in love. She read the tabloid and it has caused problems between them. Problems he hopes they can work out. I hope they can, too."

Uncle Jake released a deep sigh. "Mom is enjoying herself somewhere on her cruise, not knowing the two people she thought would be perfect for each other have fallen in love with other people." He shook his head. "She's going to be in for a big surprise when she gets back. Maybe this will shock her into realizing her matchmaking days might be over."

Victoria smiled at her grand-uncle. It was the first smile she'd allowed herself since reading that tabloid. "Do you really think that, Uncle Jake?"

He shook his head, grinning. "No. She is determined to make sure all of you are married off before she takes her last breath. Honestly, I think she will be able to accept she's made a mistake this one time, as long as the person you end up with is someone you love and who makes you happy."

When Uncle Jake parked the car, she wasn't surprised when all her brothers and cousins stood back, and it was her oldest brother, Nolan, who approached. Nolan, who'd always been her protector. Nolan, who'd been the last one to be caught in their great-grandmother's matchmaking shenanigans. And it was Nolan who'd called to warn her she was next. At the time, she hadn't cared and had been so accepting of whatever Mama Laverne did and whomever she selected. Funny, how things had turned out. Now all she wanted to do was what Uncle Jake had suggested—follow her heart. And her heart was leading straight to Roman.

Instead of saying anything, Nolan pulled her into his arms and held her for a long while before he whispered, "It will be all right, Vic. Finding out about you and RJ threw all of us for a loop, but we want you to be happy. Your happiness means everything to us."

She wiped the tears from her eyes, nodded and said, "Thank you."

CHAPTER THIRTY-ONE

VICTORIA HEARD A knock on the guest room door. She had lied down for a nap after talking with her brothers, cousins, aunts and uncles, and assured them she was okay. She'd also told them the same thing she'd told Uncle Jake. She loved Roman and not Tanner.

Opening the door, she saw it was Diamond. "Jake told me to tell you that Roman is about to hold a press conference. Do you want to watch it?"

"Yes."

Victoria followed Diamond downstairs, where their huge television was located in the family room. All her relatives, the ones who hadn't left once they'd seen she was okay, were seated around the set. At some point when she'd been napping, Christy and Alex had arrived. When Christy saw her, she crossed the room and gave her a hug.

"You okay, Victoria?" Christy asked with concern in her eyes.

Victoria nodded. "Yes, I'm fine now. I needed to rest and make a few decisions."

Christy nodded. "Do you want to watch the press conference with us or do you prefer watching it in private? There's another television in Uncle Jake's study."

Victoria released a deep breath. She wasn't sure what Roman would be saying. Would he take the out she'd offered him and say the two of them just had a vacation fling?

That would certainly help save his reputation. Double standards were double standards. It was okay if a man slept around, but it was different when a woman did it.

"No, I'll be fine watching it with everyone."

Christy nodded. "Then come sit over here by me and Alex."

Victoria had just gotten settled when the press conference began. Her breath caught at the sight of Roman. Gone were the scruffy look, jeans, T-shirt and beard. Now he was clean-shaven, had a neat haircut and was wearing a dark suit. He looked to be in the role to which he'd been born—a well-dressed, suave, debonair and sophisticated politician. He approached the podium with that self-assured walk she loved, and when he turned to face the camera, he had the smile that she adored. But this smile was lined with irritation and anger. She saw it, although he was hiding it well. She noted the room where the press conference was being held was packed. Obviously, reporters from many news outlets were present.

"Ladies and gentlemen of the press. I feel that I need to make a statement regarding my relationship with Victoria Madaris and the time we spent together in Catalina Cove, Louisiana. It's unfortunate the media painted a picture that is not at all accurate. I've known Victoria for years, as our families are close." He was looking straight at the camera, but to Victoria it seemed he was staring right at her.

"Did you know she was engaged to be married?" some reporter asked rather loudly, as if he intended to make a point.

Roman tilted his head as if to stare at the man, and the look he gave him was direct and unwavering. "First of all, that's a lie *The Tattler* fabricated. Victoria is not engaged to marry anyone. She was free to date whomever she wanted, just like I was. I'm just curious, why the interest in my love life?"

"We are interested because we assumed you were seriously involved with someone here in the DC area," some reporter responded.

Without losing his cool, Roman kept his smile plastered in place. "I don't know how anyone could have thought that when I've gone on the record several times and clearly stated I wasn't interested in a serious relationship with any woman."

"Then all you and Ms. Madaris were having was a meaningless fling?" This was asked by another reporter and Victoria held her breath for Roman's answer.

"Let me go on record now and clear up the matter. What I shared with Victoria Madaris was not, and I repeat, was *not* a meaningless fling. When Victoria and I ran in to each in Catalina Cove and began spending time together, something happened to me that I hadn't expected to happen. I fell in love. I am very much in love with her, and if I want to pursue a relationship with her, I have every right to do so. Victoria is a beautiful, intelligent and warm-hearted individual."

"What about her involvement with Tanner Jamison?"

"At no time was Victoria involved with Tanner Jamison. Mr. Jamison will hold his own press conference in an hour. He will confirm that at no time were he and Victoria involved. They haven't even dated. I would think *The Tattler* and other news outlets who followed their lead and printed the article would have gotten their facts straight before running off with a story. I'm disappointed but not surprised."

"What about Ms. Madaris? Will she be giving a press conference, as well?"

Roman looked directly into the camera. "I see no reason for Ms. Madaris to do so. The two men who *The Tattler* claimed are involved in this fictitious love triangle are speaking out and denouncing the lies. What some of you reporters want and expect is a three-ring circus, but you won't be getting one. *The Tattler* deliberately slandered Victoria Madaris's name. I demand an apology to her, a retraction of the story and list of corrections. I want to go on the record and say that I love Victoria Madaris and there's not a damn thing any of you can do about it. Nothing is more important to me than she is. Not even my being a senator. Good day."

Victoria watched as Roman, refusing to take any more questions, left the podium. It was obvious from the conversations and high-fives around the room that her family was pleased with what Roman had said and how he'd gone about defending her name and honor. He'd stated on national television that he loved her and would give up his life as a senator for her. Yet, she'd been too afraid to put up with being in the limelight for him. Now she saw how Uncle Jake was right. With love came sacrifices and compromises. Loving someone also meant falling in love with who they are, what they are and whatever problems and issues that came with them.

She fought back tears, wanting to be alone for a while. Standing, she was about to leave the room when Diamond appeared at her side. As if she knew how Victoria was feeling and what she needed, she said, "I'm moving your things to one of the guest cottages, Victoria. That way you can rest without being disturbed. You're welcome to join us for dinner, or if you prefer, I will tell Blaylock to deliver dinner to you."

There were numerous guest cottages situated around the

ranch, and Blaylock Jennings had been the ranch's house-keeper and cook for as long as Victoria could remember. She truly appreciated her grand-aunt's thoughtfulness. "Thank you."

LYRIC SAT ON her sofa and watched the press conference Tanner was holding at the CNN bureau here in New Orleans. Earlier she had watched the one with Senator Roman Malone. Now Tanner was making it clear to the reporters in that charming, debonair, yet forceful voice of his that he was not involved with Victoria Madaris, nor had he ever been. He stressed that they'd never even dated, so they certainly weren't engaged. She was a family friend and nothing more.

He went on to severely admonish *The Tattler* for printing a story before verifying the facts. The one reporter who'd tried coming back at him discovered Tanner wouldn't put up with his BS. Tanner then chuckled and said, "I'm going to suggest to the Madaris family to do this country a favor and buy *The Tattler* and turn it into a fitness magazine."

Whether Tanner was jesting or not wasn't clear, but the nervous look that appeared on one reporter's face, namely the one who'd tried coming back at Tanner several times, was priceless. Lyric had done her research and knew the Madarises were not a family to mess with.

Before ending the press conference, Tanner had smoothly put in a plug for his club, which he stated would be opening on New Year's Eve. Lyric couldn't help but laugh. He'd shown them.

But then he'd shown her, as well. He'd told her the truth. That paper had lied, and he hadn't been involved with Victoria Madaris. She remembered something else he'd told her. That he loved her.

She stood and began pacing, and knew what she had to do and where she had to go. With the decisions made, she rushed to the bathroom to shower and change clothes.

VICTORIA HEARD THE knock on the cottage door and glanced at the clock on the nightstand. It was 8:00 p.m. She couldn't believe she had slept that long, and a glance out the window told her it had already gotten dark. She had tried calling Roman but hadn't been able to reach him. Was he deliberately not taking her calls now? Was he upset with her?

Diamond had sent her dinner earlier and then she had taken a shower and fell into bed. No one had ventured to this part of Whispering Pines to bother her and she wondered who was doing so now.

When the knock sounded again, she eased off the bed, left the bedroom and headed for the door. She peeked out the peephole. She hadn't turned on the porch lantern, so she couldn't make out who it was, but could tell the person had a masculine build. Probably one of her brothers or cousins who'd come to check on her. "Who is it?" she asked.

"Roman."

Roman? Victoria flung open the door and there he stood. The beam of light from inside the cottage hit him at an angle and the silhouette nearly took her breath away. He looked just like she'd seen him on television earlier. A clean-shaven, well-dressed man in a suit and tie who was too handsome for words. An image dreams were made of.

"May I come in, Victoria?"

His question made her realize she'd been standing there, staring at him without saying anything. "Yes, please come in."

She stepped back and when he entered and closed the door behind him, in the bright lights she got a good view of his features. He looked tired but not beaten down. But even then, there appeared to be an innate sexual energy swirling around him.

Victoria wanted to rush to him, throw herself in his arms, tell him she loved him and that no matter what, she wanted them to be together. But all she had to do was remember her last phone call with him and know she had to ask his forgiveness for being so quick to cave in at the first sign of trouble.

Victoria was acutely aware of the electricity flowing between them and swore that she could hear a few crackles. Drawing in a deep breath, she said, "I tried to call you after I saw the press conference, but didn't get an answer."

He nodded. "I left immediately for the airport to come here."

"Oh. I didn't know."

"That was my intent. I wanted the element of surprise to be on my side. I wouldn't have been able to handle it if you told me not to come because you didn't want to see me."

"I would not have told you that."

He studied her face. "No?"

"No." She could see how he would have thought that after their last phone conversation.

He took a step closer. "Why were you trying to call me?"

Now it was her turn to take a step closer. She went even farther and lifted her hands to glide them beneath his suit jacket and rest on his broad chest. "I wanted to let you know that I intend to start following my heart."

"What do you mean?"

"It means since you already have my heart entirely, I am yours totally and completely. It also means I can handle anything and everything that will come with it, which includes being by your side in the limelight."

Surprise lit his features. "You sure?"

"Yes. A very wise man, namely my uncle Jake, told me today that with love comes sacrifice and compromise. He also said that falling in love with someone meant falling in love with who they are, what they do and whatever problems and issues that come with them."

She could feel the tears that fell from her eyes but didn't care. "And I do love you, Roman."

"Oh, baby, I love you, too." He leaned down and captured her lips before sweeping her into his arms and carrying her into the bedroom.

He placed her on the bed, and after removing his jacket and shoes, he joined her. "I just want to hold you awhile, Victoria."

He wrapped his arms tightly around her and said, "I got on that plane intent on coming here and pleading my case to you. I had all the reasons lined up to convince you why our love would work. Now it seems your uncle's words did that work for me."

"They did. I knew I loved you. I just didn't know how strong I could be where you were concerned until I heard you tell the entire nation how much you loved me."

"Sweetheart, if I had the chance, I'd tell the entire world how much I loved you."

Then he was kissing her again in a way that made her head reel, had her heart pounding and sent heat swirling between her legs. And when he deepened the kiss, she knew she was a goner.

When he released her mouth, she whispered his name seconds before opening her eyes. Then she saw he'd slid off the bed and was removing his clothes. She eased up and began removing hers. More than anything she wanted to be skin-to-skin with him. She wanted to make love to him and wanted him to make love to her.

Moments later their naked bodies came together when he rejoined her on the bed and pulled her into his arms. He captured her mouth again and his tongue began mating with hers, and what felt like bone-melting fire quickly began spreading through her body.

When he ended the kiss and straddled her body, she stared up at him, feeling so much love, not only in her heart, but also in every nerve ending.

"I love you, Victoria," he whispered.

"And I love you, Roman."

And then he was inside of her, claiming her and taking them on another wild adventure. The blaze of desire she saw in his eyes had her purring, and the air shimmered with sexual energy all around them. He always made love to her like each time would be their last and he intended to carry them over a tidal wave of pleasure that was destined to last a lifetime.

And as far as she was concerned, it would. Regardless of what her great-grandmother thought, Victoria was convinced this was the man intended to have her heart. No other man deserved the honor. And with every thrust into her body, he was telling her in his own way that he believed it, as well.

Every day since he'd left Catalina Cove her body had ached for his touch and now he was stroking her at every angle and she couldn't help but groan in raw, feminine appreciation. She closed her eyes, absorbed in all the sensations she was feeling, swamped with emotions, dazed in pleasure. Her nails dug into his shoulders, and she lifted her hips to grind against his every thrust.

"Open your eyes, sweetheart."

Victoria did as Roman asked and the moment she did, she felt a climax building and could sense his passion escalating, too. She saw it in his eyes, heard it in his breathing and felt it in the shaft pounding hard into her. She tilted her hips to get it all. Suddenly, she convulsed with intense pleasure.

"Roman!"

"That's it, baby. Let it go. I'm right there with you."

She watched him throw his head back as he continued to rock into her. Then he hollered her name and her hand tightened around his neck to bring his mouth down to hers.

When she released his mouth, he shifted their bodies so they could face each other. "Remember that day I told you I wouldn't give you up?" he asked, pushing a lock of hair from her face.

She nodded, clearly remembering that day. "Yes."

"I meant it. I'm not giving you up, Victoria. Doing so would be giving up my heart."

"Oh, Roman." She wanted to cry. He loved her. He wanted her. She loved him and wanted him.

And then she was kissing him again and knew that what had begun in Catalina Cove would continue no matter where their paths led. They would have to sit down with Mama Laverne when she returned from her cruise and let her know she'd made a mistake. Roman was the man who had captured her heart. Victoria knew that she was meant for him.

ROMAN HADN'T EATEN any dinner so an hour later they put on clothes to stroll over to the ranch house to get him a plate. The moment they walked through the door Victoria saw everyone had left except for Alex. He was talking to Jake.

"I'm glad to see you, RJ," Alex said, standing to shake Roman's hand, then giving him a bear hug.

"Same here. Where is that godsister of mine?" Roman asked, craning his head to find Christy.

"I took her home, which is why we weren't here when you arrived." He glanced back and forth between Roman and Victoria. "In fact, I'm glad to see the both of you. I was just telling Jake I had some information to share. Information you guys might find interesting. Especially you, Roman."

Victoria lifted an eyebrow. "What is it, Alex?" she asked, sitting down on the sofa. Roman sat beside her and took her hand in his.

"As soon as I heard about that article, I begin doing research. Luckily, I've investigated *The Tattler* before, which resulted in a huge settlement in favor of my client. Evidently Buddy Fields didn't learn his lesson."

"Buddy Fields?" Roman asked.

"Yes. The owner of *The Tattler*. He's a sleaze with no morals. He loves smearing reputations when he has no valid proof. It's a wonder he's still in business and somehow financially stable. That is another story, believe me."

He paused a minute and said, "Finding out how they got those pictures was easy. All I had to do was check the hotel rosters in Catalina Cove. Once I identified the PI—"

"Private investigator?" Victoria asked.

"Yes. Someone was hired to spy on RJ."

Roman leaned forward in his seat. "Who hired him?"

"A woman by the name of Audria Wayfare. Senator Wayfare's daughter."

A SHORT WHILE LATER, back at the cottage, Roman held Victoria in his arms. They had made love again and then gone limp in each other's arms.

Roman ran his fingers through Victoria's hair, loving how silky smooth it felt. After Alex had revealed the identity of who had hired the PI, Roman's suspicions had been confirmed. He then told Victoria, Jake and Alex that he and Audria had dated for a while, and that she'd gotten it in her head that she would make the perfect politician's wife and insisted they were meant for each other. When he'd gotten to know her better and hadn't liked what he was seeing, he'd made it clear to her that he wasn't looking for a serious relationship with her...or anyone.

"Roman?"

"Yes, sweetheart?"

"How did Audria know you were in Catalina Cove?"

"I'm not sure. She probably had my call traced when I talked to her. Mint suggested I call her to get her off his back when she showed up at his office demanding to know where I was."

"And you think she would go that far to smear your reputation?"

"Yes, if she'd convinced herself she could help clean it back up." His hands tightened around her. "To be honest, I became suspicious when she called and offered to stand by my side at the press conference today. It sounded as if she had already planned things out—or thought she had. I think she assumed I was going to save my own reputation by saying you and I were just a vacation fling, and that my true love was her."

"In other words, she felt your constituents would accept your behavior for what we'd done because you're a man, but they wouldn't accept mine because I'm a woman supposedly engaged to another man?"

"I hate admitting it, but yes. With both Tanner and I immediately publicly calling out the article as nothing but lies worked in our favor."

He kissed her forehead and then said, "With the information Alex provided, I'm contacting my attorney for a cease-and-desist. However, it seems Jake plans to take things a little further."

Victoria smiled. "Yes, it appears that way. I think he has a score to settle with that particular tabloid for how they treated Diamond when they kept insisting that she and Sterling were lovers, and she'd secretly been married to Jake. Unfortunately for them, what Tanner said at his press conference might have put that idea in Uncle Jake's head."

She turned and wrapped her arms around his neck. "Well, I thank both you and Tanner for speaking out."

"I will always do my best to protect you, Victoria. No matter what." Then he pulled her closer and kissed her.

CHAPTER THIRTY-TWO

TANNER CHECKED HIS WATCH. It was close to nine o'clock. The construction crew had left hours ago. The club was empty and it was dark outside. Why had he thought Lyric would watch that press conference and see she'd been wrong about him, and then come to him? He should not have gotten his hopes up like he had. Better yet, he should not have fallen in love so hard and so quickly.

He leaned back in his office chair thinking he hadn't been able to help it, and whether she showed up here tonight or not, if Lyric thought she'd seen the last of him, she was wrong. Dead wrong.

He sighed at the ringing of his phone and picked it up. If another one of his family members called him, he would be throwing something against the wall. He checked caller ID and his heart stopped. It was Lyric. He quickly clicked on the call. "Yes, Lyric?"

"I'm outside. Will you open the door to let me in?"

He couldn't contain his joy. She had come. "Yes, I'll be right there."

Tanner rushed through the club and practically threw open the door. And there Lyric stood, looking more beautiful than any woman had a right to look. Her thick, twisted hair crowned her face, and her outfit…

OMG…it was a very short tube-like dress that showed every delectable curve she had. His gaze roamed all over her. The dress was skin-tight, which made him wonder if she was wearing anything under it. He knew for certain she didn't have on a bra. His trained eyes could definitely detect that. And then those sky-high stilettos finished off what was one hell of a very sexy package.

It took him a moment to find his words. "Come in," he said in a deep, husky voice, one he barely recognized as his own.

"Thanks," she said, walking past him and giving him a delicious whiff of her scent. Whatever perfume she was wearing, she could definitely take ownership of it.

He watched her glance around at all the work that had been done in the club since she'd last been here. She then looked back at him. "The place looks good."

He smiled and then said, "You look good."

She returned his smile. "You think so?"

Hell yeah. "I know so." He paused to slowly take her in again. "You look good enough to eat."

The smile she gave him held a bit of naughtiness, then she said, "Glad you think so, but I'm hoping you won't stop there."

He didn't consider himself a slow person and understood her meaning clearly. Oh, he wouldn't stop there. He intended to eat her, and then make love to her until neither of them would ever think of letting anyone or anything ever come between them again.

Taking a step toward her, he began backing her against the wall. "Are you wearing anything under this dress?" He asked, barely holding back the flood of sensual emotions he was feeling.

"Umm…that's for me to know and for you to find out."

Tanner had no problem doing that. Quickly dropping to his knees, he slid her dress up. He groaned. No panties.

When he came face-to-face with her womanhood, he felt his tongue thicken in his mouth. He had gone too long without loving her this way, and before she could take her next breath, he clutched her thighs, leaned forward and slid his tongue along her seam, then thrust inside of her.

He wasn't certain how many times he made her scream. All he knew was the hunger that had built up inside of him for her seemed to take control and he could not get enough. Finally, he stood and peeled off her too-sexy dress and removed her shoes. Then he quickly got out of his clothes and put on a condom.

He was rock-hard and when he lifted her up to wrap her legs around him, he pressed her back against the wall and entered her body. Like his tongue, his manhood couldn't seem to get enough, and he kept thrusting into her. Pounding hard. Like his life depended on it. Like he couldn't get enough.

When they climaxed a few more times, he gathered her into his arms and carried her into his office. He took her again, a couple more times, on his desk. He'd never felt like the Energizer Bunny to this degree with any woman.

"Remind me never to let you go without getting some of me for this long again," she whispered against his ear.

He smiled. "Yeah, that will teach you. Should I apologize?" he asked, scooping her up to carry her around the desk to sit in his lap.

"No, don't apologize. I loved every moment of it." Then she softly said, "And I love you, Tanner. I tried to fight it. I tried convincing myself there was no way I could fall in love with you so quickly, but I did. And today when you admitted to loving me back, it was more than I could handle. I wanted to believe you, but couldn't. Will you forgive me for doubting you?"

He licked the side of her face a few times, then said, "Yes, I forgive you. Considering your history with that last guy, and my history with women, I could understand you being cautious. But things happened to me like I'd been warned they would. I was told that no matter how much I'd enjoyed my life as a single man, that I would know the woman who would bring an end to all of it when I met her."

He cuddled her in his arms. "As expected, I tried fighting it, denying it and refusing to acknowledge what I knew was true. I had fallen in love."

She pressed her forehead against his. "Where do we go from here, Tanner?"

"I want us to continue to date so you can get to know me better. Then I want you to meet my family, my business partners, my friends—everyone who is important to me."

She smiled. "And I want you to meet the rest of my family and friends, as well. Especially my godmother, who owns a bakery in town."

He smiled. "I can't wait."

And then they were kissing again.

Two days later

"Ms. Wayfare, Senator Malone is here to see you."

Audria stood from where she'd been sitting by the window overlooking the Potomac. She hadn't heard from Roman since she'd talked to him two days ago, right before he'd done that press conference and made a complete fool of himself by professing his love for a woman who had no class.

She knew he would come back to her eventually and it hadn't taken long. He owed her big-time for claiming to love another woman. She wouldn't accept less than a marriage proposal in a very public place—hmm, she would have to give that some thought. It would have to be perfect and make the newspaper.

"Send him in, Polly," she finally said to the housekeeper.

She ran her fingers through her hair and licked her lips. It had been a while since she and Roman shared a bed. It was time he agreed to stay out of anyone's bed but hers. They needed to show Washington they were a couple madly in love.

He strolled in, looking good enough to eat and lick all over. Evidently, a couple days away had helped him get his senses back in check. He probably had come straight here from the airport. Her contacts had told her that he'd caught a flight right after the press conference on Monday for Texas. She figured he'd gone home to his ranch to think things through.

She wouldn't make it easy on him. "Roman, when did you get back?"

"Today. I came straight here from the airport."

Bingo! She smiled, knowing she'd been right. "If you don't have a game plan, I do."

He raised an eyebrow. "A game plan for what?"

"Our getting back together," she said, crossing the room to rest her hands on his chest. "Of course, I'm upset about how you claimed you loved that woman on national television, but we can fix that."

Roman frowned and took her hands from his chest and placed them by her side, then stepped back. "Like you think you fixed everything else. Assuming smearing my relationship with Victoria in that tabloid would bring me to heel?"

She lifted her hand to her chest. "How could you think I'd do such a thing? I have no idea what you're talking about."

"Then let me enlighten you. You picked the wrong family to mess with, Audria. It didn't take long for a member of the Madaris family, who happens to be a skilled private investigator, to put two and two together and come up with you. Needless to say, your PI talked, and was very upset to find out you altered his report."

She couldn't stop the surprise that lit her eyes, although she tried to downplay it. "Also, Buddy Fields at *The Tattler* talked, as well, once he learned you doctored that report," Roman said.

"I don't know what you're talking about."

"Not according to Fields. We got an admission from him last night when Jake Madaris threatened to add *The Tattler* to his acquisition portfolio. The man began singing like a canary and had quite a lot to say about you. He has quite a thick file on you about all the married men you've been sleeping with, including your affair with him, your financial adviser and your chauffeur. He claims he has pictures and videos and if he loses his company because of you, he will spill all. It will be a *The Tattler* exclusive. To be perfectly honest, I couldn't care less who shares your bed. That's not my business. However, let me get this straight."

He took a step forward. "I don't want you and never have. I don't love you and never will. And if I ever get so far as to one day become president, you will never be my first lady. Nor will you be my second or third. You, Audria Wayfare, aren't a lady at all. What you tried to do—ruining the reputations of three people—is as low as it gets. I love Victoria and I plan to marry her. If I hear that you even whisper her name, unless it's to sing her good graces and praises, I will make sure everybody in this town knows what you've been up to and with whom."

She lifted her chin. "You wouldn't."

"Honestly, I really would," he assured her. "I am a man deeply in love, and I will do anything to protect the woman I love. You, on the other hand, mean nothing to me. I suggest you remember that."

Roman then turned and walked out.

CHAPTER THIRTY-THREE

FELICIA LAVERNE MADARIS sipped her tea as she gazed across at the two couples seated before her. She had returned from her cruise three days ago to be informed that both couples had requested her presence. She was more than happy to accommodate them. She knew they figured she'd made a huge mistake, but they would soon discover that any mistakes had been theirs. From the looks of it, she had planned everything perfectly.

She set down her teacup and gave the foursome her undivided attention. She ignored the fifth person in the room. Her baby boy, Jake. He was on the other side of the room, sitting comfortably in a recliner with his long legs stretched out and a Stetson almost covering his eyes. She figured he was there in case whatever the couples had to say was more than her heart could handle, and he would be needed to revive her.

"Well, I'm glad to see everyone, and I know all of you, except for you," she said to the woman sitting on the love seat beside Tanner.

"Ms. Felicia Laverne, this is Lyric Evans, a very good friend of mine," Tanner said as way of an introduction.

Felicia Laverne nodded. "It's nice meeting you, dear." She turned her attention to her great-granddaughter. "So, Victoria, what is this meeting about?"

Victoria hesitated for a moment and then said, "I think

you made a mistake in choosing Tanner for me. I'm in love with Roman and Tanner's in love with Lyric. So there's no way Tanner and I could ever be a couple."

The room got quiet and everyone stared at Mama Laverne. She stared back and smoothly answered, "No, I didn't make a mistake."

Victoria frowned. "But I don't love Tanner. I love Roman."

The older lady smiled. "I'm curious, Victoria, what gave you the idea that I had chosen Tanner for you?"

Victoria opened her mouth, then closed it, clearly taken aback. Then she said, "You wouldn't give me the name of the guy, but you led me to believe falling in love wouldn't be easy for him. So I assumed he was a man who thoroughly enjoyed his life as a bachelor." She paused, then continued, "You gave me and Tanner gift cards to the same bakery so we could run in to each other. You also suggested to Tanner that he look me up once he got to New Orleans. All of those things seemed suspect to me."

Felicia Laverne didn't say anything for a moment and then she said, "I don't see why. The man I had chosen for you all along was Roman."

"Me?" Roman said, clearly surprised.

Felicia Laverne's gaze landed on Roman. "Yes, you. I've been watching you all your life, Roman Malone Junior. Your aunt Nora and I decided long ago that Victoria would be perfect for you."

Victoria was shocked, and from the look on Roman's face it was obvious that he was, too. "You and my aunt Nora?" he asked.

Mama Laverne smiled sweetly. "Yes, me and your aunt Nora."

Victoria frowned. "I don't know how the two of you

figured that Roman and I would be perfect for each other. For years I didn't like politicians and avoided being in the limelight."

"Yes, we knew that and figured Roman was just the person to make you change your mind about both."

Roman shook his head, obviously still not understanding. "But how could you know that I would be spending time in Catalina Cove?"

Felicia Laverne chuckled. "I knew. When I met that nice young man named Mint Stover, who works for you, at that fundraiser party Jake gave you here last year, I convinced Mint that you looked tired from all that campaigning and whenever you could, that you should visit Catalina Cove. I'd heard it was a great place to rest and go fishing."

Roman just stared at her. Speechless.

"But what about Tanner? Blade told him that he was my intended. What if he had acted on it and sought out my attention?" Victoria asked.

Felicia Laverne shook her head. "He wouldn't have done that. Tanner only considered you a friend. He didn't see you in a romantic way." She glanced over at Tanner, who nodded his head in full agreement.

"But what about all those gift cards to that bakery?" Victoria asked.

She chuckled as she looked back at Victoria. "Oh, yeah. That. I was just looking out for you. I knew how you liked sweets and rarely slowed down to eat, so I figured giving you those gift cards would make sure you were eating something."

"And you gave them to me because you know how much I like sweets, too," Tanner said, grinning. He stood and took Lyric's hand in his. "Well, now that everything has been cleared up, Lyric and I will be leaving."

"Not so fast, young man. Please sit back down."

Everyone watched as Tanner reluctantly sat back down. He asked in a somewhat nervous voice, "Is there more?"

"Yes," she said, catching his gaze. "Granted, I do know how much you like sweets, but I gave you those gift cards with a purpose in mind, Tanner."

He drew in a deep breath, clearly afraid to ask, but he did. "And what purpose was that?"

"That you and Lyric would meet."

Tanner heard Lyric's sharp intake of breath and looked over at her, and then back at Mama Laverne. He returned his gaze to Lyric and asked, "The two of you know each other?"

Lyric shook her head. It was obvious she was clearly confused. "No."

Felicia Laverne said, "Although this is my first time officially meeting you, Lyric, I knew Isabelle."

Lyric lifted her hand to her throat, surprised. "You knew my grandmother?"

"Yes. As kids growing up, Isabelle and I attended the same church summer camp. I also knew Isabelle's best friend, Yvonne. Yvonne's daughter, Susan, is your godmother and owns the bakery."

"Susan's Bakery," Tanner said thoughtfully, putting two and two together and not liking what he was coming up with.

"Yes, Susan's Bakery," Mama Laverne said, nodding. "I was hoping you would run in to Lyric at the bakery, Tanner, and had no idea your paths would cross in an entirely different way. What I did know is that when you saw Lyric, you would be smitten."

Tanner frowned. "How could you have known that?"

She waved off his question. "You're Blade's friend. You

know that saying about birds of a feather flock together? Just like Blade recognized Samari as the woman for him, when he didn't want to. I knew you would do the same."

Felicia Laverne leaned back in her chair and continued. "Besides, you and Lyric had so much in common with all that charity work both of you like to do, I figured the two of you would be perfect together."

"Did my godmother know about this?" Lyric asked.

"Of course, Susan knew. For a minute there she was worried that you and Tanner wouldn't come to your senses. But I assured her that eventually the two of you would and that all would be well. Just like with Liam and Paula."

Lyric's eyes widened. "Liam? My brother?"

Mama Laverne smiled. "Yes. Isabelle was alive then and she solicited my help for that brother of yours. Lordy, the boy was worse than my Clayton and my Blade put together. Thankfully, we found the perfect girl for him. Don't you think?"

It was obvious to anyone looking at Lyric that she honestly didn't know what to think.

"Susan and I promised your grandmother before she died that we would make sure her two granddaughters, namely you and Liza, would marry the perfect mates."

Tanner, who was still finding it hard to believe what the older woman had done, asked in an annoyed tone, "No disrespect, ma'am, but you actually thought it was okay to interfere in our lives?"

"I don't see why not. Do any of you have a problem with the results?"

The two couples' silence was proof they did not.

Leaning on her cane, Felicia Laverne slowly came to her feet. "With that settled, if there aren't any more questions, it's nap time for me." She called out to her son, "Jake, stop pretending to be asleep over there and come walk me to my room."

When Jake reached Mama Laverne's side, Victoria said, "I do have a question, Mama Laverne."

She turned to face Victoria. "And what is your question, dear?"

"Is Corbin next?"

Felicia Laverne's lips stretched into a broad smile. "That was the plan. However, I will admit those gray-eyed Bannister boys do concern me."

"Gray-eyed Bannister boys?" Roman asked, not even trying to hide his grin.

"Yes, you know Marilyn's nephews. Those sons of her brother Stuart Junior. Wyatt is a good friend of Blade's. Camden is good friends with Luke. And the twins, Brenton and Branson, are good friends of Nolan's. Those four boys need my help."

"This I got to see," Tanner muttered under his breath.

Jake Madaris shook his head as he walked his mother out of the room. She had pulled off yet another one, or two, of her matchmaking schemes. He wouldn't want to be in Corbin's, Wyatt's, Camden's, Branson's or Brenton's shoes about now. He had a feeling his mother thought she was on a roll and was about to really dig in.

He chuckled softly. The next year would definitely be interesting.

Three weeks later

ALL HEADS TURNED when Senator Roman Malone Jr. walked into the Capital Ball with the beautiful woman on his arm. Every woman there thought he looked totally dashing and that Victoria Madaris was too radiant for words and her beauty astounding. And that gown she was wearing was simply exquisite.

The couple had entered with Jake Madaris and his wife, the famous movie star, Diamond Swain-Madaris; and retired senator Nedwyn Lansing and his wife, Diana. All three couples were getting attention because they looked so good together.

Roman leaned down and asked Victoria, "You all right?"

She smiled at him. "I couldn't be better." She glanced around. "There are a lot of people here." And she didn't want to say it, but it appeared all eyes were on her and Roman.

Surprisingly, *The Tattler* had done something it had never done before. They had publicly apologized as well as retracted the article and admitted they had used misinformation from an unreliable source.

After Roman's public declaration of love for her, all the romantics had come out in support of the couple. Twitter had gone crazy, trending that Senator Malone's words of love had been utterly romantic. That in itself had been a backlash to the tabloid even without a retraction.

Roman strolled Victoria around the room and introduced her to a number of his colleagues, then he asked if she wanted to dance. "Yes, Senator Malone, I would be honored to dance with you," she said, smiling.

Roman took her into his arms and they danced the night away, one song after another. She also danced with her uncle Jake and her uncle Nedwyn, while Roman danced with her aunts, Diamond and Diana.

During the night, Victoria couldn't help noticing a very attractive woman who would often stare at her. When she and Roman took a quick break from dancing and went to the buffet table to grab something to eat, she asked him if the woman was Audria Wayfare. He confirmed that it was. In a way, Victoria felt sorry for her. She was attractive on the outside, but was obviously mean-spirited on the inside.

Roman and Victoria were enjoying what she knew would be their last dance of the night when suddenly she noticed they were the only couple on the dance floor. Then the bright lights came on at the exact moment the band stopped playing.

She looked up at Roman. "What in the world is going on?"

Instead of answering her, he smiled and, holding her hand, he lowered to one knee. Gazing up at her, he said, "You are everything I could ever want in a wife, Victoria, and I love you so much. Will you marry me and share my life with me?"

Victoria fought back the tears in her eyes. Several weeks ago he had declared publicly that he loved her, and now tonight, he was proposing in front of everyone present. "Yes, I will marry you. I love you, too."

Everyone clapped and there were hearty cheers when Roman slid a gorgeous ring on her finger. Victoria held out her hand to look at her engagement ring, a beautiful three-carat French halo diamond on a white band. He then stood, gathered her into his arms and kissed her. Moments later, he pulled back and said, "One more dance before we leave."

As if on cue, the band began playing a slow number, and he pulled her close and they danced. They were the only couple on the dance floor. It was as if this song, this dance and this moment belonged only to them. Victoria felt totally happy and knew her great-grandmother had known all along that no matter what, she would follow her heart.

When the song ended, she whispered to Roman, "I'm ready to leave. I just need to tell my family good-night."

Both of her aunts loved her engagement ring and as they headed for the exit, she and Roman received many words of congratulations and well wishes. "Just so you know," Roman said casually, "I want a Christmas wedding."

Victoria's head snapped up to look at him. "A Christmas wedding? That's barely two months away, Roman. Not enough time to plan."

He grinned. "I want to start off the New Year with you as my wife. And as for there not being enough time to plan, I know the women in your family will make it happen."

Victoria threw her head back and laughed because she knew it, too.

THE FOLLOWING MORNING Victoria woke up in Roman's bed. She sat up and saw she was in bed alone, then glanced at the ring on her finger to make sure she hadn't dreamed it.

"Good morning, sweetheart."

She looked up to see Roman, dressed only in pajama bottoms, lounging against the bedroom door. He held a newspaper in his hand.

She smiled over at him. "Good morning, Roman."

He crossed the room to the bed, leaned down and placed a kiss on her lips. "I love you," he whispered.

"And I love you," she said.

He pulled back, straightened and said, "I thought you'd like to see this." He dropped the newspaper in bed with her. She picked it up. It was a copy of the *Washington Post*. A front-page photo showed him on his knee proposing. The article had the caption, She Said Yes!

"We look good together, don't we?" she asked him.

"Yes, and we always will."

She read the article, and they were referred to as the "Darlings of Washington." Tilting her head, she looked up at him. "Were you serious when you said you want a Christmas wedding?"

"Yes. Very serious."

She watched as he removed his pajama bottoms and slid back in bed with her. Victoria thought a Christmas wedding would be perfect, just like the man she would marry.

EPILOGUE

Roman wanted a Christmas wedding and, just like he'd told Victoria, all the women in the Madaris family were more than happy to make it happen. Diamond flew in a well-known bridal gown designer from LA, and her cousins-in-law, Syneda, Caitlin and Lorren, were put in charge of finding the perfect location to accommodate all the guests. Close to seven hundred people would be invited. That's what happened when you married a man destined to become president one day.

More cousins, Christy, Skye and Kenna, as well as her sister Lindsay, were in charge of the reception. And family members and family friends—Traci, Kattie, Mac, Sam and Peyton—were in charge of coordinating all the bridal showers. Ivy, Marilyn and Roman's mother, Traci, would work with Diamond to make sure the guests staying at Whispering Pines would be comfortable.

This wedding was a team effort, a family affair, and everyone was eager to pitch in to do whatever needed to be done. Everyone was happy…well, almost everyone. News had soon spread about Mama Laverne's matchmaking double whammy. To hear she had not only orchestrated a romance between Victoria and Roman, but also one with Tanner, had Corbin and the Bannister brothers shaking in their boots. They were refusing to be a part of a possible quintuple whammy and rumor had it that they were trying to come up with their own plans. Everyone was wishing them good luck with that, and suggested they might as well face the fact their bachelor days were numbered.

Christmas Day had finally arrived and Victoria looked out the church's window. People were still arriving. It would be huge with all of their Texas friends, families and a number of Roman's DC colleagues and college fraternity brothers. She had invited her friends from Catalina Cove and her boss and coworkers from the television station.

And speaking of Catalina Cove, Roman had presented her with her wedding gift last night. He had surprised her with a deed to a waterfront property in Catalina Cove. They would be building a summer home next year. He'd said he couldn't resist since the cove would always have special memories for them.

Washington, DC, would be their home for now, but she looked forward to spending time on his ranch in Austin, as well. Things were moving fast. Already she had resigned from her job in New Orleans with plans to make DC her home.

Two weeks ago, she had received a job offer as a talk show host at DC's CNN bureau and she had accepted, but wouldn't start work until sometime in January. She was excited about fulfilling her role as a senator's wife. Right now, more than anything she looked forward to spending their two-week honeymoon in Venice.

At the knock on the door, Victoria turned. "Come in."

She smiled when her great-grandmother walked in with her cane.

"Mama Laverne," she said, hurrying to get a chair for her to sit down.

"No need, dear. I don't intend to stay that long. Just wanted to check to make sure all was well with you."

Victoria's smile widened. "Yes, all is well with me."

Felicia Laverne nodded. "Glad to hear it. I just saw Tanner and Lyric. She's wearing a gorgeous engagement ring and they are planning a June wedding."

Victoria grinned. "I am so happy for them." She had also heard from Blade that all the renovations had been done and the club would be opened for business as scheduled on New Year's Eve.

Less than two hours later, Victoria walked down the aisle on the arm of her father, Nolan Madaris Junior. The look in Roman's eyes as he watched her come to him filled her with even more love. Today was the day they would remember for the rest of their lives. She was glad she had done the right thing and followed her heart.

She was exceedingly glad.

FELICIA LAVERNE MADARIS couldn't help but smile at the way things had turned out today. She loved weddings, especially when it was one of her own kin getting hitched. She glanced across the room at the groom's aunt, Nora Parker, caught her eye and winked. A Malone had married a Madaris.

Mission accomplished.

She looked around the reception's ballroom and chuckled when she saw her great-grands and their friends huddled together in a pack. The single ones had tried avoiding her today but discovered they couldn't. Out of respect they had spoken and had given her the kiss on the cheek and asked about her well-being. Then they had high-tailed it away once they'd done so.

This was the first wedding she'd ever attended where the single men refused to participate in the garter toss. How crazy was that? After taking a sip of her punch, she noticed three single ladies and several pairs of male eyes who were checking them out. Hmm...

Whether they knew it or not, three of those men were making things easy for her since the interest was already there. All of her great-grands thought they weren't ready for love and marriage in the beginning, but soon discovered how wrong they were.

She leaned back in her chair, thinking she loved helping them discover love in its purest form and with the perfect partner.

Now, on to the next.

* * * * *

ELAINA TURNED TO face him, her heart pounding again and a dozen warning bells going off in her head. She should shut down the flirting, but the look in Alex's eyes said he was willing to go with her down this path. "I've got some experience with wanting the wrong man."

"But that's all in your past now." He took a half step closer.

She shook her head. She'd never been good at not going for what she wanted. Her ego needed stroking, and Alex with his quiet understanding and empathy had shown her more care than anyone had in a long time. She'd be smarter this time. This was just to quell her curiosity. People said there was a thin line between love and hate. Maybe all their bickering had just been leading to this.

"Not quite," she said, choosing her next words carefully. She pretended to check the list in her box. "I find myself thinking about someone who I once despised. I miss clashing with him daily. I enjoy the verbal sparring. Not to mention he recently wrapped his arms around me and for some reason I can't get that out of my head." She glanced at him. "He's stronger than I imagined. His embrace comforting in a way I didn't realize I'd like. It makes me want more even though I know I shouldn't."

Alex stilled next to her. "What are you going to do about this ill-advised craving?"

"It kind of depends on him," she said. "I think he's interested, but I can't be sure. And you know I can never offer myself to a man who didn't want me." She said the last part with a slight shrug. Though her heart imitated a hummingbird against her ribs, and a mixture of excitement and adrenaline flowed with each beat.

Alex slid closer, closing the distance between them, and filling her senses with him. He pulled the paper out of her hands. "What if he wants you, too?"

His deep voice slid over her like warm satin. She faced him and met his dark eyes. "Then I'm in trouble, because I'm no good at saying no to the things I want but shouldn't have."

Alex watched her for several heartbeats. The pulse beat quickly at the base of his neck. A question hovered in his eye. Was she being genuine, or was she playing with him? She wasn't about to back down now. Not after she'd worked up the courage to acknowledge the attraction humming between them.

Before he could let common sense kill the moment she lifted on her toes and brushed her lips across his. "Tell me, Alex, am I in trouble?"

Alex's strong arm wrapped around her waist. He pulled her carefully against his body as if she were precious. Emotion squeezed her chest while a jolt of desire rushed through her. She never could resist a man willing to accept her challenge.

Don't miss what happens next in...
Careless Whispers
by Synithia Williams
Available April 2021 wherever
HQN books and ebooks are sold.

www.Harlequin.com

Welcome to Rose Bend for the first book in
USA TODAY *bestselling author Naima Simone's*
irresistible new series.

If it was only about her, she might never have
come back to Rose Bend.
But it's not only about her anymore.

Read on for a sneak peek of
The Road to Rose Bend

"Stop." Cole gently tugged on her hand, drawing her to a halt. "Look around you. What do you see?"

Sydney tossed him a look that he clearly interpreted as *what the hell*, but she still glanced around the busy downtown area, packed a little more than usual with shoppers, tourists and traffic because of summer and the upcoming motorcycle rally. But the places that marked Rose Bend as a small, close-knit community still stood, impressive in age yet humble in simplicity.

"What am I supposed to see?" she retorted. "I feel like this is a trick question."

"Do they teach suspicion in the South along with genteel manners?" He surrendered to his desire and allowed himself a gentle tug on a brown curl.

"Yes. It's free, along with the master class on the War of Northern Aggression."

"Smart-ass," he growled.

"Not the worst thing that I've been called."

Delicious. Perfect. Worship-worthy. All things he would—and had—said himself. *Goddamn, stop.* "Not touching your ass," he said, then pinched the bridge of his nose, inwardly groaning at his words.

Sydney grinned. "You don't sound at all happy about that fact," she drawled.

"Focus," he grunted.

"I was." She lifted her shoulders in a shrug, a wicked smile tugging at the corner of her mouth that completely ruined the innocence she was obviously striving for. "Then you started in about manners and asses, and it all went left quick."

He couldn't help it; he threw back his head, laughing. Long and hard. And damn if it didn't feel good. Warm and...cleansing. He brought her hand, still clasped in his, to his mouth and pressed a quick kiss to her knuckles in gratitude.

Her soft gasp reached his ears. Without his permission, his gaze dropped to her mouth. How would that puff of breath feel across his lips if he bent his head over hers?

"What do you see, Sydney?" he asked again, choosing not to acknowledge the question in those liquid brown eyes.

She jerked her head away, obeying his request. For several moments, she studied their surroundings, and when she returned her attention to him, she shook her head. "The same place I left eight years ago."

"No," he objected. He held the ice cream cone out to her, and when she shook her head, he tossed it into a nearby garbage can. Then, stepping behind her, he settled his hands on her slim shoulders. "You're looking out the eyes of that hurt, misunderstood teenage girl. What does the mature, successful woman see now?" When she remained quiet, he offered, "Let me help. See the pharmacy?" he asked, slightly turning her to the left where the store had stood since his parents had been born. "Mr. Price used to run it with an iron fist and pretty much bark at every kid who came in there. Talk about crotchety." The corner of his mouth quirked at her "hell yeah."

"But now, he has grandkids, twin girls, and you wouldn't recognize the old man. He actually—wait for it—smiles.

And his daughter helps run the pharmacy. She's enlarged the cosmetics and toy sections, and even added audio-books."

Again, he turned her, so they both surveyed the sprawl of the town and the breathtaking view of Monument Mountain and Mount Everett soaring above it.

"We have a new nondenominational church and a synagogue. The resource center hosts several advocacy programs for our LGBTQ community, to provide support for their mental and physical health, and helping them lead successful lives in an often intolerant world. We have a Puerto Rican mayor." He nodded. "What I want you to see, Sydney, is that yes, we're still the same in the way that you're still the same person who left here. But just like you've grown and changed, so have we. Just give us a chance to show you. To welcome you."

Several beats of silence passed between them, and he was about to release her and continue on their walk when her quiet voice halted him.

"What if the woman is still hurt?"

He barely caught that low whisper. It throbbed with old wounds. But he did catch it. And he lowered his head, bracing his jaw against the side of her head, her curls tickling his chin, mouth and cheek. Vanilla filled his nose, and he subtly inhaled the scent.

"That's okay. Because she's not too old to be healed. And she'll find healing right here in the very place she ran from."

Like you did.

But he ignored that taunting voice. Her situation and his were different. There was no redemption or miracle cure for him. The best part of him was buried in the cemetery behind St. John's.

He shifted from behind her, taking her hand again. This time she didn't hesitate to enfold her fingers around his. That tiny show of trust shouldn't have struck him in the chest like a fist. Shouldn't have had him battling the need to tunnel his fingers through those thick, sexy curls to tip her head back and brush her lips with a kiss of thankfulness.

Don't miss what happens next in....
The Road to Rose Bend
by Naima Simone
Available May 2021 wherever
HQN books and ebooks are sold.

www.Harlequin.com

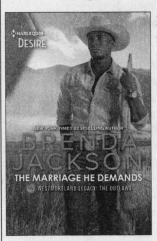

Wealthy Alaskan Cash Outlaw has inherited a ranch and needs land owned by beautiful, determined Brianna Banks. She'll sign it over under one condition: Cash fathering the child she desperately wants. But he won't be an absentee father and makes his own demand...

Read on for a sneak peek at
The Marriage He Demands
by New York Times *bestselling author Brenda Jackson.*

"Are you really going to sell the Blazing Frontier without even taking the time to look at it? It's a beautiful place."

"I'm sure it is, but I have no need of a ranch, dude or otherwise."

"I think you're making a mistake, Cash."

Cash lifted a brow. Normally, he didn't care what any person, man or woman, thought about any decision he made, but for some reason what she thought mattered.

It shouldn't.

What he should do was thank her for joining him for lunch, and tell her not to walk back to Cavanaugh's office with him, although he knew both their cars were parked there. In other words, he should put as much distance between them as possible.

I can't.

Maybe it was the way her luscious mouth tightened when she was not happy about something. He'd picked up on it twice now. Lord help him but he didn't want to see it a third time. He'd rather see her smile, lick an ice cream cone or...lick him.

He quickly forced the last image from his mind, but not before a hum of lust shot through his veins. There had to be a reason he was so attracted to her. Maybe he could blame it on the Biggins deal Garth had closed just months before he'd gotten engaged to Regan. That had taken working endless days and nights, and for the past year Cash's social life had been practically nonexistent.

On the other hand, even without the Biggins deal as an excuse, there was strong sexual chemistry radiating between them. He felt it but honestly wasn't sure that even at twenty-seven she recognized it for what it was.

That was intriguing, to the point that he was tempted to hang around Black Crow another day. Besides, he was a businessman, and no businessman would sell or buy anything without checking it out first. He was letting his personal emotions around Ellen cloud what was usually a very sound business mind.

"You are right, Brianna. I would be making a mistake if I didn't at least see the ranch before selling it. Is now a good time?"

The huge smile that spread across her face was priceless…and mesmerizing. When was the last time a woman, any woman, had this kind of effect on him? When he felt spellbound? He concluded that never had a woman captivated him like Brianna Banks was doing.

Don't miss what happens next in
The Marriage He Demands
by Brenda Jackson, the next book in her
Westmoreland Legacy: The Outlaws series!

Available April 2021 wherever
Harlequin Desire books and ebooks are sold.

Harlequin.com